Acclaim for
UPSIDE DOWN

"*Upside Down* is a refreshing and heartfelt New Adult contemporary romance." —*USA Today*

"This story shows just how frightening it is to let yourself fall in love and be that vulnerable." —HeroesandHeartbreakers.com

"Lia Riley turned my emotions *Upside Down* with this book! Fast paced, electric, and sweetly emotional!"
—Tracy Wolff, *New York Times* and
USA Today bestselling author

"Where to even start with this book? Beautifully written, Australia, hot surfer Bran, unique heroine Talia. Yep, it's all just a whole lot of awesome. Loved it!" —Cindi Madsen, *USA Today* bestselling author

"Fresh, sexy, and romantic, *Upside Down* will leave you wanting more. I cannot wait for the next book. Lia Riley is an incredible new talent and not to be missed!"
—Kristen Callihan, award-winning author of the
Darkest London series and *The Hook Up*

"A rich setting and utterly romantic, *Upside Down* will have you laughing and crying and begging for it to never end. I absolutely loved it!" —Melissa West, author of *Pieces of Olivia*

"*Upside Down* is a brilliantly written New Adult romance that transported me to another country. With vivid imagery and rich characterizations...I was completely smitten with the love story of Bran and Talia. I cannot wait for the rest of their story!"
—Megan Erickson, author of *Make It Count*

SIDESWIPED

ALSO BY LIA RILEY

Upside Down

Inside Out

Carry Me Home (novella)

SiDESWiPED

AN OFF THE MAP NOVEL
Book Two

LIA RILEY

FOREVER

NEW YORK   BOSTON

Copyright © 2014 by Lia Riley
Excerpt from *Inside Out* copyright © 2014 by Lia Riley

All rights reserved. In accordance with the U.S. Copyright Act of 1976, the scanning, uploading, and electronic sharing of any part of this book without the permission of the publisher constitute unlawful piracy and theft of the author's intellectual property. If you would like to use material from the book (other than for review purposes), prior written permission must be obtained by contacting the publisher at permissions@hbgusa.com. Thank you for your support of the author's rights.

Forever
Hachette Book Group
1290 Avenue of the Americas
New York, NY 10104

www.HachetteBookGroup.com

Printed in the United States of America

RRD-C

Originally published as an ebook

First trade paperback edition: June 2015
10 9 8 7 6 5 4 3 2 1

Forever is an imprint of Grand Central Publishing.
The Forever name and logo are trademarks of Hachette Book Group, Inc.

The Hachette Speakers Bureau provides a wide range of authors for speaking events. To find out more, go to www.hachettespeakersbureau.com or call (866) 376-6591.

The publisher is not responsible for websites (or their content) that are not owned by the publisher.

Library of Congress Cataloging-in-Publication Data

Riley, Lia.
    Sideswiped / Lia Riley. — First trade paperback edition.
        pages ; cm
    ISBN 978-1-4555-8574-8 (pbk.) — ISBN 978-1-4555-8576-2 (ebook) — ISBN 978-1-4789-0392-5 (audio download)
    I. Title.
    PS3618.I53279S53 2015
    813'.6—dc23
                                        2015008004

To anyone stuck in Fear Swamp . . .
Courage doesn't mean you don't get afraid;
courage means you don't let fear stop you.

ACKNOWLEDGMENTS

First up, a bucket of leprechaun gold to Jennifer Blackwood and Jennifer Ryan. You rescued me from a dismal self-doubting bog during this book, and for that, I'm FOREVER grateful. Also, big hugs to Jules Barnard, for not liking one chapter and pushing me to write the night surf scene, and Megan Taddonio for reading snippets and offering your blunt two cents.

Rock star agent Emily Sylvan Kim, when you loved the ending, you made my entire week—no, my entire autumn.

Team Forever: Lauren Plude, I'm so flipping lucky to partner with you on this series—your edits are always spot-on. Elizabeth Turner, you knocked it out of the park with another fan-freaking-tastic cover. Carrie Andrews, sorry to burn your eyes with my grammar abuse; thanks for making me look better. Marissa Sangiacomo, you are a publicity queen who deserves all the Aragorns.

Love nuzzles to AJ Pine, Megan Erickson, Natalie Blitt, Lex Martin, Claire McEwan, and Lexi Clemence. To all my '14 Debut homies...Bigfoot's getting the next round.

Okay, I must splatter adoration on a few bloggers—such incredible book champions—you guys rock. Momo from *Books Over Boys*, you really are the world's most adorable blogger—Fassavoy and unicorns forever. Marifer at *Maf's Crazy Book Life*, Ashley at *Books by Migs* and Vangie at *Painful Reads*, guys, gah! So many feelings. Thanks for believing in Bran and Talia. You three have such a special place in my heart.

To my family, I know, I have sorely neglected many of you while this series hijacked my brain. I promise to call more. You're never far from my thoughts.

To J and B, you two are my heart walking around outside my body. I am so blessed to call you my children.

To Nick, so this book, yeah, this is what happened to your wife during the three months she went MIA. Thank you for driving me around Melbourne and the Mornington Peninsula for research, and listening to me ramble about my characters as if they were real people. This isn't our story, but there's so much of us hovering on the fringes of the page. Our first year, in Tasmania, in the A-frame on the side of Mount Wellington . . . that was one of the best and hardest times of my whole life. I love you.

SIDESWIPED

Some of us think holding on makes us strong;
but sometimes it is letting go.

—Hermann Hesse

I

TALIA

September

Our California bungalow sits empty, a headstone for a ghost family. The rooms are tomb quiet, devoid of any comforting, familiar clutter. All our stuff, tangible proof the Stolfi family once existed, rots in a long-term storage unit. When the movers hauled off the last cardboard boxes, they took more than precious memories. They snatched my breadcrumb trail. The last stupid, irrational hope that Mom, Dad, and I could somehow find a way back together.

These bare walls reflect the stark truth. We're over. My family's done. A cashed-up Silicon Valley couple craving a beach town escape will snag the house by the weekend.

I pause near the front window and chew the inside of my cheek. Dad's Realtor drives a FOR SALE sign into the front yard. The invisible dumbbell lodged in my sternum increases in weight with every hammer strike. Seriously? Do I need to witness this final nail in the coffin?

If fate exists, she's one evil bitch.

I turn and trace my finger over the hip-high door leading to the under-the-stairs closet. Inside is the crawl space where my older sister, Pippa, and I once played castle. Now I'm the only one left, a princess with a broken crown, my home a shattered kingdom.

Pippa is gone. The result of a stupid, preventable car accident followed by a grueling year where she lay suspended in a vegetative half-life while Dad, Mom, and I clung to a single, destructive lie: She will get better.

I learned my lesson. Things don't always work out for the best. False hope destroys quicker than despair.

Mom checked out, filed for divorce, and hides in her parents' Hawaiian compound where she dabbles in New Age quackery while nursing a discreet alcohol addiction. Dad recently crawled from the rubble, brushed clear the cobwebs, and returned to the business of life. He quit his cushy job with the U.S. Geological Survey and hit the road on his own midlife escapade, giving expedition cruise ship lectures.

The day we turned off Pippa's life support, our family died with her.

Breathe.

Terrible things happen if I allow myself to key up.

Come on—in and out. Good girl.

Better to say that Mom, Dad, and I stumbled to the other side, battered like characters at the end of a cheesy post-apocalyptic flick. I wouldn't go so far as to say life is easy but there's less falling shrapnel. These days, when I brave a glance to the horizon, the coast is actually clear—or maybe I'm just kidding myself.

I check my watch—still no sign of Sunny or Beth. I love my girls, hard. They rallied, stepped up, and closed ranks when I crawled home from Australia in June, heartsick and dazed from the fallout with one Brandon Lockhart. Even after Bran flew in unannounced to commence the world's most epic grovel, they remain suspicious.

Bran.

My heart kicks into fifth gear, like it always does, responding to the mere thought of his name. Tingles zing through my spine as I cover my mouth to hide my secret smile. Tonight, at 31,000 feet, I'll cross the International Date Line. Bran waits for me in Tomorrowland. Here's my golden opportunity to rebuild a life nearly torn from the hinges by stupid fucking obsessive-compulsive disorder.

I'm getting better and I'll only grow stronger. The next few months are organized around two major goals: (1) Give Bran every ounce of my giddy, dizzy love and (2) finish my senior thesis and graduate. My UCSC advisor approved my oral history project and a professor at the University of Tasmania agreed to supervise. Once that baby's done and dusted, our future waits, ready to shine.

"Everything's going to be okay," I whisper to Pippa, as if she's listening.

Either way, the words taste sweet.

"Knock, knock. Hey, who's the creeper out front?" Sunny breezes into the hollow void, once upon a time a disorderly foyer brimming with Dad's surfboards. She stops short and stares. "Holy demolition, Batman."

"Your house!" Beth enters half a step behind and slides up her Ray-Bans. "You doing okay?"

"Yeah, I guess so." My throat squeezes, making the next words difficult. "Looks pretty crazy, though, right?" Change, even for the best reasons, is still effing scary. I'm a California girl, born and raised in Santa Cruz, except for last year's roller-coaster study abroad. When I cruise around town, people here know my name.

And all the hoary, gory details of my family's slow disintegration.

In Australia, any personal details I share will be of my choosing. There's a certain freedom in anonymity. How many people are given a blank canvas, the chance to paint a whole new life alongside the guy who rocks their world?

"Earth to Talia." Sunny waves an ink-stained hand in front of my face. "Want your good-bye gift?"

Beth rolls her eyes. "You're not really giving that to her, are you?"

"Shut your face." Sunny thrusts me a small wrapped package. "It's hilarious. Talia will appreciate it. *She* has a sense of humor."

"Careful," Beth stage whispers, nudging my hip. "Someone's a little edgy this morning. Last night, Bodhi tried to define their relationship."

"Ruh-roh. Not the DTR!" I rip the present's paper along the seam. Bodhi, Sunny's current booty call, works as a diver on an abalone farm north of town. "Isn't that a strictly friends with benefits arrangement?"

"Not even." Sunny readjusts her infinity scarf, brows knit in annoyance. "Friendship implies the capacity for rudimentary conversation. Bodhi sports lickable biceps—no doubt—but that guy's one fry short of a Happy Meal. He's hump buddy material, pure and simple."

"Was he crushed?"

"Like a grape. He cried into his can of Natty Ice."

"Ugh."

"Poor guy, don't mock him." Beth is a whopping whole year

older and seems to find life purpose in playing the mature, responsible role. Pippa used to be the exact same way.

When our trio was a foursome.

"He made me hitch home at three a.m. I swear, I'm taking a guy break for a while." Sunny opens her baby blues extra wide as if to prove she really means this oft-repeated phrase.

"Yeah, right, until when? Next Tuesday?" Beth fires back.

These two bicker worse than an old married couple. But Beth has a point. Sunny breaks hearts up and down the coast. You could almost call it a hobby.

I crumple the wrapping paper into my fist. "Seriously?" Sunny's gift swings between my two fingers—a chef's apron with BAREFOOT AND PREGNANT embroidered across the chest. "Um, thanks?"

She giggles wickedly. "That's my prediction for you. By Christmas. Spring at the latest. Except you better add getting married into the equation. I don't want my pseudo-niece or nephew born into sin."

"Riiight, because living with a guy automatically translates into marriage and babies these days. Guys, I'm moving to Australia, not the 1950s."

My friends swap suspicious expressions. After we broke up, Bran flew to California in early July and begged for a second chance. I accepted and the subsequent week devolved into wild beach sex and mad plotting for our future. Beth and Sunny only caught glimpses of the guy who'd wrecking-balled my heart. They remain guarded, like two mother lionesses.

An adorable act if they weren't so annoying.

"Come on, living with a guy is a normal next step."

"Nothing about the Bran Situation is remotely normal," Sunny mutters.

Beth nods in rare agreement.

"I've always wanted to travel, haven't I?" I stuff the stupid apron into my duffel bag.

"This is hardly the Peace Corps." Beth throws my old dream in my face. The one I had before Pippa's accident, before my brains decided to double down on the crazy.

"Forget it." Sunny jumps to my defense and tosses a loose auburn wave over one shoulder. "I just need to get a grip...still can't believe you're leaving."

I force a smile. "You guys have so much going on you won't even notice I'm gone."

Beth's lined up a PR internship over the hill in Silicon Valley, and postgraduation Sunny is...well, the usual Sunny—cashiering at a natural foods store, never finishing her graphic novels, and hunting down her next conquest like a top predator on the African savannah. I hope my smile overrules the fizzy nervousness in my belly. "Don't forget, my visa is only for four months."

"So you keep saying." Beth hasn't dropped the concerned frown. "What comes after? Have you worked out a plan?"

"No, not exactly." I roll my shoulders. If there's one thing I hate in life, it's uncertainty. "Bran says we'll figure things out once I'm there. We have until December thirty-first to wrangle a solution."

The drop-dead date.

"And, what, he's some sort of immigration wizard?" Typical Beth, pushing to ensure every *i* is dotted, *t* crossed.

"Play nice." I sling my arm around her, getting perverse satisfaction from knuckle-mussing her perfectly straightened hair. "He's nervous enough that I might get cold feet and reconsider coming."

"Oh, you'll be coming, friend. Won't she, Bethanny?" Sunny can't resist the opportunity to tickle our girl.

"Get fucked, bitches." Beth squeals, breaking free. She's a gym rat, way stronger than she looks. "What are you guys, five-year-olds?"

"Don't be a poop."

Sunny's pouty descriptor rips startled laughter from my chest.

Beth is almost freakishly beautiful. She rocks her lululemon yoga wear better than a movie starlet. And right now she's not amused. "Sunny Letman, we've known each other since we were, what, zygotes?"

"At least embryos," I toss in my two cents through a giggle. We've been pals since our mothers introduced us in nursery co-op. Sunny and I drew the short straws, mothers who failed their daughters. Mine is lost in a fog of tropical denial while Sunny's mom shacks in a Nevada desert bunker with a wackadoo prepper awaiting Armageddon.

"Maybe it's time to grow up." Beth can front prim all she wants. But underneath that perfect ice-queen exterior, she's a weirdo too.

"Her first." I slap Sunny's butt.

Her response is an awkward twerk that cracks us all up.

I'm going to miss these two.

"Anyhoo." Sunny folds her arms and leans against the banister. "Can I please point out that you're committing a drastic error?"

Seriously?

"Call off the attack dogs, okay?" I say. "You guys really don't know him."

"Whoa, settle down, Miss Defensive. I'm talking about you bailing before October. The best time of year."

"Our time," Beth adds.

"Hmmm. You have a point." October is fantastic in Santa Cruz. The tourists vanish and each morning we wake to perfect bluebird skies, followed by afternoons warm enough for bikinis. The gloomy fog-locked summer retreats into a distant memory as the entire town descends to the beaches, surf breaks, and bike paths, reveling in the coastal goodness. "Still not enough to change my mind."

I love my girls but Bran is the only person with whom I've ever fully been myself. He noticed my OCD symptoms after five minutes and didn't laugh or run away screaming. Sunny and Beth might be my two best friends but even they don't know the real reason I didn't graduate on time. How my rituals and health anxiety spiraled so far out of control that I was placed on academic probation. Even now, I can't bring myself to tell them the truth. The awful facts are beyond embarrassing. Easier that they accepted my simple explanation that I "messed up." I mean, who challenges the dead girl's sister?

Bran's the only one who doesn't tiptoe on eggshells. He treats me like I've got strength, makes me believe I can face life.

Beth checks her phone. "Hey, we need to jet."

"That's all you're bringing?" Sunny points to my backpack and duffel bag.

"Yeah."

"Shut your face. Two bags?" She's a notorious pack rat, hovering on needing a hoarder intervention. Last week, I unearthed third-grade spelling tests from under her bed.

"I decided to pack Zen, practice unattachment."

"Uh-huh." Beth's not having it.

"Do I sound like my mom?"

"A little."

I cave. "Truth? Extra bag charges are a rip."

"Aha, there's the tight-ass girl I know." Sunny grabs my backpack.

"And love." Beth lifts the duffel.

"Oh wait." I grab a small moleskin journal from the stairs and unzip my backpack's top zipper, stowing the journal. The pages chronicle random happenings, unusual incidents, and amusing stories from while Bran and I were apart. Things I forgot to mention during our messenger chats or phone calls. I miss his voice, that surly accent, whispering to me in the dark. My nightly record-keeping allowed me to play make-believe, pretend Bran was nestled on the pillow beside me. The ritual became a precaution against the what-ifs slithering around the edge of my thoughts, ever vigilant, waiting for an opportunity to strike.

What if Bran meets someone else?

What if I say something so stupid he has no choice but to accept I'm an idiot? What if he decides I'm a freak? Okay, fine, he's never given cause for these thoughts, but what-ifs and worst-case scenarios are routine in my world. My brain is hardwired for catastrophic thinking.

Evil thoughts can go suck it.

My friends head out the front door and I need to follow suit.

"Are you okay to lock up?" I call to the Realtor.

"That's my job." Somewhere a tooth-whitening ad wants its smarmy smile back.

"Lucky you," I mutter under my breath while stomping down the front steps.

I shouldn't turn around. Or look at the dormer window where Pippa and I shared a room for nearly two decades. But I do. And I can't hold back the sudden tears.

Sunny pauses to rub my back, saying nothing. If she had her way, I'd cry every morning before breakfast. She thinks it's good for my soul. I find the whole enterprise draining and messy but better than the alternative—becoming an emotionless robot that shuts out the good along with the bad.

I had a great last summer, more or less. Now Bran waits to catch me at the bottom of the world.

"Going anyplace fun?" The Realtor wipes his forehead, perving on Sunny and Beth as they toss my two bags into Sunny's black Tacoma, the Batmobile. The gnarly old truck is a random vehicle choice for a fresh-faced redhead with a penchant for fairy tales.

Two pelicans crisscross overhead. In the distance, sea lions bark beneath the wharf, the site where I made the worst decision of my life.

Fuck clutching breadcrumbs.

Time to let go.

Embrace the art of getting lost.

What can go wrong, as long as I keep heading in the right direction?

The Realtor shifts his weight.

"Yeah," I say after an overlong pause. "I'm going somewhere great."

2

BRAN

$\mathscr{I}$ unlock my office door and trip over Karma's splayed legs. The fluorescent lights, detecting motion, glare on and he uncurls from a fetal position, lips smacking. Graduate student workstations are at a premium, so we're forced to double. I'm the only guy whose office mate never goes home. Karma studies tree hollow habitat in old growth forests, and lives under his desk to expand his beer and weed budget.

"G'day to you too." I sit down and fire up my machine.

"Bloody hell, what's the time?" Karma emerges, hikes up a pair of saggy corduroy shorts, and resets his ever-present fedora.

"Late one?"

"Weasel and I cruised a benefit show at the New Republic." A popular bar in North Hobart.

"Good?"

"Ace, mate. We raged until two. I'd have invited your punk ass but you were flat out getting shit ready for the American woman." Karma fists an imaginary microphone and belts the last two words like it's that song with the same title.

"Wanker."

He leans over my shoulder, inspecting the photograph of Talia on my desk, taken during our hike at Cradle Mountain. The trip where I asked her to be my girl, and she said yes. She's looking back over one shoulder, laughing at an inside joke, blond hair glossy in the late-afternoon sun. She glows, and I put that light in there. My throat grows thick—this shot helps me survive each mundane day.

I'm the luckiest bastard on the planet getting this girl's love.

Karma rubs the air like he's whacking off. "Your chick's got fantastic tits. No surprise why you're pussy-whipped."

I stand so fast my chair tips over. "There's this thing called a line? You fucking crossed it two sentences ago."

Karma throws his hands up. He's got a few inches on me but I'm not jerking around and he knows it.

"Duly noted, dude. No talk of girlfriend. Makes Hulk angry." He aims his thumb toward the open door. "Gonna go grab a juice. I'm dry as a nun's nasty this morning. Want one?"

"Nah. I'm good." I right my seat. "Got loads to do." Honors is a specialized year of study—in my case, modeling Antarctic ice-sheet response to climate change. At the end a thesis is created, written in heart's blood. I arrive on campus by eight most mornings, not biking home until after ten at night.

I tried to get ahead in my work before Talia's arrival tonight, but I'm barely above water. My fantasy Tasmanian outdoor lifestyle, with after-work surfs and cruisy weekend bushwalks, yeah that's not happening. I'm twenty-three and a desk jockey.

It blows.

"Mate?"

I glance up. Karma's got one hand on the doorknob while the other scratches down his pants. "I almost forgot—"

"Dude, don't spread your dick juice around here."

He grins. "Asshole."

"Fucker."

Karma and I have an odd friendship but it works, mostly. As long as his filthy mouth doesn't form a syllable of Talia's name.

I shove on my headphones, a signal not to bother me unless a zombie apocalypse threatens the Geography and Environmental Studies building.

"Guess you don't want to hear how my mate got accepted as crew with the Sea Alliance. They ship out in December."

Okay, he's got my attention. "No shit? That's sick." The Sea Alliance is a marine conservation organization that uses direct-action tactics to expose and confront illegal activities on the high seas. The International Whaling Commission enacted a moratorium on all commercial whaling without any enforcement capacity. Since then, over 25,000 whales have been slaughtered under the guise of scientific research. The Sea Alliance might take the law into their own hands, but they draw attention to the crisis and make a real difference.

Which is more than I can say about most of us.

"He says there's a few spots open. What do you say? Still keen to freeze your nuts off down south?"

Antarctica has haunted my dreams since I was a kid. The place at the end of the horizon—a true last frontier. Down there, shit's the real deal. A chance to discover what you're made of.

"Serious?"

"I'll ask him to put in a good word."

But I have Talia. Honors. I slump my shoulders and grind my eyes. There's no time for chasing pipe dreams. Too much happening. Good things. Bloody important stuff. Life's about negotiation, knowing when to compromise.

I sound like Dad.

"Timing sucks, dude."

"What? Your chick's got your nuts on lockdown?"

My stomach hardens. "Don't go there."

"Hey, I named no names." Karma shrugs. "I'm adhering to the agreement—our office code, if you will."

"The honors gets dibs on my soul until March. And fuck yeah, I want to be with my girl."

"Postpone honors—your supervisor's cool. What about She-Who-Can't-Be-Named?"

Talia would no doubt support me pursuing my dream but I reject the idea of long-distance relationships. My first love dissolved into an intercontinental affair and annihilated my heart. No second chances. Talia and I are staying together. I'm not going to blow this shot.

"Thanks for the offer. But I'm good."

"Yeah." Karma scans my desk, which is buried in academic journals, scrawled notes, and shriveled apple cores. "Living the dream."

———

I complete another tour around the baggage carousel and recheck the time. Hobart International Airport needs to review its name. The last overseas flights were canceled years ago.

The wall clock taunts me. Surely more than three minutes have elapsed since the last time I checked. The distant engine drone cuts

through the terminal chatter, growing steadily louder. My scalp
prickles. God, I despise air travel. Only a few more minutes and
she'll be safe on the ground, here in Tasmania, crossing the tarmac.
Breath bottles in my chest. I rub my palms on my jeans and pull
down my hat.

Talia.

A thousand images strike my brain like sudden lightning. Her
sexy lips quirking when she's privately amused or ragging on me.
Those bright eyes and wild hand gesticulations. The way my whole
body simultaneously revs and calms from her touch.

Muscles fire down my body's length, concentrating a heated
flare in one particular region.

Down, boy.

Fucking hell, I'm nervous.

A typical bogan, red-faced and outfitted in a faded rugby shirt,
jostles against me beside the arrival door. He fails to subdue the
supersize rose bouquet exploding out of his beefy arms. "How ya
goin', mate?" he asks with a proud shrug, proceeding to mistake my
aggravation for polite interest. "Got to treat the missus right, 'ey?"

I avoid humoring this blokey conversation by giving a curt nod.

Shit.

Talia isn't expecting flowers, is she?

The thought never occurred to me. I yank a retractable pen
from my back pocket and click the button.

Tick, tick, tick.

The bogan peers through the lifeless blooms; his thick lips
frown in my direction.

Tick, tick, tick.

Never understood the big attraction in giving a girl dead blos-
soms as a symbol of affection.

Tick, tick, tick.

The bogan grumbles under his breath and moves away.

I can't help irritating dudes like him. It's a gift.

Outside the terminal, a thunderous engine roar signals touchdown. The din dials to a high whining hum as the plane taxis. It's been two months since I flew halfway around the world and begged Talia for a second chance. Despite everything, a miracle happened. She took my dumb ass back. I wondered if she'd wise up, reconsider. Moving to Australia is a big deal. Takes effort, commitment. Would have been easy to back out.

Will she ever know—truly grasp—that I died a little every day waiting for her?

The first passengers trickle in, becoming a flood. I dismiss the unknown faces.

You don't matter.

Don't care about you either.

Or you, love. Shuffle along.

The crowd shifts.

There.

Familiar copper eyes lock with mine and doubt evaporates. In three steps—four if you count me sidestepping the human rosebush—Talia is in my arms.

"Hey, you," she whispers.

I spin her around and the whole world blurs like a piece of abstract art, our lips the only concrete entities. She tastes exactly the same—warm, salty, with a hint of mint. This is a kiss of victory. Talia and I, we pulled off an impossible stunt.

My hands slide up her back. There's a keyhole opening in the fabric between her shoulder blades. Her skin is satin smooth and she smells subtly delicious, like toffee. Our tongues entwine and my mind flatlines. Her body is holy ground. Our kiss a prayer. This girl is my own personal religion.

"Mmmm. Looks like someone's happy to see me." She does this little hip shimmy grind against my quick-fire erection.

I clear my throat, ears heating. "Maybe a little. How was the flight?"

"Long. They had those movie screen thingies on the seat backs. I tried falling asleep rewatching *Armageddon* but ended in a cry-a-thon somewhere over Polynesia." She stretches and muffles a yawn. Her shirt slips to reveal a perfectly curving hip.

"Get back here." I can't stop touching her, not for a second.

"That's pathetic, right?" She nestles into my arms. "I fell apart over Bruce Willis blowing himself up on an asteroid. We're talking the big, ugly tears. So not attractive."

"Whatever you say, Captain. You're beyond beautiful." That's no exaggeration. I drink her in, from that sleepy-eyed grin to the little skirt sporting a fantastic skin-to-fabric ratio. Kilimanjaro? Machu Picchu? Grand Canyon? Screw them all. I could happily watch her, and only her, forever.

"Wow." She draws a finger over my chest in the shape of a heart. "Nice kittens, hipster." Two cavort on my T-shirt.

"Since when is it a crime to fancy pussies?"

Her eye roll is perfectly executed even as she clutches my hand for dear life.

"Steady, don't test my gangsta, sweetheart." I swirl my tongue around her earlobe in the way she loves. "I'm no one to be trifled with."

I'm addicted to her startled gasps. Their memory has been my constant companion these dreary months. I'm about to cry like a total wanker. I screw my eyes shut and try to ride through the overload. I planned to play this reunion a little cooler.

Something bashes the back of my head and knocks off my hat. The big bogan's wife wacked me with that ridiculous greenhouse as she hustled by, beaming like she'd taken hold of an Olympic torch.

"Whoa." Talia freezes.

"I know, why buy one rose when twelve hundred will do?" I tap my heels against the floor and fight to regain equilibrium.

"I'm talking about your hair." She stares at the top of my head, lips parted. "Where'd it go?"

"Oh, that." I pass my hand over my cropped scalp. "Got too long."

"Makes you look different." Twin creases appear between her brows.

"That bad?" Crap. Have I put off my girl before we've even left the terminal?

"Riiiight."

My heart needs sunglasses to withstand her megawatt smile.

"Like you don't know how hot you look." She tilts her head in careful study. "Seriously, H.O.T."

"Well, all good, then." I fist my fallen hat.

"What's this? Mr. Self-Assured blushes? Quick, call the papers."

Self-assured? Hardly. This girl has an all-access pass to my soft underbelly.

"So can I stroke the new do or what?"

"Stroke me anywhere." I want to bite her amused pout. "Anytime."

She crowns my head with her hands and rubs lazy circles. "Oh yes. Me likey."

This isn't helping the situation in my pants. "Um, Talia?"

"Hmmm?" Her pupils are huge. Each pass of her fingers chisels my restraint and drives me toward the best insanity. I haven't had this girl in two months. The fact that she's not naked on the baggage carousel is a testament to my self-control.

"If you don't stop, I'm bending you over the closest luggage trolley."

She threads her hands around my neck and rises on her tiptoes until her forehead presses mine. "Is that a threat or an invitation?" Her teasing voice drops to an über-sexy level. I tried to cajole her into phone sex a few times during our separation but she always ended up convulsing into giggles. Not that I cared all that much; her laugh is cute as hell.

"Naughty."

"But nice." She winks in a way that wakes my soul.

I bury my face in her hair and breathe deep. The sweetness sends me floating, obliterates all bullshit stress. "God, I missed you." Her hands tighten on me, let me know I'm not alone in this wanting.

"Missed you more." A tremble passes through her.

I link her hand in mine. "Doubtful."

She swings herself under my arm, executing a twirl. "Come on, let's blow this Popsicle stand. We can debate the recipient of the Most Pathetic Pining Award from the road."

"Sorry, there's no contest." I lean into her with a playful shove. "You've caught yourself a winner."

I barely notice slinging her bags over my shoulders. Talia skips a few steps ahead. Brightness pours from her. She's so fucking joyful that people stop to watch her pass. And she's mine. I shake my head.

What did I get right to deserve this shot?

We walk to the parking lot. I unlock and open the passenger door to my Kingswood. "Your carriage, m'lady."

"Why thank you, good sir." She ducks in and her skirt slides to her upper thighs. She catches my hungry stare. "How long to your place?"

"Not far." I drum out a staccato beat on the car roof. "But I have a surprise first."

"Really?" She squeaks on the endnote.

"Key word—surprise." My girl isn't big on ambiguity.

"C'mon. A teeny-tiny hint. I *need* one."

I press a finger to my lips and slam her door.

3

TALIA

I study Bran's face. The short hair transforms his whole look and the change takes adjustment. I told no tales—he's as smoking as he was two months ago. More so even—less boyish with a new undercurrent of sexy manliness. The cut gives prominence to his striking face, those eyes, the strong jaw shadowed by a five o'clock shadow.

"Touch me." He keeps his gaze trained on the road. "Prove I'm not dreaming."

The space between our seats is the distance between lost and found. I settle my hand on his thigh and muscles flex beneath the worn denim.

"I'm glad I'm here," I murmur, nervous to unmask exactly how much, appear too desperate. Truth be told, vulnerability is one freaking scary ride.

"That's the year's understatement." His contagious smile burns away my doubt.

"I went a little crazy without you."

He grabs my hand and kisses the inside of my wrist. "Me too."

"Really?"

"Every single second. But now you're here and life's all good."

One side-eye glance and I squirm in my seat.

Je-sus.

When Bran flashes me that look, everything about our crazy plan, my move to Tasmania, an island best known for a slobbering cartoon with behavioral issues, seems sensible. I sport the same goofy grin that plasters my face while watching Ryan Gosling's rain scene during *The Notebook*.

Somehow, despite my talent in rampant fuckuppery, I won at life.

Bran and I are two loose ends who found a way to tie ourselves together. Here's the one person on the planet who fills my scaredy-cat heart with the same joy normally reserved for musical theater numbers. One where characters burst into spontaneous heel clicks or dance, arms flung out, through mountain meadows. He glimpsed my darkest, ugliest places and still thinks I'm the coolest.

I faced down his scars, his bitter rage. But those times are over.

Together, we stumble toward the light.

Bran releases my hand to downshift like a boss, fingers wrapped around the gear stick. Soon he'll touch me all over, like a landscape he intends to commit to memory. The idea melts me into a randy puddle. I fell asleep every night of our separation imagining those clever hands.

Well, *sleep* is a generous term for what amounted to me tossing, turning, and doing everything but slumbering. My salvation came from a plucky little sex toy purchased in Melbourne last semester. If I didn't own a vibrator, I'd have worn my fingers to nubs slaking my frustrated lust for this boy. I shift in my seat, a hot bundle of nerves.

My layover in Auckland Airport afforded me enough time to grab a soy latte, splash water on my face, and change underwear.

What I need is a hot shower, preferably for two.

No doubt I want to do dirty, dirty deeds with Bran in the near future. But there's this whole other thing—the thing my friends don't understand—the thing I can't quite explain. When Bran is close, my brain quiets. The compulsive urges and distracting thoughts don't seem to have enough room to take root. True, we share a chemistry more explosive than a mad lab experiment, but there's more going on, a feeling deeper than the body. If you burn away my bones, my love for him would remain, tattooed in the air.

He veers the car off the asphalt and we bump along a gravel road. "What are you thinking, thinker?"

"You're the ketchup to my fries."

"Here we say tomato sauce and chips."

"Doesn't have quite the same ring."

"Heh."

Gypsy jazz croons from his iPod while the Kingswood's headlights penetrate the darkness, affording glimpses of grazing long-tailed marsupials. Kangaroos, wallabies, potoroos—I have no actual idea. My knowledge of Australian wildlife is sourced from *Crocodile Hunter* reruns and the old nursery song that goes, *"Kookaburra sits in an old gum tree, merry, merry king of the bush is he..."*

"This the way home?" Home. The word tastes sweet on my tongue.

"Nope."

"Come on, dish. Where we going?" The front wheel drops into a serious pothole and I brace myself on the dash.

"Right here." He swings the Kingswood into a tight space before a tea tree thicket. The wheels crunch over dried leaves. There's a glimpse of ghostly white sand before he blacks the lights.

I look around. "Seriously. *Dónde estamos?*"

He flings open his door. "Seven Mile Beach."

This is so random. "Got an urge for a hike?"

"Not exactly."

"What—"

"I'm going to fuck you, Captain."

"Oh, well. Okay, then." My body explodes with the same mindless high-kicking joy displayed at National Cheerleading Championships. "Right now?"

"Yeah." He climbs from the car.

Thank sweet baby Jesus I swapped underwear. Beth bullied me into purchasing a whole new sexy set at Victoria's Secret last week. I'm sporting a black thong with more lace than cotton—a massive departure from my usual plain-Jane jockeys.

I unbuckle my seat belt as the passenger door flies open and Bran scoops me out.

"Whoa, Tiger."

"Couldn't wait another second." He eases me against the hood and a sound escapes him, like he's being strangled but in a good way. "Thank you," he mutters, brushing a stray hair from my face.

"For what?"

"Coming back—and wearing this very tiny skirt." He slides his hand over my thighs and pauses when he reaches the lace. "Hello, what do we have here?"

I cock my hip. "A little somethin' somethin'."

"I gotta see." He hikes my jean skirt to my waist.

"It's so dark, how can you possibly— Holy, wow."

Bran didn't mean a quick peek, but an up-close-and-personal inspection.

My God, what if someone comes? I'm arched against his car like a vintage pinup girl and there's a gorgeous guy with his face buried between my thighs. I grapple the windshield wipers because his tongue is all over the place, and his fingers everywhere else. Oh, wow, okay, someone is coming. Right here, right now. My inner muscles seize, seconds from frenzy.

"Not yet." He heaves back and fists his shirt, tearing the thin cotton free of his head. "Gotta be in you." He jerks on his buckle. I fumble with his zipper, more hindrance than help. Seeing *him* is still a shock. Before Bran, I'd believed penises were totally bizarre. The shape, the head, the slack mouth-breathing way dudes behave when you get within three feet of one. But my life is divided into two epochs: B.B. and A.B.—Before Bran and After Bran.

To the Before Bran Talia, penises were a necessary evil, a body part to tolerate.

The After Bran Talia is a convert—I drop to my knees, can't get him into my mouth fast enough.

He rocks, once, tentative. *This okay?* I grab his hips and urge him harder. He growls, grabs fistfuls of my hair, and fucks my mouth; there's no other polite word. He takes, I give, or maybe I'm taking, he's giving—by this point coherent thought is impossible.

"You. Now." I push myself to standing, press my hands on the hood, and hoist myself up.

He digs a foil from his back pocket and tears it open with his teeth.

"Stop."

"What?" His voice is a hoarse rasp.

"We..." I hesitate, a little shy. "I'd planned on announcing this in a slightly different way but I got on birth control."

He blinks and his abs flex in one hypnotic motion. "No condoms?"

"Nope," I whisper.

Within the span of a second, my pretty undies dangle from one ankle. He's right there, nudging against me.

I pass my hand down his face and his eyes close.

"Talia." He grinds out my name like he hurts. "I love you. You know that, right? I fucking love you."

"I love you too." I'm so wet that he enters me with zero effort.

"To feel you, like this." He groans. "Bloody intense."

I dig my heels into the bumper to find purchase, angle my hips up and back until he sinks to the hilt. His moan is thickly unintelligible. I grab his ass and slam him that last centimeter home. We freeze with the realization we're closer than ever before. I don't want this second to end but an instinctive drive takes hold. We start to move, the rhythm set by the distant, inexorable waves. He takes me hard, each thrust a pounding crash. I grapple his chest and he responds to my hunger, angles his length to hit my clit in exactly the right way, urges me closer with every stroke.

"Can't. Hang. On." He bites my shoulder.

"S'okay." My fingers lock on his hard triceps as the rest of me falls apart. "I'm coming."

Behind his head is a kaleidoscope of stars but there's an entire universe in his eyes. "Fuck, Talia." The whisper breaks from him like a violent devotion.

We explode in our own private big bang.

———

Bran back-kicks the front gate closed and I stumble up the walk, delirious but blissful. He opens the front door to the weatherboard cottage—our first place. The idea shoots a thrill through my core. The porch light reveals nail marks scoring his neck, scratches I put there. I don't want to imagine how I look. My mouth feels puffy and between my legs, a sweet soreness lingers. We didn't go easy on each other.

I didn't realize our separation would be so difficult. At times, I worried I'd become an addict, desperate for a fix. We Skyped multiple times a day, exchanged instant messages, and traded saucy pictures over Snapchat. Nevertheless, the contact was the equivalent of doling methadone to a junkie.

He drops my gear to the polished hardwood floor. The golden buttery color complements the creamy wallpaper. I didn't waste much time pondering the specifics of the place Bran rented us, at least not beyond the bedroom, but I expected more squalor.

This is an adult palace.

A stainless steel fridge and pot rack gleaming with copper cookware shine from the kitchen at the end of the hall. I'm not great at math but it doesn't take long for me to conduct a dismal tally of my personal finances.

"Whoa, this place...so not what I expected."

"Great, hey? I thought you'd appreciate that the house is heritage listed."

Uncertainty gnaws my stomach. I refused to acknowledge when Mom's monthly allowance dried up in my bank account this summer. To have done so would only play right into her passive-aggressive hands. Dad's career change is an opportunity of a lifetime but one that comes with a sharp pay reduction. No way can I hit him up for cash. For the first time in my life, I'm on my own to sink or swim. Sunny wrangled me seasonal cashier shifts at New Leaf, the health food store she works at, but the depressing fact cannot be ignored. My economic circumstances are sharply reduced.

"The house is gorgeous but rent's got to be insane, yeah?"

"Mind-boggling." Bran takes my hand and leads me up the wide staircase.

I swallow hard as we reach the landing and he tugs me through open French doors. From the wide windows, Hobart's lights twinkle down the hill, reflecting on the waterfront like a fairy kingdom. "I don't think I can afford—"

"It's free, Captain."

"Huh?" My jet-lagged brain is unable to produce anything close to an intelligent response.

"Free ninety-nine."

I don't detect sarcasm but the facts aren't computing.

"Did you perform gigolo services for a cougar pack?" I'm totally kidding, except not.

Seriously, how the hell did he pull this off?

"My uncle Chris hooked us up with a house-sitting gig. He qualified for long-service leave and he and his new boyfriend, Xavier, are on a grand tour: Asia, Europe, Africa, and North America. They'll be gone six months, and Xavier didn't want his house unoccupied. He also didn't fancy the idea of renting the place to strangers."

"Aren't we exactly that?"

"Chris worked his magic." Chris is Bran's uncle, estranged from the rest of the family. He lives in Hobart near the harbor, where he's employed as a federal bureaucrat by day but is blossoming into a genteel cross-dressing mystery writer by night. Bran is the only person in his family still on speaking terms with him. They are very different but have a strong bond forged through their mutual black sheep status and appreciation for black humor.

"We owe him, big-time."

"Chris digs you, Captain." He plucks a twig from my sex-snarled hair and his eyes catch a distant streetlight. "He's not the only one."

"Ready to go another round?" I nod at the massive four-poster bed.

"You know it."

We pounce on each other, punch-drunk with promise.

4

BRAN

*T*alia passes out hard from the travel and epic sex. I'm too
amped for sleep, so I lie in the dark and trace her spine.
Can you love someone too much? No point being afraid, might as
well jump in it with both feet. I press my mouth to her neck and she
undulates, responsive even from her dreams. If miracles were real,
I'd swear we were designed to fit together.

I loop my arm around her waist and hold fast, until our breathing
syncs. I'm drifting off when she jerks—hard—once, twice. Her
body recoils as she unleashes a lung-tearing scream.

"Talia, wake up. Come on, sweetheart, talk to me." I clamber
over her, hunching protectively. "Open your eyes. It's Bran. I've got
you. I'm not letting go." I keep talking while she flays my chest like
she's drowning under ice, desperate to find a break in the surface.

"Can't breathe. I can't breathe. I...where am...oh God. Bran."

"I'm right here." I cradle her while she draws another unsteady
gasp. Her hair plasters her forehead in sweaty wisps.

"Give me a minute. I'll be fine." She pushes herself to a half-sit
and sways with disorientation. "This...this happens sometimes...

panic attacks or night terrors…whatever. They seem to come when
I drop my guard. Or, I don't know, maybe it's the meds. Those pills
make me feel like a toxic waste dump."

"Have you been bad this summer?" The muscles in my neck
cord. It shreds my guts to see her hurting. I'd do anything, any
fucking thing, to carry her pain. I don't fully understand the
inner workings of OCD but she's explained that for her, the condition comes in waves. Everything will be rolling along fine, more
or less, and then bang—a giant squid grips her brain. She fights
hard for recovery, a warrior even when she believes she's nothing
but a coward.

"No, not really." She grinds her eyes with the backs of her
hands. "I kinda danced around the edge of the rabbit hole a few
times but never fell inside."

My muscles release some tension. "Try to go back to sleep. You
need the rest. Don't worry, I'll keep watch, okay?"

"I'm sorry to be such a psych job. It's totally shaming."

"Shhhhhh."

Her chin tips down. "Can you talk to me for a little while? Get
me out of my fuckball head?"

"Hey now, I got mad love for that head, Captain." I kiss her
brow, acting chill even though I'm scared. How can I get her to
settle? Then it hits me. "I want to take you surfing again."

"Mmmm, that'd be nice."

"Picture yourself out there, in the water, on a board, under the
shooting stars."

"With sharks eyeballing me from the depths?"

"Nah, they're all busy hunting sea lions or some bloody mischief. This is you, the sea, and the sky. A set rolls in. You can't make
out the wave. The board lifts and you feel the momentum building.

There's fear deep in your belly, sensible, because you can't see what's coming or where you're going. You fight the self-protective instincts, give yourself over, and the next thing you know—you're having the ride of your life."

"Thank you." She flips in my arms so we're belly to belly. "I mean it. That was beautiful, really, *really* beautiful. I'm so excited to be here, for right now—to live in the moment. But it's like I have this...this weird mental stutter. My thoughts keep skipping over the same annoying question like a scratch on vinyl: What will we do?" Tears spill from the corners of her eyes, course silently toward her chin. "My visa."

Talia's been granted a three-month student visa to complete her senior thesis in history. In all its benevolent generosity, the Australian government expanded her time in the country by an extra month.

Four months—the sum of our allotted time.

"They'll make me leave."

"Don't believe everything you think." I wipe her damp cheeks.

"Can you tattoo that on my forehead?"

Maybe it's my imagination, but the brass alarm clock on the dresser clicks louder.

Another second gone.

Another second gone.

"I'm not losing you to some shithouse immigration policy, Captain. We will be all right in the end." I've no idea how the hell I'm going to solve this drama but I will figure it out. "We have to hope, otherwise we're sunk."

She jerks with surprised laughter.

"What?"

She hiccups and covers her mouth with her hand, shoulders shaking. It takes me a second to realize she's giggling.

"I'm funny to you right now?" This girl drives me every sort of crazy.

"I'm not laughing *at* you." She works her lips together and unsuccessfully smothers the smile. "It's—"

"Forget it." I instinctively stiffen.

"Bran the Optimist." She grabs my wrists, lifts my palms to her face, and plants a kiss in the center of each one. "I like this side of you."

"Never mind. I was being dumb."

"You were awesome." She pecks the tip of my nose. "And for the record, I love your stupid face."

I give her a begrudging kiss back. "I love yours too."

Love isn't enough of a word.

I wasted almost an entire year of my life implementing a scorched earth policy, not caring who I left burned and broken in my path.

Talia was my oasis. My salvation.

"Don't give the visa a second thought." I nestle her against me, rubbing her lower back in easy circles. "I'll sort this out, I swear to you."

Even if I don't have the first fucking clue.

———

I rouse to the oily rich smell of fresh-brewed coffee. Talia perches on the edge of the bed wearing nothing but my ratty Wilderness League T-shirt. "Morning, sunshine," she chirps, and hands me a ceramic mug. "Time to wakey wakey."

I take a tentative sip. "Ouch, bloody hell."

"Want to hear a joke?"

"No." I hand her back the mug with a grimace.

"How did the hipster burn his tongue?"

The clock reads seven-fifteen. I slam a pillow over my head.

"He drank his coffee before it was cool."

"What have you done with my girlfriend?" From memory, Talia is not a dawn riser.

She wrestles the pillow from my clutches. "I'm not wasting our time sleeping." Her smile is over-bright, like she can deal last night's shadows a knockout punch through sheer force of will.

I squeeze her bare knee before walking my fingers up her inner thigh. "It's okay to relax, Captain. We'll be all right." Captain America is my pet name for her. I can't believe I'm in a relationship with nicknames and shit. It's good. Better than good.

"Yeah, I know." She averts her gaze. "Get up and at 'em. I wanted to fix you a home-cooked breakfast but the cupboards are bare. How about a run and then a trip to the grocery store?"

"A what?"

Her ears turn pink. "I thought we could go running. I mean, you do that, right?"

"Sure, but you?"

"I'm no ultramarathoner but I've been known to pound a little pavement."

I pull her onto my lap. "You're full of surprises."

She nestles against me and her hair is soft on my cheek. "Well, I'm normally more of a walk-jogger but if push comes to shove, I could take you down faster than a shin splint."

"Sure about that?"

"Careful—I'm scrappy."

"Little trash talker." I nip her neck. "When we were apart, how much did you miss me?"

"Well, I was pretty busy. You know, running super fast and stuff."

"That's it. You're going down."

One hilarious footrace later, we square off in the produce aisle at Hill Street Grocer.

"Wait a hot second." She grimaces at the bottom of the basket. "Zucchini is a hard limit for me."

"What the fuck does that mean?"

"It's a BDSM term—means a mutually agreed upon prohibited activity."

I can't hold back a snort. Jesus, the shit that comes out her mouth sometimes. "And when exactly were you ever into BDSM?"

"I read a certain book about a Mr. Grey like everyone else on the planet." She plucks out the zucchini.

"I don't read shite." I playfully wrestle the vegetable from her grasp.

"Maybe you should." Her coy over-the-shoulder grin slays me. "Could pick up a trick or two."

"Bloody hell."

She sashays closer; the way her hips swing gets me hard in a heartbeat. "Although I must confess—you have mad skills."

I drop the shopping basket and my hands migrate to her hips. "Flattery gets you everywhere."

She tugs my belt loop until we're hip to hip. "So no zucchini?"

"Fine, you win." I shove the veggie back onto the produce stand.

"Bran!"

I turn around and there's a chick with intricate sleeve tattoos all up in my space. "Hey?"

She smiles too wide, flashing a tongue stud. "You're coming to the department barbecue this arvo, right?"

The girl looks vaguely familiar. Oh, right, what's her name? Jacinda, or Jessica—one of the conservation ecology mob.

"Shoot, we have plans. Sorry." Talia plasters to my side, her teeth bared in a faux friendly grin. It's like watching a David Attenborough documentary where a cute, fluffy animal reveals razor-sharp fangs.

"O-okay, no worries. Another time maybe?" Jacinda/Jessica stutters an awkward good-bye and hightails it to the freezer section.

"Look at you, Captain."

"What?"

"Play nice." I grab for her hand.

She ducks out of range. "I'm all sugar and spice."

"Definitely spice."

"That girl's interested." There's a weird undercurrent to her tone.

The jealousy game was fun for half a second but nothing I want to become habitual.

"She doesn't even know me."

Talia makes a derisive sound. "Like that matters."

"All I know is that I'm into you." I go for a kiss and am surprised when she responds with more than a bit of tongue.

"Same."

"Cool."

Her eyes clear and we link hands, tour the aisles, entertained by each other's preferences.

"Coffee or tea?" she quizzes.

"Always tea. Always black."

"Weirdo."

Her partiality for soy. "Milk is sick. I mean, who suckles another species?"

"What about this tub of blackberry cheesecake ice cream you got so wet for?"

"Nasty, never use that word as an adjective ever again."

"Wet?"

"Stop! Anyway, the ice cream stays. Better you accept my inconsistencies earlier rather than later."

We negotiate breakfast cereals like members of the United Nations Security Council.

"Weet-Bix?" She jabs the box with a cautious finger.

"Yeah, it's great."

"There's zero sugar content."

"That's the whole point."

"Blech. Looks like cardboard." She eyes Coco Pops with undisclosed longing.

I steer her away. "Weet-Bix tastes like magic."

"Soon you'll try and ply me with Vegemite."

I pluck a jar of local leatherwood honey from the shelf. "Okay, fine. How about you drizzle cereal with sweet stuff, hey, sweetheart?"

"God, yes, please. Sold."

We poke fun of tabloid magazine covers in the checkout aisle. Grocery shopping, normally a mundane necessity, takes on an air of amusement park giddiness. We stroll home, bags heavy, crossing roundabouts and meandering along footpaths.

"Back there in the store..." Talia mutters something indistinct.

"Sorry?"

"The pretty girl."

"Jacinda? What about her?" Was she pretty? Bloody hell, I didn't even notice. Talia's sucked my senses into some sort of black hole.

"While we were apart…you didn't, I mean you never…or wanted…er, never mind."

I got around a bit before meeting Talia. And by a bit, I mean a shitload. But I haven't thought of another girl since last January.

"I never—"

"Wait, don't answer." She stops in her tracks and shakes her head. "Please, let it go, all right? Really, it's fine. I'm sorry for over-reacting. I know you wouldn't do anything dodgy."

"Talia, I—"

She covers my mouth and points to the street sign with the other. "Forest Road, this is us, right?"

"Yeah," I mumble through her fingers. "Typical misnomer." The gentrified neighborhood is dense, packed with elegant Federation homes, renovated within an inch of their lives. The front gardens are a carefully disheveled mix of jacarandas, camellias, wattles, and roses.

Roses—my mind jerks back to the previous night and the bogan with his cheesy flowers at the airport. He'd distracted me. "Shit."

"What?"

I drop the grocery bags and slip my backpack straps from my shoulders, rummaging in the depths. I can't believe I forgot, what a bloody idiot. "Here, I got you a welcome present."

"Seriously?" She clutches the white box like it's a rare diamond. Fuck, maybe I need to buy her pretty things more often. She pops the lid and squeaks.

"What do you think?"

She lifts the necklace. It's a thin chain with a tiny u-bolt bike charm on the end. "I love it."

"It's not roses."

"Roses?" She wrinkles her nose. "I hate roses."

My heart does this funny surge. Is she for real? "No girl hates roses."

"They're ordinary, so...so"—she waves her hand as if the missing word hovers between us—"so ubiquitous. C'mon, there's zero creativity involved in giving a girl roses."

"Talia?"

"Yeah?" Her smile is uncertain.

You're bloody perfect. "Have I mentioned you're a killer girlfriend?"

"Not today." She lets the necklace catch the sunlight.

"I love you and only you, Jacinda."

Her head snaps and I shoot her a cheeky smile.

"You are such a—"

"Fantastic, amazing boyfriend?" I grab the groceries and knee open the gate to our place. "The necklace is the first in a two-part gift, Captain. Set your bags on the steps and head around the side."

"Did you buy me a pony?"

"Humph." I lead her down a winding cobblestone path, under a wooden archway dripping with green foliage.

She freezes in front of the two bikes chained together.

"Hobart's so small we don't need a car that much. Better to save the dinosaur juice."

"OMG. You got me a pink fixie?" She crouches to reverently stroke a pedal.

I kneel beside her and kiss the sensitive spot behind her ear. "I like how they're so simple, you know? Like riding as a kid used to be. I found a bike mechanic and asked him to build it to spec."

She half turns and her mouth finds mine. "I adore it," she whispers. "Seriously. You're the best gift giver ever."

I lift her to standing and settle her against the weatherboards.

"I know you said you don't want to hear it, but some things need saying. I'll never—ever—think of another person this way in a hundred million years."

She traces my lips with her finger. "I was being stupid. Blame it on the jet lag. You're a babe. Girls would need to be blind not to notice you."

"Whenever I close my eyes, you're all I see."

"Are you about to serenade me with an eighties power ballad? Not going to lie, that would be badass."

I go in for a kiss.

"Wait, can't someone see us?"

"Nah." I nod at the dense jungly bower, my pelvis anchoring her in place. "Not through all that."

"Bran."

I nuzzle her skin, so fucking hot when she moans my name.

"Stop. Bran, Jesus, stop." She yanks down her shirt, face frozen.

Behind the fence, next door, a man stands immobilized at the side entry. The bloke's in his midsixties, shirtless, with a hairy gut that falls between his hips and knees. "Don't mind me none." He raises a weathered garden hose. "Watering me tomatoes."

My fists ball. How long has he been watching? "Bloody pervert."

"Hey, now." He gives a slow leer. "I'm not the one with my tits out, am I?"

Talia covers her face. "Oh, for God's sake." Her shoulders convulse. It takes me a second to realize she's cracking up.

"Show's over." What a bloody cluster.

"Come back tomorrow," Talia calls out, and I snicker.

"Pack of nutters." The neighbor shakes his head, tosses his hose down, and ambles back inside.

"Fucking bogan." My retort is aimed loud enough to be heard

over the slamming door. I pull Talia close. "Sorry about that. Not exactly what I had in mind."

"I think we're done here, unless you want that creeper jerking in the bushes."

"My nuts crawl off at the thought."

"Can't have that."

We tear along the path, gather the groceries, killing ourselves laughing any time our gazes meet.

My phone rings while I grapple the bags at the front door.

Talia lifts the mobile from my pocket, checks the screen, and snorts. "Wow, weird. Karma is calling."

"Let it go to message."

"Is that an actual name or a joke?"

"Haven't I mentioned him? He's my office mate."

"Shut the door. You'll let the flies in," drawls a sneering voice from the dining nook.

5

TALIA

*T*he hell?" I levitate, my heart slamming into my trachea.

A striking gutter punk slouches over a beer bottle at the kitchen table. He parts his black dreads, takes aim with one finger, and fires in my direction.

"Um, hello?" I slant Bran a glance. *Who's the sketcher?*

"This her?"

"Karm…" Bran's growly tone is an ominous warning.

Karm? Oh, right, Karma—the office mate. What's with the feral sprite act?

"Hey there, I'm Talia, Bran's girlfriend." I warily extend my hand.

Karma tips back and half sings, half chants under his breath, *"There my pretty lady is, river-woman's daughter, slender as the willow-wand, clearer than the water."*

"Cool it with the Tom Bombadil already." Bran passes a hand over his dark scruff.

I'm lost and it shows.

"Tom Bombadil—minor character from *Lord of the Rings*." Bran's busy engaging Karma in an intense stare-off.

"He's the master of the Old Forest." Karma blinks first, dropping the chair legs to the floor with a dull thud.

"Hang on." My best friend, Sunny, worships Tolkien. I read *Lord of the Rings* a few years ago and vaguely recall the Tom Bombadil chapters. "Isn't he the character who prances around Middle Earth while everyone's about to get skull-fucked by the Dark Lord?"

"That's sacrilege," Karma shoots back.

"We're a grocery bag short." Bran's cough might be a strangled laugh. "Hey, mate, try not to annoy my girlfriend to death while I go grab it from outside."

Despite Karma's nonchalant smile, those unnervingly light blue eyes are straight up Judgy McJudgerson. How am I supposed to engage in small talk when the guy stares me down like I'm a Magic Eye poster?

I clear my throat. "You're a student?"

"Allegedly."

"What do you get up to?"

"This, that."

"Wow. Sounds fun."

"Maybe."

What's crawled in this guy's ass? I tap my toes inside my Mary Janes. One…two…three…

Stop it!

His sneer shows he derives enjoyment from inflicting conversational torture. I fight the urge to swat an imaginary mosquito.

"I knew a chick from the States once."

"Yeah?"

He rubs a silver ear gauge. "Native American."

"Cool, from where?"

"Montana. Her accent was great, kind of a guitar twang. Nothing like yours."

Bran comes back with the missing bag while I'm hunting for a suitable comeback.

"Did you fill her in on our 'arrangement' yet?" Karma makes air quotes.

"Have I missed some vital detail?" My head swivels to Bran. If this jerk-off thinks he's shacking with us, we're having all sorts of words.

Bran's got his head buried in the fridge, unloading produce. "Karm comes round to use the kitchen and shower."

"Plumbing problems at your place?"

Karma shrugs. "I live at the office."

"Uh, wait…at the university?" My eyebrows squish together.

"On the DL."

"How long are you planning to milk that scheme?" What a total freeloader.

He dismisses me to retie a faded black bandana around his neck.

"Don't you get scholarship money, same as Bran?"

"What are you, the uni police?"

"Dude, lay off." Bran finally steps in. "Talia just arrived. We need privacy."

Karma doesn't budge.

"Mate." Bran dials to testy.

Karma adopts an exaggerated pondering pose before snapping his fingers. "Oooh, riiiiiight. This is my cue to leave. I get it. No worries." He pauses, looking straight through me. "Hey, bro, I head out of town tomorrow for a little mischief."

"Yeah?" Bran perks.

Karma gestures in my direction.

"Chill with the paranoia, dude. She's cool."

"You sure about that?" Karma says with a smirk.

How had I initially thought this douche canoe was attractive? I've scraped better-looking chewing gum off the bottom of my shoe.

"Talia, are you an informant?" Bran asks.

"My contract work is strictly CIA."

Karm grabs a scuffed long board. "There are plans afoot to block access to a timber mill. Want in?"

"Nah. I'm good." Bran loops his arm around my waist.

"Right-o." Karma's lips press flat. "Things to do, I see how it is."

"Awesome meeting you," I chirp, hoping my little finger waggle adds salt to his sullenness.

Dang, his phony grin is as good as mine.

We all stand there smiling like freakish Cheshire cats.

"So, good-bye, then," I add helpfully, wishing time would speed up.

"I'll cruise to Weasel's pad. Sayonara, Tal-i-a." He draws out my name long and slow like it's a joke.

Except I'm not laughing. This guy puts me on edge.

Bran bites his lip as I mouth, *Weasel?* behind Karma's back.

Karma pauses and slaps his forehead with ham-handed exaggeration. "Oh, I almost forgot. I came bearing a message from our mutual friend on the Sea Allia—"

"I'll walk you out." Bran's good humor vanishes.

Karma issues me a parting salute and ambles down the corridor after Bran.

———

Bran's lost in another galaxy tonight as he braces his hands on the sink and scowls at the bathroom mirror. He grabs his toothbrush and works it furiously around his mouth. I study the Ouroboros inked on his chest, the self-eating snake—a symbol of infinity. The tattoo is half light and half dark, his permanent reminder that there's no brightness without shadow.

He stiffens, discovering me resting my head against the door frame.

"What?"

"Enjoying the show." I blatantly perv on his shirtless status.

He tosses the brush on the counter. "I haven't surfed in weeks, getting outta shape."

My gaze lasers over the cut muscles bookending his laddered abs. "Then I'm terrified by what you think of me."

"You?" His clouded expression lifts. "Whatever, Captain. You're perfect."

He comes closer.

"Um, is that a swagger?"

"Maybe." His hands slide around my waist, dip at the small of my back, and squeeze lower. My Italian heritage packs serious curve in my badonkadonk.

"Hey there!"

"You're so bloody hot."

Despite my disagreement, I refuse to demean myself with one of those pointless "But I'm so fat," "No, you're not, babe" conversations. That dynamic reminds me of my mom and dad's relationship, and homie don't play like that. Instead, I push on. "What's the deal with your new best buddy?"

"Mmmph." Bran's hands explore my ass.

I searched him out for a purpose and this isn't it—at least not yet. I break contact. "I want to discuss Karma."

A flicker of annoyance crosses his face. "What about him?"

"Besides the fact that he appears to loathe my guts for no reason?"

"He's crap around pretty girls."

"That's psycho. Still, I need to talk to you. The acoustics in this house are amazing." I overheard enough of their conversation this afternoon not to want to let things stand. "He called you a sellout."

"Don't worry about it."

"Worry is my middle name, remember?"

"Karma lives to stir shit. I'm over drama, aren't you?"

"Yes…" I've had enough for a lifetime. "But…" Bran's narrowing eyes check me for half a second before my own temper kicks into motion. "Are you trying to intimidate me?"

"No." His lips compress into a white slash.

"Hey now, don't go getting all…all Branish."

"Then leave off digging for trouble where there is none."

"What's bothering you?"

"Captain—"

"Don't Captain me unless you want to be straight."

"What the fuck?" He folds his arms behind his head. "Drop the fixation that something needs to be wrong."

Self-doubt steals into my mind. Yes, I obsess. It's what I do. But I didn't hallucinate the frustration etched in Bran's features after Karma bailed. Even now uncertainty flickers behind those soulful green eyes.

He *is* off, growing pricklier by the moment.

My muscles knot, jumpy from the undercurrent of tension.

"Want to get worked up? Knock yourself out, you're on your own." He makes to push past me, executing a classic duck and run.

"Hold it." I poke my finger into his chest.

His ribs lurch but he halts, panther-like, wary and riveted.

"Don't shut down."

"I'm not."

"Dirty liar."

I'm rewarded with a hint of a dry smile.

I don't have a clue why Karma set him off but I'm not yielding an inch. I tangoed enough with Bran's broody alter ego last semester—not a fun paradox—more like 50 percent minefield, 50 percent mind-fuck.

The boy seeks control with single-minded focus, and this very moment he's directing all his energy to closing me out. Screw that. My nail tip accidently bites into his olive skin. I push harder, disturbed by my urge to hug and hurt him at the same time.

Bran's beautiful face is impassive, his expression a little bored, but his body whispers a different tale. Beneath the scant inches of skin and bone, his heart accelerates. If anything, he leans into my touch, dares me to go rougher. The space between us charges, like the instant before an electrical storm.

"What do you want?" he growls.

"The truth. You're upset. Maybe I can help. Answer my question—what was Karma talking about earlier?"

"Screw Karma. It doesn't matter."

"How are you selling out?"

He slams his mouth shut and shoots me his best "What are you gonna do about it?" expression.

"Throw me a freaking bone already." I take a deep breath.

Can't lose my cool; he wants me to get angry so it's easier to push me away.

His right hand opens and closes in an even beat. A clue he's not quite the emotionless badass he might like to front.

I trace my tongue along the back of my teeth. A plan glimmers, one with definite legs. Sure, my plot requires a little stolen creativity and some serious bravery—at least for me—but it's all I got.

"Let's get out of here." My voice comes out calm, deceptively authoritative, even as my stomach churns.

A muscle tics on his temple. "And go...?"

"It's a surprise. Get dressed and wait by the car. I'll pack and be out in ten."

"I don't want to play—"

"I'm not the enemy." It takes everything I have not to break his gaze.

The glow in his green eyes intensifies. "I know."

"Good. See you in a few minutes."

6

BRAN

I fidget against the side of my Kingswood. The streetlight is glaring, shielding most of the stars. Talia is taking forever. What's her mysterious plan? A long walk? Some big heart-to-heart? I'm not in the mood. I stalk around the car, seconds from calling the game off, when she opens the front door and pauses—silhouetted by the hall light—dressed in my favorite black hoodie.

Hold up—why is she wearing my backpack?

"Where are your boards?" She steps onto the veranda and flips her hair.

I'm shocked into silence. She wants to surf? Now? Out of all the possible options she could have suggested, she lands on the most unexpected.

"Check it." She points to the sky. "There's a full moon—or close enough."

A rope tightens deep in my guts, a tug-of-war between pure love and self-defense. This girl gets me in a way that's scary, finds uncanny means to expose things I'd rather keep hidden. I bound onto the footpath and lean against the gate. "Come on, Captain. Let's go back inside. Get some sleep."

She skips down the steps. "No way. I don't know what's up but I refuse to sit around watching you build the Great Wall of China."

"You're cold." I lean forward and tug the hoodie cord. She's got a gray wool beanie pulled low over her forehead.

"I'm fine." She taps the backpack. "I bought a new wet suit—a fancy 4/3 job that's sealed *and* taped. Plus boots and gloves. I'll be snug as a bug in a rug, or in this case—neoprene. I grabbed your wet suit, too, and towels—don't know where you stash the boards."

The breeze ruffles my hair. The wind's a light northerly and there is a reasonable south swell on. Talia's right—the moon is almost full.

I rub the back of my neck, considering. "We could drive over to South Arm, takes about thirty minutes. Clifton's a good bet—there's a decent beach break with consistent surf."

"What are we waiting for?"

Is this real enthusiasm or bravado?

"How much did you surf this summer?"

"Maybe once a week, more than ever before." She lays her head on my shoulder.

I'm tempted. Night surfs are addictive, facing the nothingness, senses on high alert. But with Talia's skill level—she's better than she admits but isn't much past a beginner—I don't want to get her into the wrong situation for the wrong reasons.

"I'm a little nervous but all good." How does she do that—read my brain? Or maybe I'm putting out less than encouraging subliminal messages.

She's trying to be brave for me and so I need to return the favor. "Fine, we'll give it a go. The boards are in the backyard. I'll grab them."

An hour later I'm zipping the back of Talia's wet suit at the edge of the tide line. Moonlight glimmers on the black water. The waves line up perfectly, peeling clean. I breathe deep, savoring the air's briny tang and the musty smell of decomposing kelp. My awareness is sharpened by anticipation, the five senses amplified by the dark.

Talia shuffles at my side, getting antsy.

"You sure about this?"

"Yes. Well, sure enough."

Another set breaks. The conditions are choice. If she changes her mind, I might need to have a ride—a quick one.

Maybe two, tops.

"What's that noise?" She stills. "There it is again. Can you hear it?"

I concentrate and smile when a sound like a wheezing donkey drifts from beyond the breakers. "Fairy penguin."

"Shut up! There are penguins around here?"

"Sure. In the summer they build burrows in the scrub along the coast. If you stand outside a colony right after sunset, things get pretty noisy."

"Penguins." She almost whispers the word. "That's so cool."

The wash races over the sand and breaks across our toes. I figure out a plan of attack. "We'll paddle to the left shoulder where the wave's less steep. Stick with me, okay?" No one else is out and my voice feels extra loud even though I'm speaking quiet.

"Have you ever been to Rome?" She takes my hand.

"No, not yet."

"Me neither. But I can't imagine the Sistine Chapel being more amazing than this."

Besides the moon, there's zero light pollution. The Milky Way arches in a dazzling band across the sky's apex. Individual stars are indistinguishable in the brilliant haze.

"You ready?"

She squeezes my hand in reply.

We paddle out.

"Whoa!" She pushes her chest up to better peer over her board's tip. Around us the water casts a luminous green-blue light.

"Phosphorescence. Cool, eh? It's blooming phytoplankton, caused by this marine species of dinoflagellates releasing enzymes that—"

"That's enough, Sid the Science Kid. Let me retain this fairy kingdom illusion a little while longer."

"Science *is* cool, Captain."

"I never said— Oh, crap!"

Instead of duck-diving under the incoming wave, the water wall pounds her in the face. She breaks through the other side, coughing out a lung.

"We can head back to shore, don't have to—"

"I'm fine. Please. There's a wave coming. I can feel the pull. Can you?"

"You want it?"

"It's all yours."

I take off on a left break and fly down the smooth face. For a few perfect seconds, I'm right here in the moment. Rational thought is eclipsed and with it the aggravating confusion of having everything: Talia, Tasmania, honors, and still hungering for more like a greedy bastard. I paddle back to her.

"You looked great."

"That was good."

She sits, bobbing lightly. "It's not as freaky out here as I imagined."

"Fucking hell, Captain. You said you weren't scared."

"No, I never did. I'm scared by everything. But I want to do this."

We're quiet. A few more waves come but I let them go, happy to be with my girl, the stars, and the radiant water.

Hard not to believe in magic on such a night.

She clears her throat. "About what happened back at the house...if this is going to work, you can't shut me out. You're not just a you anymore; we're an us. We have to be there for each other."

I bob on my board and drag my fingers through the water. The phosphorescence lights from my touch. Finally I speak. "Karma's got this mate; he's on the crew of a Sea Alliance vessel. There's an opening for a gig, with voyages to Japan and Antarctica."

"You want to go for it?" I can't decipher her expression.

I almost say no, but honesty's easier in the anonymous dark. "Yeah, kinda. But I want to be with you more."

"Oh, Bran, that's way too much pressure."

"What do you mean?"

"Imagine coming home in a few months and I'm all vegged on the couch, watching awful reality television. Will you think to yourself, 'I could be gallantly defending the high seas but instead I'm attached to this boring anchor'?"

"Life with you is bound to be a lot of things, but boring isn't the first depiction that springs to mind."

"But life isn't always night surfing. I...I can't compete against a fantasy."

"I never said you had to."

"Isn't supporting the other's goals a fundamental part of the good girlfriend/boyfriend job description? I mean, say I always wanted to volunteer in Africa? Join the Peace Corps."

"Do you?"

"I used to toy around with the idea. Now? I'm not sure but I don't want to close myself off to opportunities."

"We can travel through Africa someday."

"Peace Corps is one of my dreams, not yours. I want you to have the freedom to pursue your own happiness."

"You make me happy." I strike my words like flint before sucking in a rough breath. "Look, I'm not a guy cut out for the long-distance thing. I hated every second we were apart the last two months."

"Bran..." She reaches out her hand and I take hold. "I won't let go."

"Me neither." I scrutinize the sky, heart clanging. Everything appears so deceptively still. In reality, the Earth careens through space. Talia and I, we're little specks of cosmic dust in the grand scheme. It wouldn't take much to blow away from each other.

"But in the future—"

"I hear what you're saying and I appreciate the support. But the only future I'm willing to discuss is the one where it's me and you—together."

Better to orbit far away from black holes.

———

The front door slams and Talia's boot heels click down the corridor. I blink into my untouched tea. How long have I been zoning? I palm the side of the mug and the ceramic is cool to the touch. She doesn't notice me hunched in the dusky twilight as she drops her computer bag to the counter with a heavy sigh and flicks on the electric teakettle.

Living with her is going great except for that one time Karma came round, hell-bent on a good rabble-rouse. We haven't revisited the idea she floated during the night surf session, doing the long-distance thing. Maybe I'm a coward but fuck it, everyone's entitled to a line in the sand.

This afternoon, I couldn't focus and eventually lost the wrestling match with my statistics. I bailed uni earlier than normal. I'm developing a computer model measuring ice-sheet change in the Antarctic. My frustration was compounded by Karma's empty desk. He disappeared to an old growth forest that's under threat from logging. I swear the dude is never working on his project.

He invited me and—big surprise—I turned him down. I need to forge ahead with my all-important research.

Yeah, right.

Everyone with a functioning brain knows the ice caps are melting. Climate change is real and human caused. We are screwing over the planet.

At first, I convinced myself this project was a way to fight back. But I'm only bearing witness to an inevitable global train wreck like everyone else. Next week, a grove of ancient trees may stand and Karma will know he helped keep them there. Meanwhile, I'll have mastered a tricky spot of advanced mathematics, and more ice will disappear.

Talia dangles a tea bag in the air, watches it swing like a pendulum, and yawns. She's flung herself full-tilt into her senior thesis and volunteer project with the National Refugee Action Project. She narrowly avoided failing her program in California. She claims to be improving, but I'm not so sure. I've done enough Google research to know OCD doesn't turn on and off like a bloody light switch. The condition is chronic, lapses not uncommon.

Talia drops the tea bag into a mug and pours hot water from the kettle. She stares into the cup and dumps the water. I'm about to announce my presence when she refills the mug and dumps again.

Alarms clang in my brain.

She drops the kettle like the handle burst into flames and unplugs the cord from the wall. She wraps her hands around her waist, face averted. I can't see her expression as she walks through the kitchen methodically unplugging each appliance. I keep having to plug stuff back in around the house but didn't make the connection until now.

Dread tears an angry hole in my stomach like an open-pit mine.

Stupid shit—how didn't you notice?

I can't fail her, need to do better. I try to think of something to say, anything to break this useless silence. But I don't speak the magic fucking language to make her shit disappear. The only word I can find is the one that matters most of all.

"Talia?"

"Jesus." She lurches with a squeak. "You scared the crap out of me."

"What's up?" No bullshit, not with her.

She finger-combs her hair and moves to kiss me on the cheek. "Oooooh, you smell good."

Quite the deflection.

Her cheeks glow pink from the early spring weather. If I hadn't spied her a second ago, I'd have imagined everything was great. Doubt sinks through my chest like a lead balloon.

How many times has she played me off like this?

"How was your day, dear?" Her cute-as-hell smile is sweetly ironic.

"The usual school shit."

"Poor boy. Want some tea? I'm getting hooked." Talia heads to the counter, the picture of innocence. Way too fucking innocent. There's a slight tremble when she pours me a cup.

She wonders what I saw.

Inspiration strikes. "I'll grab some biscuits." I walk to the pantry and rummage for the Tim Tams—Talia's favorite. This is a cheap shot, but when do I ever play fair?

I stride to the opposite side of the kitchen island and toss down the packet. "Go on, then." I brace my elbows on the granite countertop. "Take *one*."

She licks her lips and shoves her hands into her back pockets. "That's okay. I'm not hungry."

She knows what I'm asking.

The tapping, the rocking, the plugs. Her OCD is flaring and she doesn't want me to know.

I'm reduced to this test and that's bullshit.

One of her compulsions—the first one I ever noticed—is to eat food in pairs. She can't take a bite of one thing or three things. It's two or nothing. She'll starve rather than fight the urge. Her belief in magical thinking won't tolerate deviation; otherwise she believes bad things will happen. The ritual seems awkward as hell to hide, except she's skillful enough most people never notice.

Unluckily for her, I'm not most people. When it comes to Talia, I don't miss a trick.

"Don't, please." She backs away, like I'm dangerous—a threat. Not going to lie, it hurts. But I need to be there, waiting to push back in case she steps too close to the edge. It's a crappy role to play, one that she gets angry at, resents and rails against. And thanks me for three days later.

"You understand why I'm asking, don't you?"

Her chin drops to her chest. "I can't."

"When were you going to tell me things were getting bad?"

"I don't know. I keep hoping it's temporary. That I'll get a handle."

"Are you still taking your medication?"

"Yes." The word comes out soft even as pain darkens her eyes.

"Have you contacted a shrink?"

Her next blink is slow. "Not yet."

"Talia."

"I will. I'm planning to."

"You need to keep me in the loop."

"I know."

My heart stutters. "You promised."

"I *know*." Her glare is vicious.

"Talia—"

"I get it, Bran, okay? Remember, I don't choose this." She offers a brittle laugh, on the verge of tears. "God. I bore myself. I don't want you to get sick of me too."

I hate what I've got to do. But I do it anyway. "What makes you so special?"

"Excuse me?"

"Seriously." I get all up in her space.

Her eyes widen. "I've never said I'm more special than anyone else."

I'm challenging her because this is her rational brain talking. Not the part she hides. The OCD place that whispers she *is* special.

Marked.

Tainted.

I make this big show of screwing up my face.

"What are you doing?"

"Thinking about dying."

"What? Shut up. Stop."

I pop a biscuit into my mouth and speak through the chocolate crumbs. "I'm going to choke and die right now."

"Seriously, quit."

"Painful way to go, yes. But also delicious."

"You're nuts." She knows magical thinking—that a fear will manifest just by thinking it—is stupid. But what she knows and what she believes can be two vastly separate things.

"Okay, your turn."

She stops giggling. "My turn what?"

"To think a bad thought."

"Um, I'm pretty sure I'm an expert."

"Knock me out, prove your talent, hot stuff."

"That's okay, I'm good." Her gaze skitters away.

Even though I'm acting casual, like this is all a big joke, I mean every word. "Go on, one tiny terrible thought."

"You aren't letting this go, are you?"

"Nope. Might as well fold."

She blows out her cheeks and ruffles her hair so it stands up in adorable little spikes.

"You look like an annoyed echidna." I trace the crooked furrow between her brows.

"Echidna? The little hedgehog-looking dudes?" She rumples her hair. "Wow. Way to make a girl feel special."

"I love those guys. They're prickly but petable."

"Hah. Okay, you're on. One tiny bad thought." She delicately breaks a Tim Tam into two equal halves. "If I only bite one, something bad will happen."

"Like?"

She shrugs. "You'll resent me for being here, screwing up your life."

This is the closest she's come to revisiting the Sea Alliance position.

"Not going to happen." I point to the Tim Tam. "Take one bite. Only one."

She stares at the biscuit. For a second I'm positive she'll refuse but she shoves the single section into her mouth and chews with her eyes closed.

I want to kiss the crumbs scattered on her lower lip.

She opens one eye. "Ugh. I'm a hot mess. Why do you even like me?"

"I don't."

Her pretty mouth falls open. But I hate the resigned expression in her eyes. Like she isn't surprised.

"I fucking love you."

"Why?"

"Are you really going to ask me that?"

"Yes. Because I seriously don't have the first clue."

Am I really going to admit this?

"I've got fifty thousand reasons, but let's start with one. Your hair."

She stares at me like out of all the reasons in all of the world, I landed on the most random.

Crap. My palms are sweaty.

"IknewIprobablylovedyouwhenIcouldn'tstopthinkingabout yourhair."

"Huh?"

"Look, when we met in Melbourne? You drove me crazy. I didn't know what was happening. I remember driving you to that beach house party. We were bickering and you were a pain in the ass. But I couldn't stop noticing your hair, how pretty it was, with all those different colors."

She's biting the inside of her cheeks. But hey, her eyes dance with new light. That's worth any pain and suffering.

"Guys don't think like that without cause, I promise." I grab her waist and ignore her high-pitched protest as I settle her ass on the counter, step between her open legs to nuzzle her cheeks, still cool from the walk home.

"I want a brain transplant."

My butterfly kisses travel over her forehead and her brow unclenches. I'm dying to promise her that I'll fix everything. But this isn't a fucking fairy tale. I can't rearrange the way she's hard-wired. She needs to deal. Otherwise she'll crack and what if there's a time I'm not right there to pick up the pieces?

7

TALIA

*I*f I squander five more minutes of life deciphering this video software manual, I'll throw an adult temper tantrum. I'm in the University of Tasmania library working on my senior project that is going like gangbusters except for my pathetic lack of technical prowess. My thesis is on the importance of oral history, using the National Refugee Action Project as my case study. To work with the organization, I needed to agree to volunteer, gather digital footage for interviews. After a crash course in camera training at the NRAP office, I've gathered some raw footage and need to practice editing the material. I'm supposed to produce the few clips available for streaming on the organization's new website, give Joe Public a window to the exile experience, with the aim to break down xenophobia and build understanding.

As a lowly undergrad, I stick to preauthorized questions, designed to draw people out without crossing cultural red lines. Project participants are from protracted refugee situations, meaning they've been displaced in Australia for over five years. They come from places synonymous with horror and war: Afghanistan,

Burma, and East Africa. I've been assigned people who volunteer around the office, ones who self-selected to participate.

Even though the participants are friendly, the situation is still awkward. Or maybe that's just me. I'm much better interacting with a computer than speaking to strangers sitting a few feet away—always terrified I'll say something wildly wrong. Blurt out a question that will open scars or trigger unnecessary trauma.

To help settle my nerves, I've figured out a few tricks to loosen things up while I'm fumbling with the lighting and microphones. Food talk seems to work best. Memories of taste have yielded incredibly rich conversations. For example, tips on selecting the ripest mangos in a Hpa-an market; musing over the heady fragrance of caramelized sugar, saffron, and garam masala in a traditional Afghani rice pilaf; and rhapsodizing about the rich, spongy goodness of *injera*—the national dish of Eritrea.

There is such beauty in the world, and yet, once I start asking my few basic questions, there are glimpses of so much pain, so much sadness right beneath the smiling surface. My own life has been laughably safe and privileged by comparison. I devote insane amounts of time to stressing over imaginary what-ifs and fantasy dooms, when these people faced the actual abyss: physical torture, loss of homeland, family slaughter.

I sit back in my chair and try to swallow. Guilt sinks sour hooks into my belly, creates the opportunity for festering anxiety.

Here we go, trying to make everything about you. So lame.

Sometimes I hate myself. I really do.

I settle my hands on my thighs, slow my quickening breath, and focus on a centering image.

Bran, always Bran.

I don't want to be a screwed up annoyasaurus stomping around his life, chased by fictional tyrannosaurus rexes. He deserves my best self, not a train wreck who counts to feel normal, checks and rechecks electrical sockets, or scans their body for signs of terminal illness before opening their eyes in the morning.

Stop focusing on the shit. Find the goodness...

Life with Bran has its share of surprises. Once you get past the prickliness, he can be quite sweetly domestic. He knows his way around the kitchen way better than me. Turns out he spent a significant chunk of his childhood pestering his family's chef. Yeah—a personal family chef. I mean, my family is loaded, at least on Mom's side. My great-great-grandfather made a killing by literally killing the coastal redwood forests in the nineteenth century. But I've got the sneaking suspicion Bran's family puts my yuppie mother and grandparents to shame.

I've never met any of them, although Gaby, his older sister, calls every Sunday night. His parents are based in Singapore and spend most of the year traveling for business. Bran has been estranged from them for years. Ever since he chained himself to a bulldozer at a logging site funded by a company his dad financed. The protest received media attention and when his picture hit the papers, his parents viewed the action as a fundamental rejection of the Lockhart name. Bran renounced his expected destiny of hedge fund investments and Scrooge McDuck money baths to embrace environmental studies.

I wonder if I'll ever meet his family. The idea scares the crap out of me.

One Somali woman I interviewed yesterday, Amina, described her fractious relationship with her in-laws. Her father-in-law once beat her for overcooking a goat. So, really, in the grand scheme of things, I've zero cause to fret about an encounter with Bran's parents. Besides, they're hardly in-laws. Bran and I aren't in a rush to get married. We're in our early twenties. The topic is not even up for discussion. That's mental territory to ponder, too psycho even for me.

I tip forward, thumping my forehead on the thick manual.

"G'day. Seat taken?" Phil—Dr. Conway technically, but he's all "call me Phil"—slides into the chair opposite me at the library table. He's got a warm smile plastered across his broad, whiskered face. I'm not sure why he likes me so much but I'm grateful for his kindness. He did me a solid when negotiating with the University of Santa Cruz history department's powers-that-be to sponsor my senior thesis project.

He really, *really* didn't have to help me.

We met at a pub when Bran and I took an impromptu trip to Hobart last semester. Phil shares my interest in oral history, serves on the board for the National Refugee Action Project, and is keen for me to get my feet wet with what to a professor and researcher of his clout amounts to an insignificant side project.

"How're you going?" Phil places his travel mug on the table and crosses his hands over his impressive belly, looking like Santa Claus's amiable younger brother.

"Great. Awesome. Everything is coming together swimmingly."

"Really?"

"Uh-huh." I beam my shiniest, most confident smile.

"Then you won't mind me asking why you were headbanging the table a moment ago."

Shit.

"You saw that, huh?"

"Are you going to enlighten me?"

"Don't worry, it's nothing." Crap, it's impossible to look into such a kind face and bald-face lie. "Well, nothing to do with school."

"I'm listening."

"Why you'd subject yourself to twentysomething ramblings is a mystery."

"We were all there once upon a time."

"First off, the videos are coming along great. Sure, there are few little bumps." I drum my fingers on the video-editing manual. "Techno kinks. But I'm getting better." And as soon as I say the words, truth infuses me. I *am* pretty good at this. The interviewees are opening up to me, getting comfortable, and being real. I have a good instinctive sense about when to ask a follow-up question or when to pull back if we stray too close to a hurt that's not ready to be opened. The thesis is basically writing itself.

So why am I struggling?

"Is it possible to have a quarter-life crisis?"

"Go on." He takes a sip from his coffee.

"It's just that I...I don't know what to do."

"With?"

"The rest of my life." The words spill out in a cathartic rush. "I'm almost an official college graduate. Meaning I need to *do* something—ideally a noble endeavor filled with satisfying purpose and a good income. Underlining the situation in slashing red marker is the fact that my boyfriend is Australian and cannot work in the U.S. and I am American and can't pursue legal employment in Oz."

Sucks to hear the situation spelled out in black and white—the perfect cocktail for a bender leading nowhere but the world's worst hangover.

"Surely you've considered pursuing a career in international development?"

"Sorry, what?" My outburst spiraled me somewhere in the outer reaches of the Milky Way. Phil's question yanks me back to the present at warp speed and I'm a little disoriented. "Development?"

"You'd be a natural."

"I used to imagine doing the Peace Corps, our version of Australian Volunteers International." A beam of hope flares in my brain's recesses. "Wait, maybe they have projects here? In the country?"

"Australia's the first world, love." Phil dashes the dream with a bemused shake of the head.

"Right. Crap. Sorry, I mean that's good and everything. For you guys." Just shitty for me. The Peace Corps—my old dream with a snowball's chance in hell for actual attainment. I mean, how would that work? I'll go dig water wells in the sub-Sahara and shoot Bran the occasional postcard? Yeah, that'll go over big with Mr. No Long Distance.

Since when do you base all your life decisions on a guy?

Since I fell in love, stupid brain.

Bran refuses to broach the subject but I know he wants to work on the Sea Alliance. That crew posting would be the opportunity of a lifetime—

"All I'm saying is think about it." Phil checks his watch and stands. "Have I ever told you about my daughter?"

I smother a smile. It's a standing joke around the history department how Phil introduces his daughter into almost every conversation. She's his only child and he's a crazy proud dad. She works with an aboriginal community in Arnhem Land, as out as a person can expect to get in the outback. Phil carries a photo of her in his wallet from when she was five and has a face coated with chocolate ice cream. The sweetly corny gesture reminds me of my own dad and for a second, tears threaten.

"Sharon had a fella back in uni—a nice kid. Good bloke. They were mad about each other."

"Why am I sensing this isn't going to end well?"

"She was offered a posting in Alice but turned it down."

Alice, as in Alice Springs. A small town near the country's center.

He waits for me to ask why.

I'm incapable of refusing. "What happened?"

"Her fella wanted to live in Sydney, the big city life. She didn't want to lose him, so she followed. Now, are you curious how long things lasted?"

"They're married, live in the suburbs, and have a pack of ankle biters?"

"Two months." He raises the same number of fingers to emphasize the point.

"That sucks."

"Indeed. But she learned a valuable lesson. If a bloke isn't willing to sacrifice for your dreams, he isn't worth a single sand grain from your hourglass."

"Pretty poetic, Phil. I'll keep that in mind."

"Please do. Well, I'm off, department meetings call. Take care, and remember, Talia, my door is always open."

"Thanks, Phil."

He shuffles away, the thinning patch on the top of his head

reflecting under the skylight as he heads down the stairs, giving him a spiritual, prophetic aura.

I return to my manual with a muffled groan. I like being in Australia. Love living with Bran. But my visa expires soon.

What's going to happen?

I can't very well go all illegal alien. I won't be able to find work. Bran can't support us on his scholarship, nor would I ever go for that. A thought flickers in the back of my mind—we both come from families with more money than the average bear. I immediately snuff out the idea.

No way. That's *so* not an option. Neither of us are trustafarians. If this experiment is going to work, it's got to be on our own terms.

I spend the next hour staring sightlessly at text, seeing instead African savannahs, South American high deserts, densely tropical Southeast Asian rainforests.

Why not dust off the Peace Corps plan? I don't want to spend my time watching *Kardashians* reruns, bitching about the government, and obsessing over my sparse résumé.

I want to *do*.

Bran has his honors, a passion for environmental activism. I don't want to be the lame girl who sits back while her guy charges forward.

I need a focus more important than the shitty wiring in my head.

But I *want* Bran too. Life without him is inconceivable. We've gone through so much in such a short amount of time.

Gah.

I shove my books into my bag and march out of the library, straight into a cold drizzle that perfectly matches my mood. I unchain my bike and start pedaling, with no particular direction. Any movement is welcome to release this muscle tension.

The mist transforms to a steely volley, needling my eyeballs. A coffee shop sits on the corner—the cheerful retro décor stands as a promising beacon from the storm. I jump off my fixie and u-bolt the frame to a bike stand. I have to recheck the lock seven times before it feels right to walk away. By the time I reach the door, hands over my head in a failed self-umbrella attempt, I'm soaked.

I wipe away my soggy bangs and place an order—soy cappuccino—with the charmingly gay barista and decide desperate times call for a massive slice of flourless chocolate cake. The only open table is in the far back beside four elderly chaps engaged in intense conversation.

I take a seat and can't help eavesdropping given the men's propensity to holler rather than use indoor voices.

"I'm going to go ahead and share a piece of advice, Graham." One man pauses for dramatic effect, pours a cup of tea. "Involve your ego less."

"My point exactly." Another adjusts his spectacles with a sage nod. "See here, Graham. I must speak to your constant attempts to wall off the world. What's the worst that could happen if you take a chance? You'll find yourself banging around like a bloody pinball machine?"

The poor guy they're ganging up on, presumably Graham, squirms in his chair.

"All I know is if you don't make a change, you'll have a stroke, be a goner like Baz."

You and me both, buddy.

What is this, a grumpy old men support group? Their standard-issue uniform is baggy khaki pants, suspenders, and fanny packs. I fight the urge to give the gang a collective cuddle. They are pretty dang adorbs.

"Change—a big word, easy to say, hard to do. Who here has the will to plunge boldly into life?" Graham jabs his finger in my direction. "That girl there?"

I'm forking a massive bite of cake and resist the urge to duck when eight eyes squint in my direction. Yeah, that's me they're talking about.

"That one? Nah, she's probably too busy thinking about her boyfriend."

"Adventure is wasted on the youth."

Touché, Old Man Grumpy.

I open my MacBook. I'll read about a few Peace Corps programs, take a little look, that's all.

Show these grumblers I'm no one to be trifled with.

Sure, I think about my boyfriend. When did that become a state crime? I didn't throw away my life for a guy. I moved across the world to be with Bran. The two points are so hugely different they don't even invite comparison.

Sunny and Beth might have their doubts, but they're my friends; their job is to watch my back. Sure, Bran messed up a few months ago. But I mess up too. All the time. What matters is that together, we create something beautiful from the chaos.

My friends don't get that there's no one like Bran, not for me. My whole body sings when we're close. He gets me on a basic, instinctive level.

Should I care what a table of old, crusty men think about me?

No.

My friends?

No.

I came to Australia for me, because Bran's a choice, not a dependency.

And a month from now, what will you call it?

No way around it. In a month and a half I'm SOL. I'll have a nice bachelor's in history, a perfectly useless qualification in a country that doesn't want me. I can't twiddle my thumbs on a tourist visa, cook and clean for Bran. Anyway, I suck in both those arenas.

My calf twitches.

No—maybe I imagined it.

Wait, shit.

There it is again, except farther down, close to my ankle.

What the eff? Multiple sclerosis? The first sign of ALS?

Or me being an idiot.

There we go, the most likely diagnosis.

This is what my body does at the first whiff of stress. Goes into total Kermit flail mode until I have no choice but to seek comfort in compulsions—counting, reassurance seeking—ritualized behavior in an attempt to change the paradigm.

Why is this happening? I take my medication. No, I haven't made time for therapy yet. Why? Because I'm an idiot. Everything is fine for me until it's not.

Shit a brick.

Shhhh. Breathe. Just breathe.

Remember Bran's words. When he asked what makes me so special. Why do I need to be the one struck down with a rare mystery illness? I'm fine—just hate ambiguity. After a shaky sip of coffee, fear releases the death grip on my lower abdomen and slithers away. I resist the urge to fist bump.

See? I can handle this.

I can beat this.

Google stares at me, cursor blinking with expectation. I'm not going on WebMD, so I one-finger type, *How do I become a Peace Corps volunteer?*

There's nothing wrong with information gathering.

Right?

8

BRAN

October

 alia and I proclaim Sunday an unofficial study day. October snuck in like a thief in the night and our school demands are mounting. We arrange workstations at the dining room table, clatter our respective keyboards, play barefoot footsie, and listen to Nick Drake.

"Argh!"

I raise my head, brain function mired in a statistical swamp.

Talia grimaces. "My contacts are itchy, driving me insane."

"Did you sleep in them again?" She misplaced her glasses and hates being unable to see.

"Yeah." She blinks. "There, better."

"You only have one pair of eyes, Captain."

"Okay, Dad."

"No worries. You'll be a hot blind chick."

We resume typing. After another hour she heads to the fridge and pokes around.

"What's that?"

She glances at her glass bottle. "Kombucha."

"Do I even want to know what that is?"

"It's like a fermented tea."

"There's weird shit floating in the bottom."

"Oh, that's just part of the SCOBY, a collection of yeast and bacteria."

"And you want to put that into your body why exactly?"

"This stuff's super good for you."

"Sounds like snake oil."

She huffs in the way that shows she doesn't really have a good retort. "Here, try a sip. There's a slight vinegary odor but—"

"Uh-uh. No way, it smells like old man piss."

"I don't want to know how you can make that claim with any sort of confidence."

"Seriously, get the bottle away before I puke."

"Suit yourself, you big baby."

"How am I supposed to kiss you with that in your system?"

"I'm sure you'll figure something out. Hey, wait!" She slaps her forehead. "Oh shit, is it the tenth?"

I check the calendar icon at the bottom of my screen. "Yeah."

"Crapballs, I spaced paying off my credit card. This sucks, I'm too broke for late fees." She slouches and scrunches her nose. "Fact. I pretty much suck at adulthood."

"Huh?"

"You know, being a functioning grown-up."

I trace my foot along her calf. "And what do adults do, in your expert opinion?"

"Pay their bills in a timely fashion? Buy potpourri? Maintain a ready supply of clean hand towels in the bathroom?"

"Doesn't sound optimal."

"I know, right?"

"Fuck it, want another coffee?"

She grins. "Yeah."

I make the brew extra strong and when I give her the mug, I peek down her tank top. Any motivation to wrestle data evaporates into a rush of lust at the sight of her black lace bra.

I search out her secrets with my lips and tongue—the addictive hollow above her clavicle, that sensitive inch of real estate behind her left ear. These places outrank Machu Picchu or the Taj Mahal as wonders of the world. Rain, intermittent all morning, comes down harder, rattling the tin roof.

"What is something you haven't done?" She pulls back, her gaze thoughtful.

Her eyes are the exact shade of a perfectly brewed cup of tea.

"Sexually, I mean," she continues. "You've been with, what, like a hundred girls?"

"No." Not quite. Besides, I'm done with all that. Last year was one long rage, each body a distraction spiraling me farther from myself. I despise that guy. After I met Talia, I drove a spike into his heart, buried him under the crossroads. I hate when she mentions those other girls. I want to forget ever touching someone who isn't her.

"I've slept with two guys, and a drunken beach hookup should only half count. That leaves you as the sum total of my experience."

A chill zings through my spine. "What are you saying? You want permission to screw the footy team, boost your numbers?"

"No. I mean I want to push myself."

"Sex sex is nothing. Love sex is better." I nuzzle her throat, hoping this crafty maneuver throws her off track. "Talia sex is unreal."

"Why is this a big deal? I just want to know I'm the first person who ever *did* something with you."

"Oh, you've done something, little girl." Why doesn't she get it? She's the fire in my frozen heart. The hello in my long good-bye. The best goddamn thing that ever happened to my shithouse life.

"Hang on." She ducks from my kisses and her fingers race over the laptop keys.

I'm horny as hell and she's doing…what? "You better not be updating your Facebook status."

"Here, wow, what about this?"

I glance to the screen and freeze. "For fuck's sake, YouPorn? You're joking."

"This is strictly for research purposes." She bites her lip, regarding the grainy gyrations like they are nothing more than complicated dance maneuvers. "Whoa, so to pull this off you'd have to slide in and twist to a one-eighty. Dude, check it, you can even keep going for a full three-sixty. Who dreams this stuff up?"

She catches my hesitation.

"Oh my gawd, you've done this? Seriously? What are you, MacGyver?"

"That guy must be ancient these days."

"True, so you're the younger hyper-sexualized reincarnation."

"Hardly."

"Okay, what about this one?"

The cheesy action in the soft-lit video seems convoluted but in reality it's not that hard to pull off.

"Yes or no?"

I groan. "Yeah, I guess. Look, I don't want to—"

"I'm starting to freak out here."

"Exactly. Back away from the porn, Talia. Real life is best." I slide my hand down the front of her shirt and tease her sexy bra.

"Wait, wait. I got it! Here's my Hail Mary pass."

I give the screen a reluctant glace. And do an immediate double take. "What the...? I don't even know if I *could* do that."

The level of determination on her face is unsettling. "Let's try."

I circle her nipple. "I'm good with the usual."

"We're not even a quarter century; we shouldn't have a usual." She runs her thumb over her lower lip in the way that means I'm screwed, going to agree to anything.

"We don't—"

"Pretty please with kisses on top?"

"Fine. You know I can't resist that cute-as-hell face."

Five minutes later we're both buck-ass naked in front of the refrigerator. Her thighs clench my neck while I brace myself, swaying like we're on a ship under storm.

"You okay?" Her face is right in my dick. "You're being quiet."

"I'm trying to focus, don't want to drop you."

"The blood is rushing to my head."

"Ready to admit defeat?"

"Never, we are doing this."

"I want to have sex—not be a bloody circus monkey."

"Okay, I'm going in." She sucks me halfway into her hot little mouth. My back muscles tense. This is crazy shit, but not bad. Maybe she has a point. She's right in my face, so I start to kiss her back. She squeaks in a good way. We keep it going for a minute or two. It's fine, borderline great, but it's not—

"Bran?"

"Hmmmm."

"I think I prefer our usual way."

I lower her down. "Thank Christ."

So we do the typical on the kitchen floor, and as usual, it's extraordinary.

———

Our study day turns into a study-each-other's-body day. By nightfall we're half asleep on the couch. I'm in my boxers and she's in my shirt.

"It's chilly," she says, warming her frigid feet on my stomach.

I suck in hard. "Why are girls always so cold?"

"Why are guys always so hot?"

"Do you really want an answer?"

She giggles. "I kind of walked right into that one, huh? Rubs, please."

I massage her feet. "We should move."

"Yeah."

"I can't."

"Me neither." She relaxes into my touch and snuggles against the throw pillow. "This is exactly what I hoped for, coming here."

I kiss her big toe. "Me too."

"Except for one thing."

I still. "Yeah?"

"Why don't Australian houses have freaking central heat?"

"Some places do. But most of the time people wear jumpers and get busy with space heaters."

"What's a jumper?"

"Knitted, long-sleeved garment thingo?"

"Oh, a sweater. Why do you call it a jumper? Do you jump around in one?"

"A sweater is better? Sweat? Makes me think of moist dampness."

"Moist? Sick." She nods at the fireplace. "That thing work?"

"Probably."

Her eyes are all warm and sexy. "Ooooh, be manly and build me a big Cro-Magnon fire."

Twenty minutes later, we are wrapped in quilts on the floor in front of a cheerful blaze. While I chopped wood, Talia made hot chocolate and discovered a beat-up version of Monopoly.

"No," I say. "Don't even think about asking me to play."

"What? Who hates board games?" She stares at me like I announced a talent for drop-kicking kittens.

"I have never liked games. Ever."

"Cards?"

"Even worse."

"Please, please, please, play Monopoly with me."

"Stop batting those lashes. I'm not digging the capitalist gleam in your eyes."

"Oh my God, you're like two seconds away from breaking out a creepy Guy Fawkes mask, aren't you? I'm talking Hasbro, not *V for Vendetta*. Come on, I *love* me some Monopoly."

"What a capitalist—typical American."

"So speaketh the prodigal son of a captain of industry." She pokes out her tongue. "Stop trying to occupy our living room. Monopoly is my favorite. We're playing—right here, right now."

"You are the only person on the planet I let talk to me this way."

"And you are the only person on the planet who matters."

My ribs ache as if her words bruised me. The way she so freely throws out her love, sometimes I'm unprepared and the sweetness packs a mean punch.

At night as we go to bed, I plant a kiss on her shoulder. "Today was good."

"Hells to the yeah, I won Park Place *and* Boardwalk."

I tickle around her belly button.

"I know what you mean." She cuddles into my arms, words running together as she drifts to sleep. "Everything's better with you."

9

TALIA

I'm in St. David's Park, a lush walled-off green space fringing downtown Hobart. For fifteen minutes, I've contorted myself into sun salutations beneath this blackwood tree. I should snap a yoga selfie and send it to Mom, might make her proud.

Yeah, right.

My monkey brain shows no signs of assuming a half-lotus. Serenity is one elusive bitch. I squeeze my eyes shut and try to flash-freeze my mind into smooth ice, impervious to stimulus, but all I see is the e-mail from this morning—the one I printed because reading the words on my laptop didn't feel real.

The Peace Corps wants to interview me.

I'd filled out the online application as a game, my special-edition version of "What Can Talia Do with Her Life?" Pressing SEND was the equivalent of playing dodgeball with the universe. I suck at dodgeball, never hit anything. There wasn't supposed to be an actual response, especially not within days.

I take an *Ujjayi* breath through my nose, deep and diaphragmatic. Air percolates to my lower belly, then my ribs, and finally my chest and throat. I exhale in the same measured rhythm. Better. The nearby traffic mutes beneath the sound of tree branches squeaking in the wind. A magpie warbles and a skateboard clitter-clatters along the sidewalk, halting abruptly, right in front of me.

I lift my head and an involuntary groan slips out. Inner calm escapes me faster than a released helium balloon.

"G'day to you, too, sunshine." Karma hops off his long board, knocks his dreads behind his shoulders, and quirks his mouth into a bitter smile.

I drop into downward-facing dog, thrust my hips to the sky, straighten my back. Maybe if I look like a serious yogi, he'll leave me the hell alone.

"Where's your man?"

"At school, working." I don't add, "Where you should probably be," but it's there, hanging unspoken in the air.

"You're really into him, huh? Think you're all in love?"

Like I'm going to answer such a mocking tone.

"It's his big dick."

"Excuse me?" I fall to my knees.

Karma grabs his crotch. "Don't tell me he's not rocking a baby's arm down there. No way, my boy's probably got a thick, fat—"

"Please tell me you didn't equate genitalia to the limb of a baby."

"All I'm saying—"

"Enough." I stave him off with a warning hand. "Sweet Baby Jesus, I threw up in my mouth a little."

"Aw, I'm tensing you?"

My temples pulse with a sudden headache. What if I call him out for being an A-grade asshat? He'll get snarky and I could get agitated. Lose control. Rant. Everyone in the park will stare and that's it, I'll snap—go ballistic…bonkers. People will be called. I'll be restrained in a straitjacket and deported to a psychiatric ward where medication and claustrophobia will spiral me in a viciously crazy yet inescapable cycle. In thirty years, I'll be a haggard old woman feeding pigeons dried breadcrumbs, chattering to them like they're my best friends, which of course they will be.

"Talia?" Karma gives me a weird expression, almost like he gives two shits. "You all right in there?"

How do I even respond?

Oh, don't mind me, just catastrophizing again.

Instead I opt for, "You must have better things to do than annoy me. I mean, isn't there a door nearby you can slam your head into?"

The momentary concern I glimpsed on Karma's face must have been another figment of my hamster-wheel imagination, a mere fleck of dust in his unnerving eyes, the same empty blue as a glass of water. He reaches under a thick dread and untucks a roll-your-own from behind his ear. "You can bend over again." He shoves the cigarette into the corner of his sneering mouth. "Go on, don't mind me."

"You have got to be joking."

"I never kid about a hot ass in yoga pants."

"Wow. How'd you like me telling Bran about this convo?"

"Knock yourself out, love. Here's what he'll say: 'Fucking hell, Karm, don't make me kick your punk ass.'"

I got to hand it to him, that deep-timbered snarl was perfectly Branish.

Karma rummages a lighter from his patched-up corduroys and lights his cigarette.

I wave away the stinky smoke. "Riddle me this, you want to fight Big Timber?"

"Yeah?" He eyes me suspiciously.

"What about Big Tobacco? You keep them in business and what do they peddle? Death."

"Culling."

I set my hands on my hips.

He exhales a smoke ring and pokes his finger through the center. "Humans are a disease, a canker sore on the planet. I'm doing my bit."

"Killing yourself with lung cancer? Way to fight the system." I stand and wipe the grass from my butt. "Because I think—"

"What's with Americans and talking? You lot never shut up."

"Why do you hate me so much?"

He looks surprised. "Who said anything about hate?"

"You've despised me since day one, but I've done nothing to you."

"Not to *me*, that's true."

"Who?" Then it hits me. "You don't like that I'm with him?"

"I assume you mean Bran."

"Yeah, that's it, right?"

"I don't like watching a restless Yank, a little Dorothy, skip off to Oz, hoping to find better days over the rainbow. She latches on to my mate—who's bloody brilliant by the way—and hijacks his life."

This is more or less exactly what's been causing me so much stress. I don't have a grand plan for my life, so I focus on the one bright part on my map, Bran, rather than figuring out my own direction.

"We love each other." My voice is too testy. I bite the inside of my cheek and turn away, muttering, "Not that I expect your reptilian brain to grasp such a concept."

"Everyone loves to be loved. But there's bigger things at stake than you getting the requisite number of bedtime cuddles."

"Fuck off, Karma."

"Looky here, the kitten has claws. All I'm saying is there's plenty of fish in the sea who'd love to tap that ass, take you for picnics, listen to all your deep thoughts. But someone like Bran, he's meant for more—"

"Are you in love with him? I mean—that's fine, no judgment."

"Me? A homo?" He laughs for real this time, rips off his fedora and knocks the brim against one lanky leg. "Should I invite you back to my place and show you how wrong you are?"

"I'll assume you mean the office, at uni, the one you share with my boyfriend? I'm not sure that qualifies as an actual place."

He grunts, resets his hat.

I lift my bike and toss my leg over the seat. "I'm going to pretend this conversation never happened. But if you ever run your mouth off like this to me again—"

"Dropped something."

Shit, he's holding the printout I made from the Peace Corps e-mail.

"Give that back."

"Must be important, how curious."

"It's nothing."

He opens the paper and I can see his gaze scanning the words. "Hmmm. Look at you, going all Choose-Your-Own-Adventure like a big girl. Maybe I pegged you wrong, Na-ta-li-a."

I hate how he drags out my name.

"Volunteering in Africa? Funny, I didn't expect Bran to be cool with that sort of arrangement."

"He doesn't know. My visa expires December thirty-first. I need to keep my options open."

"Curiouser and curiouser. You might not be as shithouse for him as I imagined."

"Wow, thanks for the glowing recommendation."

"Did Bran tell you about the Sea Alliance position?"

"Yes."

And by yes, I mean he communicated the bare minimum required by the English language.

"He'd be a perfect candidate, what with his small boat certificate, competent waterman skills, and the fact that he speaks bloody Japanese."

Japanese?

"We're discussing all options," I say, resisting the urge to cross my fingers.

"You in the Peace Corps, Bran in the Sea Alliance—might be a happy ending after all."

"I'm stumped as to whether you're actually a nice guy or a total prick."

"Prick? Nah. More like a hard, throbbing—"

"Okay, okay, I get the idea. Can you resist the urge to tattletale about this e-mail?"

He mimes locking his lips and hands me back the paper.

"I'm serious." I shove the printed e-mail into my backpack. "This is important."

"So am I. I'm no rat." He says this with unexpected vehemence.

"I'm not sure if I like you."

"No worries, no one does."

"I'm probably not going to do it."

"Why would you?" He hops back on his board and pushes off, calling over his shoulder, "You've got Bran's coattails to ride!"

10

BRAN

J keep a solid rhythm along the trail's stony incline. Earth underfoot, fresh air in my lungs. I'm free for a change from the sterile death trap masquerading as an office. I duck under a drooping tree fern and leap onto a boulder to catch the panoramic view. In the distance, hilly peninsulas stretch toward the Southern Ocean. I let my head fall back and suck in a deep inhalation. There's more breathing space in the wild.

And no sound behind me.

The trail's empty. Talia's fallen back. Rather, I raced ahead too fast. My heart's still pounding—a good effort. My calves twitch, urging me to push on, go harder. I wasn't made to sit at a desk. But really, is anyone?

I pop the straw from my CamelBak into my mouth and suck. We're on the south side of Mount Wellington. The hulking mountain behind Hobart taunts me daily, miles of choice trails at my fingertips. A playground I ignore to run an academic merry-go-round.

Only one thing saves me from losing my shit. And here she

comes, rounding the bend. Her cheeks are flushed, hair wild from the ridge climb. I'll swap any vista for the sight of Talia breathing hard in a clingy sports tank. I jokingly flex my biceps.

She flashes me a weak smile and pauses to fish a muesli bar from her backpack.

"Well, you look happier."

"I'm great." And I mean it.

"You've been stalking around the house like a caged tiger. I debated throwing raw meat at you and making a getaway."

I jump off the boulder and land on the path in front of her. "All you ever need to do is throw yourself at me."

She unwraps her bar. "Is everything going okay? Sorry, I've been a little checked out the last few days."

Foreboding flares in my stomach. This is one of the reasons I invited her for a hike. I've become a boring bastard, but that's no reason to drag Talia down. I need to keep her happy, not give her cause to stress. She seems improved, more relaxed, but that's no indication. Maybe she's figuring out sneakier ways to hide her symptoms. What can I do but give her the best parts of myself, dark as they might be? There's no denying—I'm brightest out here.

"Bran?"

"Yeah, sorry. I'm good." I brace my foot on a rock and stretch my calves. "School's not what I thought it would be."

"How so?"

"I don't feel like I'm doing anything, you know?"

"No." She takes a vicious bite from her muesli bar and licks crumbs off her lower lip. "I don't, actually."

My chest tightens as I try to gather my thoughts.

"You have so much going right, you don't even know. I mean, after honors you're pretty much guaranteed a fast-track to a PhD."

"Four more years chained to a desk? Frying my brain cells on computer models for a world I no longer see? Yeah, a regular charmed life."

"Oh, please. Do me a favor and put away the violin, all right? Your supervisor freaking loves you. What about last week when I came to have lunch in your break room? After you left, she cornered me by the stairs, raved you were some boy genius."

"I feel like a fraud." The admission stings but it's the truth. "Maybe this is the wrong path."

"Wait, are you talking about me?"

"Jesus, Talia, come on. Everything isn't about you."

She withdraws into herself, a bright bloom that closes when darkness falls.

My tone was harsher than I intended but she's acting like I scored a golden ticket. I'm halfway through my honors—no backing out. I need to see the project to completion. And she's right about one thing. I do have a clear shot to a PhD. A scholarship is already in the works. My supervisor talks like I'll have a quick ascendency into the new Department of Climate Change. Like becoming a high-level bureaucrat is the ultimate life pinnacle.

Someone might as well take me out back and shoot me now.

"What if I'd rather do something else?"

Talia grabs her hair in two fistfuls. "You really don't realize how lucky you are!"

"This is the first time I've spent outdoors in weeks."

"But your career is moving forward. Obviously there are going to be trade-offs."

"I'm twenty-fucking-three. I shouldn't have to trade a goddamn thing."

"Oh, but I should?"

"Here you go again. This isn't about you."

"Yes, it is. Your head's so far up your own sorry-for-yourself ass that you don't even notice."

"Fill me in. What am I missing?"

She looks like she could mouth punch me. "What am I going to do?"

Right. That. My arms fall limp to my sides.

"I track classmates from UCSC online. Everyone is scoring jobs or landing awesome internships." Her posture is rigid. "I'm falling behind."

"She'll be apples."

"What the hell does fruit have to do with anything?"

"It's an idiom, means no worries."

"*Everyone* says that here. No worries, mate." She addresses the massive peppermint gum overhead. "Screw the *hakuna matata* bullshit. How will I get money? My savings sucks and there is no way I'm going begging to my mom."

"Can't you find some work under the table?"

"Doing what? Being a nanny? Awesome. Great. Way to dream big. I don't even know if I ever want to have kids."

"You don't?" The idea slams into me with unexpected force.

"What if I turn out to be one of those serial-killing moms?"

"Hang on—"

"I'm sure those women never planned to go all psycho, right? What if I wake up one morning holding an ax?" She mimes a swinging motion. "Everyone dead?"

"Settle, sweetheart. You haven't murdered your hypothetical family."

"I know. I know! But knowing the truth doesn't stop my brain. Haven't you figured that out by now?"

"Come here, kid."

"No." She buries her face in her hands. "Do you speak Japanese?" she asks after a pause.

"Pardon?"

"Japanese, the language? Do you speak it?"

"Yeah, sure. A bit."

"Why didn't you tell me?"

"I also speak Spanish, and better than decent Italian and French. Sorry I didn't give you a memo."

"Another reason why you'd be a perfect fit for the Sea Alliance. You can talk to the Japanese whaling ships and international media."

"Sure, whatever."

"Holy crap, listen to yourself! First you're set at university, with a full graduate school scholarship in the wings. But that's not all. Behind door number two waits a second amazing option, a kick-ass environmental organization inviting you to the Antarctic—your dream destination. Sorry, I'm struggling to organize a pity party."

"It's not that simple."

"I can't sit around while you count your options. I need to figure out my own life."

Her words rip through me like a hail of bullets. "What are you hinting at, Talia?"

"Maybe—I don't know—if we took some time…"

Despite everything, I'm not enough, can't keep her. My face must look like hell because her eyes widen and her expression softens.

"Whoa, Bran, calm down. I'm not saying anything about breaking up, not even close. It's just…I never imagined I'd be the kind of girl who followed a guy. I'm almost done with school and I need to make some plans."

"Fine." Maybe she doesn't want to end things right now, but suddenly, the possibility is fucking real and I don't know how to save us. "I need a moment."

"Alone?" She eyes the bush with trepidation. "You can't leave me here."

All my emotions are getting dangerously out of whack. I need to break away from here, get a handle on myself before I seriously lose my shit. I dig into my hip pocket and pull out the key chain. "Take the car. Go home."

"No way! I can't drive on this side of the road."

"You're a smart girl, figure it out." I turn up the trail, pound the earth, run away. The forest is too tight. Got to be higher, where the trees thin out. Need more room. More headspace.

"Bran!" Talia yells. "Bran." I run until her voice grows faint, disappears.

Why am I even surprised? I lose everyone in the end.

———

Night's dropped when I return down the trail. My headlamp illuminates a wallaby nibbling leaves along the edge of the path. It doesn't move as I pass, probably because I'm calmer. Spent a few hours wandering the giant dolerite columns on top of the mountain. I gave my thoughts over to the stillness and as usual an answer emerged. Not the solution I expected but still the beginning of a workable plan.

I don't need to let Talia go or ask her to abandon career ambitions.

The idea is crazy but it smacks of genius.

I pick up speed, need to be home, with her. I'll have to hitch but that's okay.

I found us a way.

"It's the way. It's the way." I repeat the words while skittering down the moss-lacquered steps to the parking lot.

I'm jarred for a few heart-thudding seconds. A cherry-red Holden Kingswood is parked in the corner.

My car.

Bloody hell, Talia didn't march down the mountain in a snit, did she? Headlights suddenly burn my retinas.

I'll take that as a no.

I shield my eyes and draw closer. A safe bet she's stewed in the car for hours.

"Idiotic motherfucker." Talia jumps out of the car, tears in my direction. "I told you never to shut me out again."

This isn't going to be fun.

"Hello to you too."

"What part of I can't drive stick on the opposite side of the road do you not understand? And may I remind you of another fun fact? There are snakes out here—big, poisonous ones. What if I got bit? Who would have helped me? The venom would have coursed through my body by the time I managed to flag a car down. And I couldn't even begin to identify what type of snake, so the hospital wouldn't have known the appropriate antivenin to administer. I'd have lost precious minutes. And those are the ones that count when a life hangs in the balance."

"You saw a snake?"

"No, but they're around, smelling my fear."

"Sorry you were scared." I mean, what can I say when she lays undiluted irrationality at my feet?

"Scared?" Her voice cracks. "That's what happens when someone reads Stephen King or spies a clown. I was t-e-r-r-i-f-i-e-d.

Google the word and you'll find a picture of me, alone, abandoned by you in the forest. Go ahead, do it. I can wait."

"Finished?"

"I've barely warmed up. But my ass is freezing and I want to get home, eat soup, and spend the night not speaking to you."

She storms to the passenger side and slams the door so hard the pane rattles.

The Kingswood is almost fifty years old. A ride that needs to be treated with the same TLC reserved for venerable older ladies. I open my mouth to tell Talia to take it easy but reconsider. Chances are high she'll strangle me with my vocal cords. I get it, okay? I left her alone, not cool.

Our drive is silent. Even still, the idea I had on top of the mountain keeps me in good spirits.

I found us a way.

I give her a glance at the stoplight, careful to keep my smile on the inside.

She juts her chin forward. "The light's green."

I ease my foot onto the gas. A horn sounds. My foot finds the brakes before my brain can issue the command. The world contracts into oncoming headlights. Talia's scream is overwhelmed by the sickening sound of rubber squealing on asphalt. All I know is that the scream means she's still alive, that I'm alive. We jerk to a stop, flying forward until the seat belts yank us back.

"What the cocksucking shit?" Adrenaline scours my veins. A utility truck ran the intersection's red light, missed plowing into us by a meter.

"Bran. Holy crap." Talia's eyes fill her face. She unclicks her seat belt and throws herself over the console, patting my cheeks. "Are you okay?"

I pull over to the curb and cut the engine. "Fine." I blow the air from my cheeks. "Everything is okay." I repeat the words and reach for Talia's hand as the truck speeds off.

Dickhead.

"What if we—"

"We didn't."

"But—"

"No harm's been done."

"Maybe it was a sign."

"Indicating what?" This isn't my first dance with disaster. Far as I see it, the Earth does a mad spin and we hang on for the ride. "Talia." I interlace my fingers with hers. "I never should have left you alone on the mountain. I'm sorry. I got scared."

"I know. I'm sorry too. For freaking out that being here with you is keeping me from being me." She kisses my brows, one and then the other. "Being with you is when I am the most me."

"My thoughts exactly."

She tilts her head forward until our noses touch. "I'll do better."

"I shouldn't have bailed."

"Everything can change in an instant."

She's remembering her sister, Pippa, whose life ended in such a way.

"I'm not taking you for granted, Talia. Ever."

"Me neither. I love you."

We crash together, a tangle of lips and tongues. Before I met Talia, my foot was on the gas—in the wrong-ass direction. She stepped into my blind spot when least expected. I didn't have time to duck or avoid her. I tried a few defensive maneuvers but nothing could change the irrevocable course of our collision.

Sometimes, an impact can hurtle you down a path you never expected, to the exactly right place.

We drive home in silence, each preoccupied by our own thoughts. When I pull up to the curb, Karma is sitting on the front porch.

Talia lets out a heavy sigh. "Why are you friends with that guy?"

"I don't know; he doesn't take shit."

"And you do?"

I climb out and shout a greeting. "How's it going?"

"All good, mate." Karma reclines on his elbows and stretches his legs over the front stoop.

"I'm confused," Talia says. "Why aren't you scavenging our pantry?"

"Hello, hello, Talia. Nice to see you're charming as always. You look tense. Maybe you should consider yoga."

"Aren't you cold outside?" She looks smug.

Karma's smile shrinks. "The front door key vanished."

"Oh, crap." She walks to a flowerpot on the veranda. "I moved it a few days ago. Whoopsies."

Sucks the two people I like best on this island want to carve each other's throats.

"Hey, Captain." I wrap my arms around her waist, lean so her feet dangle a few inches in the air. "We had a bloody day of it. Why don't you jump in a hot shower and I'll have a quick beer with Karm."

Karma flips off his fedora and twists a dread. "Got anything harder?"

"Talia brought duty-free bourbon."

Karma nods. "Whisky makes me frisky."

We head inside and Karma veers toward the hall bathroom. "Going to hit the loo."

"Why does he get under my skin so bad?" Talia grumbles as we enter the kitchen.

I fetch two glasses from the cupboard. "If it makes you feel better, I think the feeling is mutual."

"It's like he's a jealous wife."

"Hardly." I pull out the bottle and pour a few fingers into two tumblers.

"Do you think Karma is in the closet?"

"No, I don't. Nor do I believe nine-eleven was an inside job, that the government is poisoning us with chemtrails, or that the world is secretly ruled by alien reptiles masquerading as humans."

"The hell?"

"I'm interested in truth. You should be too. The shit-giving needs to stop, on both sides. Now scoot, I want to imagine you upstairs, all hot and soapy."

Talia lifts a glass from my hand and takes a sip, screwing her face. "Ew. How can you drink that straight? Tastes like Listerine."

"I shouldn't fix you a drink?"

"No, thanks." She leans in for a kiss. "Enjoy *Senor* Pain in My Ass."

She slips away before Karma saunters to the kitchen, drops into an open chair at the dining table, and pats his lap. "Right here, baby, saved you a seat."

"What the fuck?"

"Dude, your house is an echo chamber and your girl talks louder than a bloody cockatoo. Give me that drink and I'll suck your dick."

"Steady on, mate." I hand him the glass and he shoots it back. "About what Talia said—"

"Your chick clearly wants my shit and thus pretends to despise me."

"Shut it." I don't like his words, even in jest. "What brings you around?"

"I'm out."

"Out?"

"Broke from bondage, dude. I'm calling off the honors. I told my supervisor before coming over."

"But you only have five months to go, same as me."

"I'm leaving for the Ancient Forests Campaign camp tomorrow after I pack up."

"For real?" He's moving to the antilogging camp. The situation is growing intense as more and more Greenies arrive and disrupt timber crews.

"Weasel and I are hitching in with a couple of girls from an anarchist commune over Perth way."

"Shit, Karma. I don't know what to say."

"Sitting inside on computers all day isn't natural. I'm done. No more time wasted on mental masturbation, man."

"I hear you." This could be me talking.

"You should come along. Seriously. You're smart...for a dumbass."

"Thanks. But I've got to stay."

"Oh, right. I forgot about the ball and chain."

"Hardly."

"Whatever, mate. She's hot, I'll give you that. But so what? You have time for domestics later. Right now is our time—a chance to right wrongs. You want the same thing. Be honest with yourself."

Temptation ignites in my belly. No, I won't be a traitorous bastard. "Everything I need is upstairs." The image of Talia's hot, soapy body floods my senses and I stand. "I'm going to get back to that."

"When you reconsider, you know where to find me."

We bump fists. "Take care, mate. Stay outta trouble."

"Pretty hard when that shit's my middle name." He strolls to the corridor and pauses to glance over the fancy, custom-built kitchen. "I give you another month playing Barbie Dream House. Two months max. See you soon, my friend."

11

TALIA

*A*fter our narrowly averted near-death collision, I wait for the inevitable anxiety spike. The entire week is spent trying to ignore the way Bran watches me, his shoulders braced like he's facing down a hurricane. But oddly enough, fair mental weather seems to be the forecast. Inexplicably, my OCD symptoms have slunk away. Maybe there's a strange watched pot refusing to boil phenomenon at work—unanticipated but, hey, no complaints.

I hunch at my favorite library table putting the finishing touches on my thesis's introduction section when an instant message pops in the corner of the screen.

Bran: What's up?

Talia: Kicking my paper's ass

Bran: That's my girl

Talia: I AM QUEEN OF THE WORD

Bran: Better than being the Court Jester of Stats. Any weekend plans?

Talia: Besides downing a liter of moonshine and streaking the
     Saturday Market?

Bran: A little shadier than my suggestion but hey, I'd watch...

Talia: What are you proposing?

Bran: Me. You. Camp trip.

Talia: Do go on.

Bran: I want to check out Ship Stern Bluff on the Tasman
     Peninsula. Forecast is for no surf this weekend so should
     have place to ourselves. Supposed to be a quick hike.

Talia: Define quick

Bran: Even your nana would agree

Talia: Under 8 hours?

Bran: Less than one

Talia: Sold. When do you want to jet?

"I'm kidnapping you right now," he whispers from over my
shoulder.

I jump, cursing softly as my knees crunch the desktop.

Bran half sits on my table, shutting his laptop. "You okay?"

I massage my leg. "That's a dubious talent."

"What?"

"Sneaking."

"I am a man of many skills."

"The thing is, I don't even think you're joking."

He sweeps his hand over himself. "What can I say, I'm all ninja."

"Or a shit."

"But you love the shit out of me?"

"For some weirdo reason."

He goes in for a kiss.

"Oh, get a room," some girl hisses under her breath.

Bran gives her the finger and she huffs, returning to her notes.

"You should really consider writing a book," I mutter, sorting my backpack.

"Advice on being awesome?"

"I'm thinking the sequel to *How to Win Friends and Influence People.*"

He smirks. "I don't like people as a general rule, Captain."

"What am I, a baboon?"

That earns me a laugh. "You are a person, Talia. *The* person."

Lightness sweeps over me as we amble from the library. This is what I missed—our casual banter and easy companionship. It had been absent after the trailside fight and subsequent near miss. Even our sex has been careful—uncertain—as if we both long to say something but don't know how to put it in words.

Tell him about the phone interview.

No, not yet.

Not when things are getting back to normal. Besides, I'm not even sure about the Peace Corps. No point stirring more drama on such a gorgeous day.

We reach the Kingswood and I eyeball the two backpacks in the rear seat. "You packed for me?"

"I estimated my chances of convincing you were a hundred percent," Bran says, adjusting the rearview mirror.

"Wow, tell me what you really think."

"Why would you say no?"

I shrug, a little petulant.

"Captain." His thigh squeeze ignites my nerves. "We need this, sweetheart. I want to be close to you."

My center melts to ooey-gooey goodness and I roll down the window. "Proceed."

"Atlas?"

"Thank you." I smile to see he's turned down the pages marking the planned route. I get uptight in cars, overfocused with the need to know exactly where we're going, how long the trip will take. I conduct a quick internal scan but my body remains quiet. There's only silence—beautiful, beautiful silence. No subtle demands I touch all the radio buttons or click my seat belt three times to feel right.

I sit on my hands, though, just in case.

Bran flicks on Triple J. There's a catchy, emoish tune playing and he immediately tries to change the station.

"Nuh-uh. No way. Leave it. I love this song."

"My ears, they burn."

"Embrace the dark side." I settle back and let the lyrics and odd pop rhythm lull my senses. Fields, forests, run-down country towns, and snatches of ocean blur past. What if everything could always be easy? Is this how life feels for normal people? I wish I could remember.

The drive doesn't take long, around an hour and a half. Bran pulls the car into a big field, empty except for sheep who appear more interested in the grass than our presence. We load our backpacks and head along the well-defined trail, which disappears between the trunks of towering eucalyptuses.

A cloud drifts overhead, becomes a turtle, and then a dragon that eats the turtle and it seems like such a waste of time to ever die.

Bran's right. This is *exactly* what we needed.

He buzzes, his pace quick on the trail. I love him happy. The dynamic changes when we're outside. He loses his edginess and the tightness around his eyes vanishes with each step. His body relishes physical exercise and it certainly doesn't hurt me to study the way his long-sleeved gray shirt hugs his leanly defined chest. My senses kick in as I inhale the forest's minty scent and memorize the way his thumbs idly trace his pack straps. The memory of those thumbs tracing me in other ways causes a shiver.

"Warm enough?"

"You could say that." I grab for my water bottle. I need to chill. If I want to get jiggy with Bran, better to wait for his tent, rather than dragging him into a nearby tussock. The local snake population is no doubt wiggling with glee over the arrival of American girl flesh.

The trail slopes downward and the ocean appears between the trees.

"Come on." Bran hooks my pinkie with his. "Almost there."

Our camp spot nestles in the thick heath hugging the rocky beach. Above rises a cliff wall—Ship Stern Bluff. No creativity muscles were pulled establishing that name. The rock juts toward the ocean like the proud bow of a boat. The place is deserted. Not even a fishing boat is in sight. The empty sea looks inviting, even though temperatures must hover at a stomach-clenching midfifties.

"Fan-bloody-tastic." Bran opens his pack and hefts out a tent.

"Need help?"

"Know how to set one of these up?"

"Sure. I've got mad skills."

"Uh-huh."

"You click sticks together. How hard can it be?"

"First off, they're called poles, Captain." Bran digs out a red apple, polishes the fruit on his shirt before tossing it to me. "No worries, I got this. Go poke around. I packed your camera. You can take arty pictures of the rocks or some shit."

"What a ringing endorsement of my talent."

"I want you relaxed, ready to do my bidding."

"Are you turning Paleolithic out here?" I pound my chest. "Me big man. Me build shelter."

"Keep going and I'll drag you to the bushes. Show you Neanderthals do it better."

"Oooooh. You smuggling a big club under that loin cloth?"

"Freak show." He shakes his head, chuckling under his breath.

"Fine." I snatch my camera and poke out my tongue. "I'll go take a bunch of selfies down by the beach."

"If you get your tits out for a few, I won't object."

"Pervert."

"Where you're concerned? Definitely."

I blow him a kiss and turn down the path.

"Talia..."

I glance back, surprised at the uncertainty in his voice. "What's up?" Bran is so rarely anything but 100 percent confident.

"It'd be cool if you met me around the corner in, say, fifteen minutes." He points his chin at the bluff. "Follow the rocky shelf—it extends all the way around." He doesn't offer any more information.

O-kay.

"Yeah, sure, no problem."

"Cool." His smile does funny things to my girly parts. "See you soon."

"It's a date."

I mosey along, beach-combing. The sheer variety of shells is mind-boggling. On the horizon, two big-winged birds tilt and circle, riding the currents. On impulse I throw out my arms, cupping my hands like tiny sails to catch the wind.

I'm making it. Surviving. Thriving, even. My heart is full.

No matter what happened in the grisly past, I broke through, found my version of a happily-ever-after.

"Hey, Pip." There's never been a shred of evidence my sister listens from the other side. I'd love if she kicked me some sign, even the odd poltergeist haunting, anything—except creepy bathroom spying. But that's not really her style.

"Just thought you should know, I'm making good on that promise." I'd sworn while she was stretched out, unconscious, on her hospital bed that I'd live enough life for the both of us. "Not sure what you'd think about Bran, but he's good for me. Really good."

My sister always preferred the super-nice guys. Or at least one super-nice guy.

Tanner.

He was her one and only love.

Beth e-mailed a few updates yesterday. Word is Tanner's talking about retiring from professional skateboarding. Not sure of the specifics. I didn't want to search for news, better to leave some sleeping dogs down for the count. Beth didn't reveal more than the barest facts. She hasn't quite gotten over that I slept with him, her dead best friend's boyfriend.

I don't need her guilt trip when I have my own. I knew—better than anyone—what Pippa and Tanner shared. I used to bear daily witness to the PDA. Theirs was the kind of love that left those around them supremely lonely.

Wind caresses my face with subtly increasing force. A few heavy clouds rear on the horizon.

Oh, those don't look promising.

Bran checked the weather forecast before we left, right? Freaking hope so. I glance toward our campsite. The orange tent is easy to spot but there's no sign of him. Crap, have fifteen minutes passed? I scramble along the beach to the wide rock ledge that hugs the cliff and spreads a good fifty feet to where the thick waves crash. Spray catches the breeze, lashes my face.

When I round the corner from our sheltered cove, the wind barrels into me with double-down force. I cross my arms. My pullover fleece gets a big fat fail for taking the edge off the frigid blast. I squint through tight lids over an ancient landscape carved by eons of waves, lashed to spare beauty by the world-famous storms that made this region famous.

Amazing.

Everything is eroded around me. Massive boulders dot the shelf, rivaling the size of semitrailers. I stand by a tree, trunk gnarled from the elements, thick roots fastened around the last stones of the world. The sea gnaws in discontent, fastening to land with insatiable hunger. Bran's nowhere to be seen.

"Hey!" I cup my hands to my mouth and call. "Bran!" The gale snatches my words like a child with a new toy. I must have missed him around camp.

I return to the tent; the nylon snaps in the gusts.

"Bran!"

No response. The wind shrieks and the rocky beach is under assault from the whitecaps.

I swallow a knot of panic. I'm being irrational.

Come on, think.

There aren't many options for where Bran can go. He must be on the ledge, probably behind one of the boulders, and I didn't see him.

I retrace my steps. This time when I shout his name, there is no ignoring the shrill note in my voice. I circle rocks that rise over my

head by a good twenty feet. When I reach the end of the shelf, and am still alone, paralysis threatens.

Bran wouldn't have ventured close to the water, would he? Edge dance right where the waves crash in a cacophony of mindless rage?

Of course he would.

As if to confirm my fear, a rogue wave arrives, at least eight feet higher than the rest; the crushing water wall startles a flock of gulls hovering on the previously dry rock. Certainly Bran would respect the ocean's number one rule: Never turn your back on the waves.

But when did Bran ever believe the rules applied to him?

"Bran!" My scream tears my throat and I wince, ignoring the pain.

This is my crazy thinking, right? Bran's fine. But if he's not, I could be wasting his last precious seconds by dithering. I skirt closer to the ledge and leap back as another heavy wave pounds, a fist that could easily grab a body into the ocean's clutches, drag someone down to the deep, indigo places of the world.

"No, no, no, no, no, no." I chant the words as if a mantra will make it so.

Should I race back to the parking lot? Go find help? What do I do? What do I do? I'm so fucking useless. All the shit is going down and I can do nothing but utter these quiet little animalistic moans.

"What's going on?"

I almost collapse.

Bran hunches against the wind, hands shoved deep in his pockets. He removes one to tousle my head. "I've been watching you peck around the rocks like a mad chicken."

"I thought…I thought…oh God, I thought you were…" I burst into tears. I'm not a delicate crier. My sobs are raw and choking. My nose runs.

"Whoa, settle down. Where's the funeral?"

"Where were you?" I hurtle into his open arms, burying my face in his chest and inhaling the perfectly Branish scent.

"I climbed up there." He nods to the tallest boulder. "Wind's a bitch but there's a killer view."

My shock fades. "You watched me? I thought you died."

"Huh?"

I batter his shoulders with my fists. "I thought you were dead."

"How in the hell was I going to die?"

"You went to the edge and a wave took you." I wipe my nose with my hand, another loud sniffle escaping. "I couldn't find you." I resume crying. "I looked and looked but you were gone."

"Fucking hell, I had no idea. I'm sorry, sweetheart."

My skin tingles as sweat sheens my chest. "I don't know if I should kiss or choke you."

"My vote's for the former."

I take a deep breath, try to regroup before I do something sick like vomit from sheer relief. "So what?"

"What the what?"

"You asked me to come out here for a reason."

"Oh, right. That. Never mind."

"You totally freak me out and now you've got nothing?"

"Not nothing, Talia." His tone is weird. "Everything."

"Huh?"

"Let's go back to camp. We'll talk later. The wind's crazy and you need a drink. Or five."

We finish off the last of my nasty duty-free bourbon that Bran

packed in his Nalgene and nibble dried apricots and cheese. The sky shifts through a contusion of colors—gray, black, bone, and purple, reflecting the same bruised hues in my heart. The hard alcohol, not normally to my taste but welcome for now, takes effect and loosens my neck muscles. I dig my fingers into the pebbly beach while the ocean throws itself against the cliff, time and time again. It can't do anything different. That's the nature of things. Sometimes you don't get a choice in how to act.

Bran settles his head on my stomach. "This right here? My favorite place in the world."

I release a fistful of coarse gravel and let the grains catch the wind. "Have you ever watched a sand mandala get made?"

"No."

"Tibetan Buddhist monks visited my campus one time. They worked for a week, started in the center, moved to the periphery, drawing the most intricate geometric shapes on the ground. Then they used special funnels and scrapers to fill the image in with colored sand. I skipped so much class to watch the process. When they finished, the piece was the single-most beautiful thing I'd ever seen. And then they destroyed it, ritualistically, piece by piece. So much effort for the sole purpose of being obliterated."

Bran doesn't say anything but his eyes never leave my face.

"Nothing stays the same, does it? I get so caught up wanting to keep life under control but that contradicts the natural order of things. Change is inevitable."

"There are things I'm never going to let change." Bran shifts on his side so he faces me. His cheeks are wind-burned. Impossibly, the rosiness makes his irises more jade.

"Yeah?"

He hugs my waist. "This. Me. You."

"But we'll have to." My fingers ramble through his hair. I need to tell him about the Peace Corps interview. How? I'm not sure I want to do it, but the idea might have merit, be a possible avenue worth exploring. "Bran—"

"I found a way. *The* way." Bran pushes himself up to kneel beside me. "For us, with the visa—you staying here."

I slam my mouth shut.

"What if we got married?"

The fast-spoken words slam into me with such force my brain is leveled; no coherence remains. He can't be serious but there's no trace of humor in his intense expression.

12

BRAN

*T*alia locks her arms around her knees, staring at me like I've declared an ambition to become an oil baron. "But... what? You can't casually lob sentences like that into conversations."

"I'm serious. Let's get married. Think about—"

"All I can think is that I want to strangle you."

That's not excitement shining in her eyes. She sniffles and a few tears escape. She takes a huffy breath, scrambles to her feet, and half runs toward the tent.

A gull swoops and lands, regarding me from a few feet away.

"Well, that went over fucking great."

If birds can smirk, I swear that's exactly what it does. A drop of rain hits my face. Another lands on my arm. The clouds seem close enough to scoop with two hands and sea foam flies off the back of restless waves.

When I unzip the tent, Talia's on top of the sleeping bags, curled in a fetal position.

"Hey."

"Go away. I'm serious, Bran. I need a second."

I climb inside. "We have to talk."

"About drinking unicorn blood? Slaughtering nursery tale characters?"

"What?"

"This is going to be hard for you to comprehend, but here's a little life lesson—girls like their illusions of romance." She raises a cautionary finger before I can open my mouth. "Look, I'm not demanding Hallmark cards, roses, or whatever the hell. But everyone has limits, and you've hit mine."

I'm lost, without the first clue how to get back to where we were five minutes ago. The wind grips the tent, screaming like a drunken banshee. Rain batters the nylon like the storm wants to tear its way inside.

"A prank of this magnitude...it hurts my feelings, all right?"

"Who said I'm joking?"

"Please. I beg you—be serious."

"I am fucking serious. More than I've ever been about anything in my entire goddamn life."

The wind shrieks as if to accentuate my point. Talia goes silent and stares like I'm a stranger.

Out of all the imagined outcomes, a big, fat rejection was not factored into my calculations.

Her lips move. "You're serious?" At least that's what I think she whispers. The downpour drowns her words. She might be telling me to eat shit and die. I slam into protective mode, battening the hatches.

"No, Talia. I ask all the girls to marry me." I pull away as orange flames alight behind my eyes. "Fucking hell, contrary to popular opinion, I'm not a clockwork toy. Break me open and guess what? There's a heart in there—maybe not the biggest, or the brightest, but it's real and it bleeds and right now you're knifing it."

"I'm sorry, okay?" She reaches her hands to search out mine. "I'm so sorry. You shocked the hell out of me."

Her heartfelt tone extinguishes my sudden fire to a cinder.

"Or into you. You've been a hell demon since I made the suggestion."

"A suggestion? Really? I don't think so. Proposing to spend our entire lives together is another animal. A whole other genus."

"What did you think we were doing here?"

"I—"

"You thought you and I were temporary? A bit of fun?"

"No, but—"

"This playtime for you?"

"Of course not. I—"

"Shoot straight, kill me quickly."

"Shut up! I'm not against the idea but I'm trying to process."

Okay, you're still in with a chance.

I take a deep breath, simmer down a notch. "It's mad but if you'll hear me out, I think you'll agree the plan has merit."

"Marriage." Her tongue brushes her top lip, tasting the word. "I mean, I guess I imagined something like that for us. Someday. But I'm twenty-one. You're twenty-three."

"Let me break it down. It's a simple question of whether or not we should play the system. The answer for me is without a doubt."

"I'm not following."

"The Australian government—the machine—doesn't decide who stays in the country based on compassion or human happiness. No, the machine needs to know that the correct cogs turn, the right boxes are ticked. In this case you're an American on a student visa with an expiry date. But if we can give you a different identity, the machine will be forced to accept you, let you remain here with me—even grant you work rights. We play the game, Talia, but on our terms."

"Play the game," she repeats, dazed.

"Exactly." Excitement hastens my words. "Marriage is a piece of paper, an institution, right?"

She presses her lips together so tight the edges grow bloodless. "Yeah, I guess so."

"I don't want anyone telling me we can or cannot be together. We do this and everything can go on status quo." I'm talking fast now, throwing out words, hoping they stick. "The only difference will be paperwork saying we're married, a legal document that will let you get a job, live here, keep us together."

"You've researched all this?"

"Yeah."

"I haven't seen awesome things happen with marriage. Look at my parents."

"Or mine. Or my sister. I don't know anyone married who seems happy."

Her expression is pensive. "Um, shouldn't that be a red flag?"

"Hell no. This is subversion; we're rebelling against the system."

"What about love?"

"Love?" The word trips on my tongue.

Her gaze softens. "Yeah, shouldn't marriage be grounded in love?"

"I love you like crazy, Talia." I press my forehead against hers, willing my brain to transmit exactly how much. "I don't need to put a ring on your finger to know that fact."

"So get married and fight the man?"

My lips brush hers. "Yeah, sure."

"And I'll really be able to legally work?"

"Uh-huh." I run my tongue along the seam of her sexy lips. "I want to be with you. Nobody can tell me that's not going to happen."

"Just a piece of paper?"

"That's it. Nothing more. We don't have to tell anyone. Hell, later, when the time's right, we could do it again. Get the dress, have the big deal whatever-you-want party. Come on, sweetheart." I tickle her ribs. "Say yes."

A nervous giggle bubbles from her throat. "This is for real, for real?"

"You and me, kid, against the big bad world."

"Marriage as revolution."

"Exactly."

Her laughter is deeper, more natural. "I'm surprised I was surprised at all."

"What's that mean?"

"You're one crazy cat." She lays one hand against my cheek. "Yes."

"Yes, like yes yes?" She's got to feel my heart accelerating into overdrive.

"Yep, pretty much."

I know what I said.

Marriage is an institution.

A meaningless piece of paper.

A way to play the immigration game, win on our own terms.

But when I ease her down against the sleeping bags, my body isn't dealing in intellectual abstractions.

Mine.

Possession heats my skin as my mouth covers her, desperate for a sweet fix.

Mine.

She responds with similar urgency. Our tongues speak a language our bodies instinctively understand, a top-secret version of the Rosetta stone. We act like if we push hard enough, we'll break through, get to the other side, the place with all the good stuff. A place in the heart that for too long I imagined was fictional, the result of collective Kool-Aid drinking, fueled by those who profit from selling romantic bullshit.

She drags her fingers down my lower abdomen. I know where she's going and nearly die by the time she closes around my thickening dick.

Right. This is so fucking right.

There's only one place where I belong and it's with Talia. The storm's cold front sends the temperature plummeting. I cover her exposed body with mine while the wind attacks the tent poles as if the whole world is hell-bent on destroying whatever this thing is we're building together with uncareful hands and impulsive deeds.

There's a danger in being too happy. I don't share Talia's fear, that thinking something will make it true. I don't even believe in fate. But I know joy can cut a deep groove in a human heart, and I know how sorrow fills those cracks after the happiness is gone.

I jerk her yoga pants off her hips, loving the sounds she makes when my fingers find her center like a heat-seeking missile. I drag my tongue across her skin, writing my name on her body, the story of us, a future infinite with possibility. With one glorious thrust I'm in, and we both cry out. Maybe it's the wild storm or the fact that no one is around for miles, but Talia is louder than she's ever been.

I grab the soft skin behind her knees and angle her legs over my shoulders. There's a thrill in seeing how far you can go. I want to travel into Talia's most unfathomable, hidden depths to a place without names, where I've wanted to go with her ever since she stopped to help my punk ass on Lygon Street. She's revolutionized my life in ten short months, colored everything with her sweetness, her light, the way she finds the courage to love despite everything.

She's close; her breath holds a ragged note. I'm chasing after her like a fool or a genius; there's bugger all difference separating the two.

"Come for me, sweet girl." At my command she's there, and I'm right behind her. Our shocked gazes connect as we share the profound experience of seeing—truly seeing—another person.

There is nothing like it. And nothing like her.

"We can do this forever," she whispers, fighting to catch her breath.

The wind screams.

Go on, world, do your worst.

"We're invincible," I respond, tracing her heart-shaped chin. "Unstoppable."

13

TALIA

J wait to reschedule my morning meeting with Phil until after Bran bikes into campus. My lips are puffy from his lingering good-bye kisses. He hasn't lost this radiant beam—unparalleled in the history of fantastic smiles—since we returned last night. I twist the u-bolt necklace between my fingers and realize I'm quietly giggling. Yeah, I'm totally unfit to be viewed by the general public in this dreamy state. My plans for the day can be summed up on three fingers: wander the house in one of Bran's old T-shirts, drink coffee, and smile at inanimate objects.

Incredible. Bran did it—he found a way for us to work. The idea is cliché, without a doubt, but also watertight.

We made a pact while driving from Ship Stern Bluff to tell no one about the not-a-marriage, our nickname for the audacious plan—mostly to keep my friends and my father from freaking the eff out. Marriage...sounds as foreign and adult as discussing mortgage interest rates and retirement accounts. The institution is so heavy, weighted with tradition, expectation, and a low rate of success. Mom and Dad are casualties on that particular battlefield. So are most of my friends' parents for that matter. Sure, Bran's folks remain together, but he describes them as more like business partners than a happy couple.

A cool, creeping sensation slithers across the back of my neck. What will marriage, even of the not-a-marriage variety, do to us?

Two nights ago at Ship Stern Bluff, after Bran's proposal, I woke to my pulse pounding in my ears. It wasn't from night terrors. The storm had retreated and the ocean was calmed to the point of near silence. Bran didn't stir when I climbed from the tent to pee. I started walking, marveling at the night sky, the world a new place. The moon was nearly full and the beach bathed in a pale, silvery light, covered by flotsam and jetsam. I deciphered bits of tangled fishing line, logs the size of my body, and, half hidden in sand, the sharp gleam of a shark's fin, no doubt hurled to shore during a recent Southern Ocean storm.

I crawled back into the tent but even Bran's arms couldn't squeeze away the sense of foreboding—a looming danger. Even now the ominous memory is shiver inducing.

I shake my head; I need to stop hiding from imaginary monsters.

We're not sure of a wedding date. This is so weird; after all, we're not having a *real* wedding. I mean, it will be technically legal but that's where the similarities stop. Someday, maybe in another seven or eight years, we'll actually do all the ceremonial pageantry. But then again, maybe we won't. I don't know. What does marriage even mean? It's not like a ring or a white dress will make me love Bran any more.

When I was younger, I dreamed of my wedding day. My mom filed away a worksheet from some ancient elementary school homework, the answer to the question, What would you like to be when you grow up? My answer: Be married. I stumbled on the picture while packing the house.

Why didn't I want to be an astronaut? A veterinarian? Hell, even a member of the royal family? I mean, come on, Tiny Talia, dream big.

Big dreams notwithstanding, my eight-year-old self had the day dialed to the last detail. I'd wear a purple dress with a glittering tutu flaring at my waist. My lucky husband-to-be would don a velvet suit, and together we'd eat vanilla raspberry cupcakes and build the world's biggest sand castle.

Ten months ago, when I landed in Melbourne, I was afraid of everything and was a meager percentage point from flunking out of school. Now here I am, not even a full year later and back on track. My bachelor's is so close to being finished, and I can start applying for jobs. The Peace Corps plan can remain where it should—a pipe dream. Getting married will fix everything.

Married—there goes that funny shiver again.

I pace into the kitchen. Bran forgot his iPod on the counter. I pop on the headphones and crank the volume, curious about the last song he played. I smile to discover it's "Sweetness" by The Waifs. The dreamy, folkie groove settles my nerves and I pad into the pantry to hunt down the remnants from Sunny's recent care package. Despite her horror over my sugar consumption, she did me a solid and included a few packets of Pop Rocks. She won't touch candy unless it's crafted from boiled kale and sweetened with stevia. I don't mind keeping my food on the healthyish end of the spectrum, but occasional crappy food binges are critical to my overall well-being.

I try not to look at her BAREFOOT AND PREGNANT apron hanging on the pantry door.

Mrs. Brandon Lockhart.

"No way," I whisper to myself. If we ever do name changes, he can become Mr. Natalia Stolfi.

The window seat in the breakfast nook looks inviting in the morning light. There's a cheerful view to the boxy backyard, dominated by an apple tree in full blossom. I sit in a sunny patch, wrap Bran's shirt around my bare knees, and pour the last of the Pop Rocks onto my tongue. The sweetness explodes in a satisfying sizzle.

Our backpacks prop next to the table, exactly where we left them last night in our fight to reach the bedroom. A battle we mutually lost—or won, depending on your definition of what went down on the stairs.

I cover my face with my hands, hiding my smile and blush. My belly flutters like I've trapped a thousand butterflies in mid-flight while the muscles between my legs contract with slow deliberateness.

Winning. Yeah, definitely winning.

I slide my fingers along my thighs in a restless caress.

The shrill ring from the landline phone jars me from my delicious squirminess like microphone feedback. I vault to standing, but the T-shirt is still tight around my legs and I half fall while grabbing the receiver.

"Talia speaking," I announce with a giggle, copying the formal way Bran answers the phone. No simple "Hello's" down under.

There's a pause—wrong number. I'm about to hang up when I get the urge to try one last time. Can't shake the feeling someone's there. "Hello?"

There's a definite sniffle.

"Who is this?"

"Talia?"

I sink back to the floor. "Mom."

We haven't spoken since July. She blames me and my stupid, fucking OCD for killing Pippa and I'm not sure she's wrong.

"I wasn't sure you'd be there..." She trails off midsentence before rallying. "Different time zones and everything."

"This is a great time, actually. In case you, I don't know, ever want to call again or whatever."

Muteness. Is she still on the phone?

"Mom?"

"He met someone. Of course, I suppose you knew that."

"I know nothing. Who are we discussing?"

"Don't play coy. I'm talking about Scott."

"Dad?" My heart does an awkward *flump*, like an unco frog flopping from a lily pad. Mom divorced him when we were reeling from Pippa's death. She fled to Hawaii, claiming she needed to heal but really she couldn't deal.

Neither could Dad or I.

I've spent enough rage on Mom, lit that candle at both ends and burned it to a lumpy ball of hardened wax.

"My dad? He's met someone?"

"Who else would I mean?"

"Whoa, whoa, whoa. Don't jump down my throat." My cautious politeness disintegrates. "You haven't said a single word to me in months, Mom. Months. I guess when you took my name off our shared bank account, you figured that served as message enough."

God, two seconds into the conversation and I sound like a spoiled baby.

"I was angry, Talia. I'm sorry. If you need money—"

"Fuck your money."

"Language."

"Deal, Mom. I'm all grown up. I live with a man. I do what I want. And if I need to say fuck, I say fuck."

I sound like a child play-acting an adult.

"I didn't call to debate your use of profanity." She heaves a heavy sigh. "Have you been keeping up with your father?"

"Not much, occasionally the odd e-mail. He's been on boats for most of the summer. Last I knew he was in Greenland, or Baffin Island, or Iceland, I don't know."

"He was tagged in a bunch of pictures. By a woman."

Mom is Facebook-stalking Dad? Someone punch me in the face and put me out of this misery.

"Sorry, I wouldn't know. Dad and I aren't Facebook friends."

"You're not?"

"No. It's weird and creepy for Dad to spy on my life or vice versa. I doubt he wants the nitty-gritty on me and I sure as hell don't want his. That's why I unfriended you. Besides, I don't even like Facebook anymore. I mean, Nana's on it these days." My dad's mom, my eighty-year-old grandma. "If that's not an image to sear the brain, I don't know what is."

"You should look him up. This woman, she's pretty."

Is she slurring?

"Mom, seriously. Leave it alone."

"I should write to him, don't you think?"

"Absolutely not." I've seen my stoic dad cry two times in his life. Once when we turned off Pippa's life support. The other when he told me Mom was divorcing him. "If he's finally finding happiness, don't you dare ruin it with some bullshit jealousy."

"I was only going to say I was happy he found someone."

"Riiiiiight." My mom is incapable of selflessness. "Let the sleeping dogs lie."

"She's pretty, and so much younger."

Yes, that's a definite slur on the *s*. She probably won't remember this conversation when she sobers.

That fact gives me the courage to confess what's burned in my chest the past twenty-four hours. My drunk mom is the best thing I have to a confessional booth. "I'm getting married. Bran and I are doing it so I can get a visa, stay in Australia. I mean, obviously we're crazy about each other but—"

"Marriage isn't a game, Talia."

Crap, she sounds way more coherent all of a sudden. And way more like my mother, from back when she cared about the job description.

"Try not to be too happy for me."

And drink a glass of water while you're at it.

"Where did I go wrong?" She starts to cry.

Typical. So effing typical. She turns everything around to her.

"You're pregnant, aren't you?"

I punch the countertop. "Classic, Mom. Fucking bona fide classic."

"You're only twenty-one."

"Twenty-two in a couple more weeks. Maybe you should write that down. My birthday?"

"Don't patronize me."

"Mom, look at this conversation from my point of view. You call me, drunk—"

"I am not drunk—"

"You're wasted." I'm not ceding her an inch. "And you whine about the fact that there's some photos online of my father having fun with a woman. This bums you out because you want dibs on his happiness. You can't stand the idea he might have finally moved on."

"Are you finished?"

"I haven't even started." I squeeze the phone so hard my fingers go numb. "You didn't hurt Dad. You came close to ruining him."

"You don't understand—"

"Remember the glass rose you used to keep on your bedside table?"

"I'm not sure what—"

"When Pippa and I were little, you warned us not to play with it, again and again. Pippa listened, of course. But I couldn't help myself. That little knickknacky piece of shit was the most beautiful thing I'd ever seen. One day, no surprise, I broke it."

"I barely remember."

"Really? Because you freaked out big-time. Here's the important part—my whole point. The glass rose never meant much, not to you. It was a thing you kept around because it had been yours for so long it seemed kind of pointless to give it away. But when it broke, holy hell, did it ever matter."

"You've grown so cruel."

"Not cruel, Mom. Honest. You snipped Dad's heart like a loose thread off a jacket."

"You and I, Natalia, we're not so unalike." She switches gears, going for toxic sugary sweetness.

"You straddle the brink between wrong and insulting."

"Birds of a feather," she croons, half singing the words.

"Then I can see why a gathering of crows is called a murder."

"You blame me for leaving."

"You ran away."

"Who left their friends, their family, their entire country?"

"Are you for real?"

"Denial, such an obvious defense mechanism."

"Wow, you fit your entire vocabulary into a single sentence, well done. Let me set the record straight—"

"I have better things to do. This was a mistake to call, one I don't plan on repeat—"

"Shut up and listen!" I scream.

"Talia?" I jump at the sound of Bran's voice.

He takes the phone from my grasp. "Who is this?" he demands. "Hello? Hello, is anyone— Oh, right, hello, Bee." He stiffens, his anger mutating into something cold and formal. "Uh-huh. I see. Yep. Yes. Sorry you feel that way."

He drops the phone on the counter and turns with open arms. "Come here, you."

I melt against him, bawling like a kid who can't find her mommy in the grocery store. Even though the woman grew me inside her body and raised me under her roof for two decades—I've lost her.

"Hell, kid, glad I came back for one last kiss." He squeezes me hard as if he can inject love straight into my deadened heart. The facts are indisputable. I no longer have a relationship with my mother—the person whose job it is to love me unconditionally. My core collapses in an internal avalanche, burying my hope—my light—in a crushing place devoid of air or space.

Against mounting panic, I kiss Bran hard, knocking off his hat, launching his sunglasses halfway across the kitchen bench.

He's got to dig me out. Save me from myself.

He braces my face between his hands. "You gonna tell me what's going on?"

The panic squeezes my lungs, flattens me into two dimensions.

"I need to feel good. Please..." My voice breaks mid-beg. "Make me feel so good."

He hesitates as my tears soak his palms. I can tell he wavers, fears taking advantage.

If he won't give me what I want, I'll take it for myself.

He's wearing bike shorts and I jerk them down but I don't get the boxers. No matter. I'm between his legs, sliding my mouth over the plaid cotton.

"Talia."

I shake my head, burrowing in closer to his heat. I suck hard right through the fabric and his grip on my shoulders changes from trying to tug me away to bracing himself upright.

"Bloody hell." He grabs his hair like he's in pain.

Tears distort my vision.

"This is messed up. Even for us."

I tease his waistband lower, lick the join of his strengthening erection, trace my tongue down so the velvety skin is slick before working him double time with my hands.

"I can't do this." He rips his hips back, out of my grasp, and squats in front of me.

"Come on." I wiggle against him. "I need this."

"You're bloody sobbing."

"Make me feel good. You can, I know you can."

"Then we do this my way." He lifts me to my feet. Before I can even let the relief settle, he hikes my ass off the ground so I have no choice but to lock my legs around his waist. I instinctively grapple for the counter.

"It's okay, I got you."

"I know." He shoves my T-shirt up, exposing my lower ribs. He's right there, hard and ready, pressed to my plain white underwear. He holds me with one arm like I weigh nothing and shoves my panties to the side, filling me before my next breath.

I close my eyes as the hollowness retreats. I'm full in heart and body.

He angles into me in the best kind of way. Maybe it's my desperation for escape, or this position, but I've never gotten here so quick. I fling my arms around his neck as he walks us backward, until we collide with the refrigerator door. I lose track of where my body ends and his begins. Every way he grinds is exactly right.

"Look." He runs his tongue along my cheek, over the tears. "Look."

I try to focus on the feral gleam in his green cat eyes.

"No." He shakes his head. "At us, Talia. Bloody look at us."

We both drop our heads forward and he enters me inch by devastating inch.

Only one word materializes in my hazy mind. "Beautiful."

"You're beautiful."

"We're beautiful."

He slams to the hilt and holds as my muscles rock him as much as he rocks me.

"Talia." He sounds angry but I know he's not. Whenever he gets too full of emotion, it's like he's furious. "What the fuck do you do to me?"

For a few panting moments, we don't move.

"Open your eyes," he says hoarsely.

"I'm afraid to."

"Why are you crying?"

"What must you think of me? I'm so sorry."

He kisses my wet mouth. "You owe no apologies to anyone, least of all me."

I open one eye. "I owe you the world."

"Blood hell, Talia. You are my world."

As he slides out, I remember how once the continents were joined. Over time, through plate tectonics, they let the distance carry them apart. What Bran and I are building is an uncharted country, one I'm never going to let slip away.

14

BRAN

November

I mess around on the computer in a failed attempt to ignore how quiet the house is without Talia's laughter. She's out for the evening recording the last of her oral history interviews. The calendar shows November arrived. This not-a-marriage idea came at exactly the right time and dodged us a serious bullet.

Everything is working out.

I kill time visiting Karma's blog. He posted a heap of photos from the protest camp deep in the old growth forest. Jealousy creeps along the edge of my guts as the phone rings. Gaby...my sister's name flashes on the screen. I'd texted her earlier. She's the closest thing I have to a parent. Talia agreed we should fill her in on the plan, although with a cautious hesitation—after all, telling Bee was a bloody disaster.

"Big sister!" I answer, and break the news in the same way you pull a Band-Aid—quick with minimal fuss. It's going to suck anyway, so might as well get right to the point.

"Are you mad?"

I hold out the phone as Gabriella shrieks at the same decibel as a sandblaster.

The front door slams. Talia calls out a greeting and announces she's jumping in the shower—a more tempting activity than getting harangued.

I tune back in to the conversation but Gaby's still ranting. "You're dumber than a stick horse. I swear you have shit for brains—hold on a moment...Sorry, darling. Yes, I'll just pop outside." She drops her voice to a theatrical whisper. "Joe thinks I swear too much in front of the girls."

"Fuck him."

Her giggle is wickedly infectious. "He's worse than usual. I swear he's on the rag more than me." She might be over a decade older, and more an actual mother than our real one, but every once in a while she drops the holier-than-thou act. There's a metallic click. She does love to sneak the odd smoke.

"Look, Gabbles, it's not what you think."

"You've got another girl up the duff?"

Her words punch a fist through my sternum and squeeze my heart empty.

"You didn't, did you? Brandon?"

My lips work soundlessly.

"It's not twins, is it? Oh good Lord, I can't wait to smack you in person next week."

"No twins." I clear my throat and make my voice as offhand as possible. "What's all this rubbish about next week?"

"Hello? The AGM?"

"Oh shit, I completely forgot." The AGM—Annual General Meeting—is our family gathering. Most families come together for Christmas or maybe Easter. My parents return once a year right in time for the first Tuesday in November—Melbourne Cup— Australia's biggest horse race. Fancy Thoroughbreds and champagne breakfasts are superior to anything as tedious as a family dinner or actual holiday.

Whatever. That's all old news. I'm not going to act like a whiny bitch because my parents didn't love me enough. Life is life and everyone gets on with it the best way they can. The last thing the world needs is another rich white wanker boo-hooing about how hard he's got it.

Sucks for Gaby's girls—my nieces. Would be nice if they could have grandparents who gave two shits, attended their assemblies and dance recitals. My own granddad, the tough-nosed bastard who founded Lockhart Industries, was a total cock. My uncle Chris says that's why Dad acts the way he does, because he didn't have appropriate male role models. Uncle Chris is one of the best people I know, so I call bullshit there.

But whatever. Like I said, I don't even care.

"Brandon?" My sister's voice brings me crashing back to reality.

"Yeah?"

"Welcome back to the conversation. Are you planning on telling dearest Mummy and Dad about this marriage or is that my fun-filled assignment?"

"Tell Mum and Dad? No. Fuck no—absolutely not. I told you, it's a secret."

"Why?"

"Rock me mama like the wind and the rain, rock me mama like a southbound train..." Talia strolls into our bedroom in pigtails and a pair of flannel pajamas. Her top is unbuttoned to the navel. The effect is hot, and wrong, on so many levels.

I press a finger to my lips.

"Who's there?" Gaby has a phenomenal nose for sniffing out things I want to keep hidden.

Talia doesn't know any of this. Instead, she makes a big show of rubbing her arms. *Cold*, she mouths.

I make room on the bed and lift the covers, patting the space beside me.

She burrows underneath the blankets, cursing under her breath about Australians' moral opposition to central heating.

"That's her, isn't it?" my sister barks, eager to inflict permanent ear damage. "Your little American?"

"Gabbles—"

"Shhh, I got this." Talia pushes herself onto one elbow. "Hello?" she says into the receiver.

Stunned silence. "Natalia? Fabulous! How lovely to meet you, darling. Bran shared the most surprising news." Gabriella switches from shit-talking big sister to polished socialite so fast I've got whiplash.

"Did he?"

"I was inquiring why our parents were being kept in the dark with regards to the happy event."

"Oh, well, this isn't a marriage marriage."

"Well, thank goodness. What are you doing? Exchanging rings or a charming bit of poetry?"

"No," I interject. "It'll be legal—for Talia's visa."

"Then you're serious."

"You promised you wouldn't freak. And no way can Mum find out. What if she pushes for a big show, the opportunity for pictures in the society section?"

Talia is the picture of horrified.

"There was nothing wrong with my wedding." Gaby bristles.

"You're right. When Joe got sauced, did the worm, and broke his nose, that must have been my imagination."

"I ordered a collective memory loss about that moment, remember? Fine. I won't breathe a word about this stupid plan to anyone...on one condition."

"You won't make this easy."

"Nonsense. My stipulation is simple. You come to the AGM."

"I don't want to make promises."

"Very well. I'm sure Mum and Dad will be ecstatic to learn you're planning *another* wedding to yet *another* foreign girl."

Talia goes so stiff I'm half tempted to check her for rigor mortis. We don't speak about Adie or what happened in Denmark. Talia knows the grim details and that's enough. The topic isn't an elephant in the room—not exactly—more like a tiger snake, elusive, poisonous, and best kept at a distance.

"I'm serious, Spunk. Don't leave me hanging, not right now. Joe is being a right prick and I can't face the parents on my own. There's something up with them. I need you here."

"Talia is trying to finish her thesis."

"It's okay. I've only got to finish the bibliography and proofread. We'd love to come," Talia pipes into the receiver. Her face has lost some of its tightness from a moment ago.

The snake is back in the shadows and the room feels safe again.

"You're growing on me, darling." Gabriella's tone is all begrudging sweetness—about as good as things get where my sister is concerned.

Once I hang up the phone, Talia drops her head on the pillow. "Sorry, I freaked out a little, huh?"

"It's okay, but you don't know what you've agreed to." I pretend like she's talking about committing us for a Melbourne visit, not Adie.

She goes along with my act. "Will it be that bad?"

"Picture the worst thing you can imagine and go ahead and make it ten thousand times worse. That's an optimistic take on meeting my parents."

"I was so stupid." She covers her face with her hands. "I wanted your sister to like me."

"She'll be crazy for you."

"Or think I'm crazy," she mumbles.

"Hey." I peel her fingers off her cheeks. "I'm in one hundred percent support of the Talia nutjob. At least your version carries sweetness. My dad, though, he can't help himself—he's a bastard Lockhart through and through. Like my sister. Like me."

"How's that?"

"Assholes, the lot of us."

"And your mom?"

"I noticed you didn't deny the truth."

"Come on now, I'm not getting into verbal battle over how big of a jerk you are. That's almost as pointless as getting into a land war in Asia."

What is she talking about?

"*Princess Bride* reference." She slides her toes onto me.

A block of ice hits my leg. "Fuck."

"Heat me up, Scotty." Her toes inch over my legs. "Can I do it, please?"

"Bloody hell. You are torture, you know that?"

She settles her feet on my abdomen. "Aaah, thank you. You are a human furnace."

"I burn for you, baby."

"The sun to my Pluto."

"That doesn't make sense."

"I know, right?"

We snicker at our capacity for stupidity, giving each other googly eyes from opposite pillows. I rub her ankles while she surprises me with a ridiculously adept rendition of "Sexy and I Know It" in a Cookie Monster voice. I've given this girl my whole heart, might as well throw in whatever soul may or may not be lurking around for good measure. I've never experienced so many good moments until Talia came into my life.

"I'm kind of looking forward to Melbourne."

"Masochist."

"Your family can't be *that* awful."

"Awful? No, I guess not. That would imply a capacity for actual emotions."

"Well, I'm excited to meet them."

"Famous last words."

That night Talia wakes screaming.

15

TALIA

A crisply dressed man stands in the airport baggage claim with a simple sign that reads LOCKHART in black marker. "I'm guessing that's not your dad." Bran hasn't seen his parents in a whole year and they hire a limousine service?

His answering laughter is resigned, but I'm grateful for any response. He's barely spoken since driving to the Hobart Airport. I hate the shadows under his eyes and the lingering pallor beneath his olive skin. He developed aviophobia—a fear of flying—two years ago. Pretty normal considering the commercial airliner he was traveling on suffered catastrophic engine failure, leading to the loss of all flight controls. The crew pulled off the impossible— a perfectly executed forced landing at high airspeed—with zero fatalities. The media dubbed the incident "the Miracle Flight."

My nana is fond of saying, "There are no atheists in foxholes." But Bran proves her wrong. To his way of thinking, why would God pick and choose where to intervene? Why tweak the fate of his plane but allow a genocide to occur in Rwanda or gang violence to continue in Chicago? It seems perverse for divine intervention to save him, but not all. I don't get the feeling Bran was ever exactly religious, but his experiences in Denmark and then the doomed flight took him to the edge of a void, and when he looked down, he saw nothing.

He never talks about that time but as the plane wheels launched from the runway, I gripped his hand and promised not to let go. And I didn't. Yeah, it was awkward to hold hands the entire flight but the arrangement kept Bran's shoulders from hanging out with his ears. I'm not sure what I believe about life, the universe and everything, but I don't want him to feel so alone.

The driver expertly whizzes the Mercedes around cars on the congested CityLink, one of the main traffic arteries pumping through Melbourne. The downtown skyline comes into view and I identify the starkly arrogant Eureka Tower and the Rialto. Bran links his pinky finger with mine. We have history here—from the first awkward meeting on Lygon Street to the final crushing good-bye outside Flinders Station—we spent a wild semester falling in love in this town.

I like the place. Overshadowed by Sydney's over-the-top natural beauty and on a world stage by better-known cities like New York, Paris, London, or San Francisco, Melbourne just is. The city is cool and doesn't really care if you notice or not, except that it totally does.

And I get that.

I so get that.

We zip around the Eastern Shore, catching the odd glimpses of container ships on Port Phillip Bay. Eventually the rolling hills give way to the swanky resort towns. Traffic slows as we reach the Mornington Peninsula, the narrow land strip separating the calm bay waters from the wild Bass Strait. Finally, welcome to Portsea,

Australia's most affluent postcode—Bran's hometown. The car slows in front of a boxy modern-style mansion that could be mistaken for a sun-drenched resort except for the sliding security gate and four-car garage.

Bran presses lips to my ear as the driver comes to a stop. "You'll always be my girl?"

Before I have a chance for reassurances, he beats the driver to the punch and opens his own door.

"No worries, mate. I got these." He grabs our bags from the trunk.

Bran is quick to put distance between him and his former privileged status. His family's money is rooted in investments like coal and uranium mining. After he chained himself to a bulldozer at a work site financed by Lockhart Industries, their relationship whittled down to this AGM. To hear him describe it, the week is worse than having a chimpanzee yank out your eyelashes.

We visited this house once before, when no one was home, and he showed me the family photos he hides under his bed. My heart aches for the little boy trapped inside the surly young man, privately yearning for a family who loves and respects him.

Bran heads toward the house. "There's an outstanding chance no one will be home." His voice is tight, nervous. "They have to put in all the appearances."

"One can hope," I mutter as we step inside, not daring my voice to echo off the Italian marble. My mom doesn't exactly hail from the wrong side of the tracks but whenever I visit my grandparents' place in Carmel, at least I feel welcomed. Sure, there's opulence, like hundred-dollar bottles of wine casually uncorked over dinner. Spa visits. Leisurely lunches in charming bistros where meals cost more than our weekly grocery budget. Still, Gramps drives a fifteen-year-old Outback and their conversations trend toward upcoming philanthropic events with the focus being the cause not the guest list.

Bran's house is something entirely different. I've been here before but it's startling—even the bling has bling. I take in the sunken living room with cinema seating and avoid making eye contact with the tiger rug growling from behind the open doors of an adjacent study. Bran's grandfather shot the poor creature on a big-game hunting trip to the Indian subcontinent back in the fifties. The décor is mobster meets Martha Stewart and makes me feel like I've got a split personality. On one hand I want to slip into a gold-embossed minidress and sip Cristal, but on the other hand, I'm compelled to wear a cashmere twin set, cross my ankles, and nibble crudités.

"Brandon?"

I whirl at the sound of the strong, male voice and pray my face remains blank. Bran's dad is shirtless, wrapped in a plush towel that reveals a gym-toned body that's pretty dang good for a dude of a certain age. I expected from photos that Bran's dad would be a handsome, older version of his son, not that they'd look almost identical. I also didn't anticipate the weird physical reaction of seeing Bran's eyes set in a slightly more craggy face.

Crap, really? Do I have to be such a freaking creeper? Look away. Look anywhere else.

I catch the tiger's gaze. His scowl matches the master of the house.

"You're early. Traffic must have been light."

"Sorry to be an inconvenience." Bran's tone couldn't be more facetious.

His father clears his throat and hitches the towel tied at his waist. He's not naked under there, is he? Please God, no. Otherwise, go ahead and smite out my eyes.

"We'll unpack," Bran mutters the exact same time his dad says: "I'm having a sauna."

Tempting to clap my hands and crow, *Jinx.*

I'm the first to break the awkward silence. "Hello, Mr. Lockhart. I'm Talia. A pleasure to finally meet you." I automatically stick out my hand. Good manners toward adults have been drilled into me since infancy.

"I'm sure." The look he gives me is pure sardonic Bran but his handshake is perfectly firm.

I wait for him to say, "Call me Bryce" and dispense with my polite formality.

"If you'll excuse me, I'm feeling rather rubbish at the moment—damn this flu."

I manage to resist the overpowering urge to wave an imaginary wand and shout, *I damn it, sir!* Prove to all I'm an awkward freak show at heart.

He continues through the French doors to a landscaped garden where an infinity-edge pool and tennis court are clearly visible.

Wow. At last, someone who makes Bran look like a shoo-in for Mr. Congeniality.

Bran gives me a look like, *Told you so.*

I dig out my tact and decide to let the issue drop. Who knows, maybe he really is under the weather.

Bran leads me up the spiral staircase. "He's usually more polite to strangers. You are clearly tainted through association. Sorry."

"Tainted?" A gorgeous woman leans over the railing. Another familiar face from pictures—Bran's sister, Gabriella.

"Gabbles," Bran says in greeting. She embraces him in an

awkward side hug while he pecks a kiss on her perfect cheekbone. "Where's Jocko?"

"Joe hates when you call him that."

"Good."

"He's out to drinks with the boys. I stayed back to take some time for myself." Her smile doesn't match the flinty look in her eyes.

"And the girls?"

"At home for the week."

"Alone?"

"No, there's this delightful invention called an *au pair*."

"When do nominations for Mother of the Year open?"

She swats him in the chest. "You see Dad?"

"Yeah."

"He's been in bed all morning. Mum says he has muscle pains." She rechecks her sleek chignon with a frown.

I want to say, *Don't bother, you are perfect.*

Looking at Bran and his sister together, it's not fair. They share identically elegant bone structure, flawless olive skin, and thick dark hair. In comparison, I'm a toadstool—or maybe the worm scrounging beneath the toadstool.

Gabriella gives me a quick once-over and takes in my messy bun and messenger bag with an inscrutable expression—apparently a Lockhart family trait.

"Talia, correct?"

"Hey." I give a little finger wave and resist the urge to flinch.

OMG—a wave. Can you geek out any more?

"Where are you from?"

"The U.S."

She gives me a patient smile.

"Oh, yeah, you already know that. Um, I'm Californian, born and raised."

"Lovely." Her eyes briefly meet mine, the same polished jade hue as her brother's. "Excited for the Cup?"

"Sorry? Oh, right, that's the big horse race. Yeah, sure, I guess."

Her laugh is tinkling, like silver spoons on champagne glasses. "You'll have to show me your frock later."

"Frock?" I glance at Bran, befuddled.

"*Brandon*! Tell me you informed your little American about the dress code?" Gabriella stares at my Chuck Taylors as if they'll burst into Jimmy Choos with a sprinkle of pixie dust.

Bran grips my elbow and steers me down the hall. "Come on, Captain. Let's get to my room, bar the door."

"I packed a skirt," I say over one shoulder.

"A skirt?" Gabriella sounds like I just informed her of my intention to become a nudist.

Are those Bran's teeth I hear grinding?

"At least you brought a hat?" She hastens after us.

"You mean like a ball cap?" I mimic tipping the rim.

"Are you joking? It's hard to tell." She blinks so fast it's as if she's got black butterflies attached to her lids. "What's your dress size?"

"An eight?"

"In American or Australian?"

"There's a difference?"

"If you're a size eight in America, you are a ten here."

"Okay, a ten it is." Wonderful, I upped a dress size in the span of a minute. Bran opens his door and gestures like he's about to pull the drawbridge over the moat. I step inside.

"I'll see what I can rummage but don't expect a miracle," she calls after us, sounding less than optimistic.

Gaby would probably be a size 2 back home. There's no way even half my booty would fit into anything in her closet.

Bran slams his bedroom door and braces himself against the frame like marauding tigers give chase.

"Wow. That was—"

"What did I tell you?"

16

BRAN

*A*fter an hour, the house remains quiet and I sneak Talia through a side door for a neighborhood walkabout. We stroll past the golf course toward the dunes, blanketed by dense tea tree thickets.

"I still can't believe this is where you grew up," she says as we reach the paved walking track.

"Why?"

"We haven't seen any little kids. Only tourists and old people."

"Yeah, pretty much." We pause at the London Bridge Lookout. The rocky arch juts from the turbulent waters like a lonely sentinel. A persistent wind blows salt spray in our faces, smells like brine and kelp—of home.

"Feels like the world's end." Talia nestles under my arm.

"Nah, Tasmania's right there, beyond the horizon."

"Hard to believe."

"I used to imagine stealing a yacht and sailing over Bass Strait. Running away from everyone."

"Tasmania was the promised land?"

"A bit like that."

"Well, you made it in the end, didn't you?"

"Yeah. I did."

She squeezes my hand. "With no boat thievery required."

We follow the trail through melaleuca groves to the wide swath of sand. A few intrepid surfers catch rides on head-high breakers.

"Portsea Back Beach," I say.

"There's uncharacteristic affection in that statement."

I bend and choose a turbo shell, running my thumb over the spiral. "Guess this place is special. As a kid, I ran feral around these parts, from here all the way out to that land tip, Cape Schanck."

We watch a surfer flail off a wave and eat some serious shit.

"The current is full on. Check out that rip!"

"We lost a prime minister down the point, over Cheviot Beach way." I point toward the rugged cliffs to the west.

"You're joking! Countries don't up and lose their leaders."

"Australia did—happened back in the sixties. Harold Holt. He went for a swim and was swept away."

"Holy crap."

"There's a memorial to him in Point Nepean National Park. They never recovered his body."

"Shivers. What's with all the dead birds?"

"Short-tailed shearwaters. They migrate here from Alaska and feed and breed along the coast during the summer months. The trip's long and most are extremely weak by the time they arrive. Many don't make it."

"They come all this way only to die?"

"A natural phenomenon."

"Morbid." She stares at the moody clouds skirting the horizon. "This place was your boyhood stomping ground?"

"More or less. Not the National Park so much. Nepean was used as a military firing range for decades. The place is riddled with unexploded ordnance."

"So what do we have? Disappearing world leader? Check. Ticking time bombs? Check. Dead birds? Check times a thousand. Freaking idyllic."

I brush a lock of hair off her forehead and kiss the worried wrinkle. "And to think you haven't even partaken in a family dinner yet."

———

Talia jumps in the shower after we return home. I wander to the kitchen for a rummage. Dad perches on a barstool, glaring at a spreadsheet open on his iPad. He hears my footsteps and looks up without a smile, scouring the skin between his brows with two fingers.

"G'day." I pour hot water into a French press and grab a still-warm croissant. The best part of my parents' house? The on-site chef they hire for the weeks they are in town.

"Hello." He dabs his nose with a handkerchief and blood smears the linen. What's going on there?

I clear my throat. "Everything okay?"

"Fine." He pockets the cloth without a glance in my direction. "How's uni?"

"Good."

Silence.

If I'm not getting an MBA at INSEAD, he's not interested.

I toss the uneaten pastry in the rubbish; it's a waste, but I've lost my appetite.

"Brandon? We'll need to schedule some time during your visit for a conversation."

"Fine." Didn't he spend the last few minutes ignoring me? "Check your busy calendar and pencil me in for a suitable time."

"Right." He acts as if I'm being earnest. "Looking forward to it."

"Bonza." I grab another pastry for Talia and tear upstairs.

She's sprawled belly-down on my bed, hair wrapped in a towel. "There you are." She closes the surf mag. "Uh-oh. Who got to you?"

I punch the dresser beside me. The rage enters and leaves my body so fast I'm not even sure it was there at all, except my knuckles hurt like fucking hell.

"What the— Are you all right?" She pushes to her knees.

"I'm fine."

"Let's talk before you destroy whatever delicious baked good you're carrying in the nonviolent hand."

"Don't want to."

"Fine, go ahead and Bruce Lee the furniture."

I pass her the tart.

"Seriously, what went down?"

"We should have stayed in Tassie. There's nothing here for me. But what do I care? I made my peace with all of that a long time ago."

"That's debatable." She holds out her arms and I crawl over to rest my head on her chest, close my eyes, and focus on her heartbeats.

"I have a home here, with you."

She presses her lips to my throbbing knuckles. "Poor little hand."

"Make it better." I reach for her breast. She's not wearing a bra.

"Not so fast. You need a hug, not a booty call."

"Heal me." My voice is sarcastic but I mean those two words from the badlands of my barren soul.

"Cheer up, Charlie, I got your back." She removes my roving hand from under her shirt and clasps it instead. "I get it, trust me, you know I do. Family isn't for the fainthearted."

"Bloody oath."

She wiggles the pastry in my face. "Now you must tell me, what is this magical creation?"

"Fig and mascarpone tart."

She takes a careful nibble. Her eyes close as she chews with reverence. "Oh my God, I'm having a taste bud party." She opens one eye and offers me a bite. "Sure you don't want an invite?"

"No."

"Seriously, you don't want to miss this. I'm having some sort of a religious experience. I'll probably start speaking in tongues soon."

"I'm not hungry." But I tear off a chunk because she gives that cute-as-hell smile, trying her damndest to cheer me.

She wipes crumbs from her lip. "Hands down, that's the best thing I ever put in my mouth."

"Should I be offended?" I pop the bite into my mouth—not bad.

She sticks out her tongue. "That tart sky-rocketed to the top of my getting-stranded-on-a-desert-island pack list."

"Good luck with that. You'd be dead from scurvy within a few months."

"Okay, Smarty Man, what would you bring?"

"Coconuts, beans, kale."

"Must you be the most literal person on the planet?"

"I'm surprised you can even hear me from Hyperbole Mountain."

"You can shut it and watch me gobble the rest of this like the goddamn Cookie Monster."

A blob of jam smears on her cheek. "Let me get that for you." I give her a slow lick.

She heaves a blissed-out sigh.

"You good?" Would be nice if one of us was doing okay.

"Truth?"

"Always."

"I'm happier than a Disney movie." She kisses my cheek. "You know I'm addicted to this dimple? It's kind of getting to be a problem."

I tickle her and she shrieks as the sharp sound of heels in the corridor passes my closed door. Mom. We fall silent but the foot-steps don't slow a beat.

I gather Talia close and lock my chin on the top of her head. "Make some room in that happy place, Captain. We need a fucking hideout."

———

Talia and I hole up in my room for the rest of the afternoon. We cuddle, nap, and read my old stash of comics and surf magazines. I regain control. Whatever storm raged through me has retreated by evening.

Talia rolls from the bed and heads to her suitcase, removing her T-shirt in favor of a dressier top.

"Don't change for them. No one in this house is worth half of you."

"I'm going into battle, need armor." She applies a light lipstick.

"You don't need any of that. You're a knockout." And I mean it. Talia looks better first thing in the morning than most girls who spend an hour in pointless primping.

"What's she like—your mom?"

"Blend emotionless with robotic and drizzle the result in expensive hair products."

"That bad?"

"Worse." After I made the front page of the paper getting chained to the bulldozer, Mom seemed finished with me. It's hardly as if she'd been doting. She did have me late. Gaby was already a teenager. A baby probably felt like a pain in the ass.

But a baby can't help getting born.

"When it comes to Dad, well, he's got blood on his hands. But the fact of the matter is, we all do, this whole family. Rampant environmental exploitation has been financed by Lockhart Industries dollars, with irreparable impacts. This is a firm that invests in natural resource and timber companies not only in Australia but also throughout the developing world. We aren't in the heart of the beast—we *are* the bloody beast. All this stuff, the money, the upperclass bullshit privilege, and the trappings—promise you won't ever ask for it."

"I would never—"

"I'm serious." I sit back on my knees. "Don't be flippant. Someday in the future, shit will go down one way or another. An event will occur that means we need my family for connections or money. We can't. I made that promise five years ago and I've stuck it out."

"I'm not with you as part of a secret billionaire fantasy plot."

"Maybe not now, but someday you might change your mind."

She looks down at her wrist, where I hold on tight.

"You are starting to freak me out. I get it, okay? My dad never wanted to touch my mom's family money. He wanted them to make their own way. And they did, until Pippa was in the hospital. Sometimes there are good reasons to break rules."

I jump from the bed and start to pace. "Being in this house..."

Nothing dramatically terrible happened within these walls. No physical abuse. No alcoholism. Not even raised voices.

Silence and inattention aren't torture. They leave no outward bruise.

"You have a sucky family life, Bran. Happens to the best of us."

"*You're* my family."

"And you're mine."

"Sometimes I want to keep you in a box, away from the world."

"I get claustrophobic, remember?"

"I know. I just fucking love you so much."

"I love you, too, but don't watch me sleep."

"Why not?"

"It's creepy and Edward Culleny."

"Edward who?"

She rolls her eyes. "Never mind."

The door flies open and Gaby bursts in. "Are your pants on, lover boy? We're all waiting."

"Remind me, how old are you these days, Gabbles? Fortyish? About time you learn doors were made for knocking?"

"I'm still very much a thirtysomething, prick."

"Congratulations."

"Talia, we need to sort out what you're wearing tomorrow, darling. After dinner we can rummage through my closet. There's not much, unfortunately, mostly old leftovers from school formals and footy functions."

My sister used to serially date Australian rules football players, mostly so she could preen over photographs of herself in tabloid magazines.

"We'll be down in a sec."

A few minutes later, we wander toward the stairs. Her husband, Joe, is mouth breathing into his phone from the landing. He flicks his hand in greeting, a fat watch glinting from the chandelier light. "Got to run." He clicks the phone off and shoves it into his pocket.

He's shorter than me, a former jockey sporting middle-age spread and a hard glint to his eyes.

"Brandon! Mate!"

"Joe."

Cheating, fucker scum.

I busted him sexting five years ago, right after Ruby, their second daughter, was born—quite the stand-up guy. I'd been crashing with him and my sister in those heated days after the whole chaining-myself-to-a-bulldozer photo debacle. Uni wasn't starting for two more weeks and I had nowhere to go. He convinced me of the wisdom of not telling Gaby. Even intimated she messed around too.

My fake-but-real marriage is going to be better than theirs. My parents' too. Word is Mum and Dad don't even share the same bedroom in Singapore.

I love sleeping with Talia. Why would I ever want to miss out on the cute noises she makes as she drifts off? Or the way it feels to wake in the morning, skin to skin, her sweet smell filling my senses?

Did my parents ever have that? Or Gabriella and Joe?

If so, how did they lose it?

Because I'm never losing Talia. I'm not going to dick around. Or put up with us on opposite sides of the bed, giving each other the cold back before eventually retreating into parallel lives.

"Hi, I'm Talia."

Joe looks at her like she's a chocolate truffle.

Talia clears her throat, offers a hand. "Nice to meet you. I've heard so much about the girls."

My nieces. Those girls are the only ones in this whole family circus who are halfway normal. Why aren't they here? Gaby better not consider shoving them off to boarding school too.

Dinner is silent.

"This, uh, fish is really great," Talia says.

"Yeah," I add after a ten-second pause when no one else chimes in. "Delicious."

Mum gives her a foggy look. She must have spent this afternoon with her Xanax prescription. "You're Canadian?"

"Me?" Talia looks around like maybe there's another North American who can rescue her. "Oh no, just American. California exactly. The Bay Area?"

"Oh." Mom's tone could mean any number of things. None of them positive.

"Silicon Valley?" Dad glances from his e-mail.

"Nope, that's over the hill. I was raised in Santa Cruz, a little beach town that—"

"Okay." Dad returns to his e-mails.

"California." Joe braces his elbows on the table. "Like *90210*? I had a thing for Donna." When he grins, there's spinach stuck between his teeth.

"The television show?" Talia looks confused.

Gaby glares at a wine bottle. "Enough already."

"You stop, that chick was hot. I love blond girls."

My sister's hair is almost black.

"I have a migraine." Gaby jumps from the table but Joe doesn't budge a muscle.

"I might pop down to the pub after tea, have a few cold ones with the guys."

My sister makes a rude noise and leaves.

Mum hasn't blinked and Dad doesn't look up from his screen.

"Hmm, *90210*. Donna?" Talia snaps her fingers. "Wait, it's coming to me. I think you're referring to the original version. Sorry, can't help you—that one started before I was born."

She catches my gaze and winks.

I grin. "Showing your age, Jocko."

"Don't call me that, mate."

He always acts like we should kiss his ass because he used to ride horses. He can go fuck himself. In a stable. With a pitchfork.

"We're done. Good night, Mum, good night, Dad."

"So nice to meet you both," Talia says.

Dad grunts.

"Be ready by ten, Brandon," Mum replies. "The drivers will arrive then. It will be a big day."

"I'm sure it will."

17

TALIA

*I*t takes me .01 seconds to grasp that the Spring Racing Carnival, with the Melbourne Cup as the headlining event, is an Event, with a capital *E*. Impossibly chic crowds throng the entrances to Flemington Racecourse, decked out in styles found in this month's fashion magazines. I haven't seen so many gorgeous hats in one place since I watched Kate marry Will. These women are dressed to kill—in a literal sense. TSA agents back home would confiscate most of these heels for lethal potential. I smooth my flouncy, tiered skirt and yank the beaded tank, the fanciest items I could conjure from my suitcase.

While the fact that Joe bailed last night seems a Very Bad Thing, he did prevent an hour or so of shaming. Gaby's retreat into her childhood bedroom saved me from admitting I couldn't squeeze my curves into her petite wardrobe. Ahead, a silver BMW maneuvers into the valet station. When the driver opens the back door, Gaby and Joe emerge looking happy enough. Bran's parents strut from the Bentley behind us, coolly elegant, wearing the most stylish item of all—identically bored expressions.

Bran doesn't budge until our own driver opens the door and waits. "Sir?"

"We're up." I scruff my fingers over the back of his head. "And don't forget to smile. Who knows, we might even have fun." I'm using the same voice parents put on when they tell their kids to eat mushy peas or overcooked Brussels sprouts.

"You're the history major. Does medieval torture amuse you?" Bran mutters.

"Come on, Spunk," Gaby calls from the curb, surreptitiously checking her lipstick in a hand mirror.

Bran gets out and reaches for my hand. He's not dressed any fancier than me—gray slacks, no tie—but holy hell, he looks like a model plucked from a sexy cologne advertisement. Put him in a rumpled collared shirt and it's not hard to imagine him dining with nubile heiresses in Monte Carlo.

Quick, someone give this boy a yacht!

I smooth my frizz, failing to ignore the cougar stares from the surrounding women. Yes, ladies, he's totally paw worthy.

If anyone does pay me any attention, I know they're wondering the same thing as me. Why is a guy like him with a girl like me?

His family turns in unison on some invisible signal and moves toward a private entrance.

Bran makes a weird growling noise, a cross between a warning and frustration.

"You okay?"

His teeth clench so tight he'll need a trip to the dentist when we return to Hobart. "I hate this." He jerks his head at the milling crowds, preening like expensive peacocks. "I fucking hate all of this. Such a bloody waste." He's not spouting vitriol; his entire body is rigid with blatant dread.

Any awkward self-consciousness evaporates. Who cares how I'm dressed? Bran needs me.

"I've got your back." And he'll have mine. He doesn't want me in a designer dress. He made that obvious last night. From the look in his admiring eyes, he gives me exactly what I need to fight insecurity. "I won't let go." I link my fingers with his and squeeze.

"You're amazing."

"You owe me."

"Big-time."

"Massive."

"Ready?"

"Holy crap, are those photographers?"

"They're only interested in my parents, and Joe and Gaby. He used to race, remember?"

The camera lenses pivot in our direction.

"Hang on." I clutch his hand.

"Let's show the bastards." Bran's panic attack is apparently under control, for the familiar surly edge returns to his voice.

"It's paparazzi, not a firing squad."

"Same difference." He shoves on his sunglasses and saunters forward, leading me straight through the horde. His cocky posture makes it seem like he's got this scene down to a red carpet science, but really I know it's because he couldn't care less. Me, on the other hand, I'll probably be in papers tomorrow looking like a deer on the interstate or a special feature for *What Not to Wear*.

Do I have food in my teeth? What if I trip? Or someone asks me a question and I say something totally stupid?

But Bran's right. We're photographed yet generally ignored. We end up in a plush box, right in front of the finish line.

"You guys nab the cheap seats, hey?"

Bran eyes the full complimentary bar. "I need a beer."

Gaby breezes in with two flutes filled with pale yellow bubbles.

"You survived! Cheers." She hands me a glass. "Keep calm, drink champagne. That's how you do the Cup."

"You actually enjoy this cluster?" Incredulity tinges my words.

"Today is tradition."

"You sound like you're ready to start singing *Fiddler on the Roof.*"

"Mmmm." Gaby wipes away an invisible mascara clump, either not listening or not caring. No problem, I'm only anxiously talking a bunch of crap.

"Who've you bet on?" she asks, brightening and switching on a supernova smile.

"Um..." I actually hadn't given it the first thought. "Should I—"

"We're here under duress." Bran steps in to my rescue. "Remember?"

"Yeah, yeah, Spunk. Whatever. Oh, look, there's a potted plant over there who might find your complaints entertaining." Gaby dismisses her brother as if he were nothing more than a bothersome fly and turns back to me, staring over my shoulder, twin lines putting in a brief appearance on either side of her mouth.

"Is everything—"

Gaby throws back her neck, exposing her slim throat, and laughs like I told a hilarious joke. Which I didn't—I didn't say anything.

I turn around and restrain an immediate gag because there's Joe trading toothy grins with a server on the wrong side of twenty. He makes this grand douche baggy show of deciding which finicky appetizer to select. After about an epoch, he pops a quinoa cracker with Brie and salmon down the hatch, chewing with seductive slowness like he stars in his own personal soft porn movie. No way—he's totally licking his plump fingers. Sick.

The whole scene is cringe-worthy.

Joe clearly entertains delusions that he's hot shit, even though his looks are fading faster than wallpaper in a sunny room. I mean, Gaby is a bona fide beauty queen while Joe's hair thins in the back, the buttons slightly strain over his abdomen, and his nose is one shade of red over attractive.

Why is he allowed to get away with such dickish antics?

Gaby shuts off her laughter like a faucet and grinds out a blandly polite excuse to sashay toward an attractive man with salt-and-pepper hair. Apparently my role as a stage prop wasn't satisfactory to whatever scene she's acting. I'm left in her dust, still giggling uncomfortably for no reason.

"Brandon?" Mariana struts into the room with two well-heeled women. She repeats her son's name as if she can't place him for a moment. "Oh yes, Brandon. He's still at university."

There are a few polite murmurings.

"Bran's doing so great—his supervisor is basically obsessed with him. You should be really proud." I throw in my two cents and resist the urge to duck when all heads swivel in my direction.

Obsessed? Great, I made a respected professor sound like a serial killer.

"Yes…uh, this is…" Mariana's voice fades.

"Talia. I'm Talia." I bite the inside of my cheek while automatically giving a polite smile. I don't think the gesture is particularly attractive. Everyone stares at me. Pins and needles shoot down my legs.

"She's American." His mother recovers, waving her hand at me like I'm an interesting piece of art she's compelled to explain. "Californian, from near San Francisco."

There's an invisible band around my head growing tighter and tighter.

Please stop looking at me.

I'm bailed out from an unlikely quarter.

"Brandon's in the middle of his honors year," Bryce pipes in, waving off a tray of food. "We're expecting a first-class result before he moves on to a PhD."

"What business did you say your father was in, Talia?"

I didn't.

"He's a geologist." Thankfully Bran decides to return from wherever he's zoned off to at an opportune moment.

"Geologist?" One of the men perks, turning his head in my direction. "What game is he in—mining?"

"My dad?" I laugh at the idea. "Oh God, as if!" Wait, aren't a few of these men iron ore tycoons? "Sorry. I mean...ahem...no nothing like that."

"Talia's father currently works in ecotourism but his main interests center on the impacts of global warming in coastal communities," Bran says before I can utter a word. I love the shape of his mouth but not when it's bent in this frown.

After that, the comments fly fast and furious from all sides. It's pretty much open season.

"Bring it on. My beach house is at a hundred meters. Give it another twenty years and I'll swim from my front door."

"Rubbish. Climate change is fodder for socialist journos determined to peddle their propaganda to the masses."

Bran studies climate change, too, but no one in his family utters a word to our defense. Mariana examines her nails like they are engraved with the meaning of life.

"How about it, Brandon? Still think profit's a dirty word?" a fleshy-faced man near the bar calls out, smiling nastily.

For fuck's sake, we're being swarmed in this snake pit. Why can't Gaby come to the rescue? Nope, she's too busy trying to give Joe a mental vasectomy. Bryce stands near the giant windows giving an Oscar-winning performance in obliviousness.

"Don't bait him, Boris," a Stepford wife chides with a laugh after the pointed silence threatens to poke out my eardrums.

Eventually the pack retreats to debate threats such as the Green Party and carbon taxes.

Bran and I stand on the sidelines surrounded by people considered wildly successful by most standard measures. Imagine if Bran had followed his parents' plan? Joined this world? I know more about hedgehogs than I know about hedge funds. I don't want this—any of it.

Bran's dad catches my gaze while polishing his wire-frame glasses. He has his son's eyes but with none of the soulfulness. He seems to weigh me, measure my worth, and decide I'm lacking.

"Son," he calls. "A word, please."

"We need fresh air." Bran slides open a large window.

"Brandon, stop fiddling," Mariana says coldly. "The air-conditioning is on."

Bran looks tempted to send his sneaker through the glass.

I rest my hand on his lower back, the muscles tight beneath his shirt. "Walk with me?"

"Fuck yes." He grabs a champagne bottle on the way out.

"Son—"

"Later, Dad. Later."

His mother doesn't give us a second look.

We escape the private box with the canapés, plasma televisions, plastic people, and recycled air in favor of the crowds and the sun on our faces. Bran forgoes a glass, drinking the champagne straight from the bottle.

"Easy, tiger."

He pulls the bottle from my reach. His shirttails are untucked, and with that scowl and mussed-up hair, he resembles a pirate whose ship's been plundered.

I'm desperate for any distraction. "I don't even know how a horse race works." I point at the posted odds by the TAB bookies. "What does this stuff mean—quinella? Each way? Place bet?"

"Do you seriously care?"

"We're at a horse race. What else are we going to do? Talk about how bad your parents' friends suck?"

"See, a firing squad is more fun."

"Well, nothing we can do about it. So cut out the pity drinking and throw me a bone." I yank the bottle from his hand and pass it off to a pack of blondies who can't be over eighteen. "Ladies?"

"Thanks!" one says, and they huddle around giggling.

"Fucking hell, Captain."

"This trip is hard enough without you going drunk-ass." I hook my thumbs into his belt loop and bring us hip to hip.

"Why do I ever have to do anything besides look at you?"

"Let's play a game. You and me, we're superheroes against the world."

I let his hands perfectly mold around my ass; at least life returns to his eyes.

"What's your special power?" I tease his dick with my thumb.

"You play a dangerous game."

"You could use a distraction."

"Bloody oath." He smiles at my eyebrow waggling. "Tell you what—let's get out of here. Hail a cab, go home, and fuck each other brainless. No one will be home for hours."

"But won't they—"

"You were struck down with the flu." He presses his hand against my forehead. "They'll believe it. My dad's been sick, remember?"

I rub my bare arms. "I have chills, and the muscle aches are excruciating."

"I need to rub your back, bring you medicine."

"You were devastated to miss the fun."

"Careful, we can't take it too far; otherwise they'll know it's bullshit."

"True."

"Blimey, if it isn't Brandon Bloody Lockhart. Haven't lost your touch, mate."

Crap, we almost made it out alive.

There's a youngish guy playing the grown-up in an Italian suit. He fingers his overgelled hair and brandishes a self-satisfied smile.

"Davo!" Bran says with forced cheer. The guys exchange a complicated brotastic handshake. "We went to boarding school together," he tells me as an aside.

"The old times were good times, hey, man?" Davo talks too close. He gives me a blatant up and down with bloodshot eyes. "So tonight, after party at my new place. Bring your little hottie."

"Girlfriend," Bran says, laying claim.

"Talia," I add.

"A pleasure." Davo grabs my hand and kisses my knuckles

like they're a treat to be savored—he's so smooth I can barely hang on.

Bran makes his murdery face. Impossible boy. How could I want to do anything more than wash my hands after Davo's skeezy touch? Seriously, I'm about to go hunt down hand sanitizer.

"Sounds like a plan. See you later tonight, Talia?"

I'm not digging his self-satisfied smirk.

"Gee, I don't know." I manufacture a pathetic black lung cough. "I'm a little fluey."

Bran snorts and this guy chuckles like he has a clue.

"We've got to go place a bet." I tug Bran's hand, lean toward the bookies.

"You guys are crazy. Catch you later. Tonight's going to be off the hook." Davo bails with a cheesedick wink.

"I'm willing to wager that guy's herpes has herpes."

"The odds are in your favor," Bran mutters.

The lines are long in the betting area. "You feel lucky, punk?" I put on my worst mobster accent.

"No."

"Come on. Not even a little smile?"

"I'm not in the mood, Captain."

"I don't blame you. This place is Douchebagland. I've changed my mind. No ducking and running. We stay, dig in our heels, and not let the bastards get us down."

"Really?"

"What the hell."

"Correction: We're in hell."

"For sure. So what can go wrong?"

"Fine, but for the record, I'd rather be copping a feel in the back of a cab."

I scan the horse names. "Beam Me Up, that guy sounds promising."

"My vote is for Chip on His Shoulder."

"Ha, big surprise. Oh, look. This one!"

"Rooster?"

"Yes, check out his odds."

"They're awful."

"A dark horse. I like it. Rooster by a nose."

Bran's smile disappears. He's frozen, statue still.

"What?" I've suddenly got chills.

"Rat bastard."

He's gone, bulldozing through the crowd. Bodies fly from his path.

What the hell?

I tear in his general direction but the heaving bodies block my vision. Luckily I'm in flats so I can duck and weave through the crowd with the velocity of a fresh-shot marble. Elbows and shoulders jab in reply.

There, I see him. Beating the everlasting shit out of his brother-in-law, Joe the Jockey.

Bran is strong with a naturally graceful agility that is anything but right now. He's bobbing and weaving trying to land another quick punch. He must have gotten a good one in because Joe's lip is busted and bleeding.

I run forward because no one else raises a finger to stop this shitshow. The bloodlust is palpable.

"Get back," Bran orders me, not taking his eyes off Joe. "This cheating scumbag's earned a shit-kicking."

"I don't think—"

"Talia…" He spares me a warning glance and that's all it takes for Joe to seize an opportunity. He dives forward, grabs Bran in a tackle hold, and lunges to the ground. But Bran flips over and lands a solid face punch. There's a wet sound like a mallet striking meat. My stomach turns inside out.

"You're her fucking husband, a fucking father. What's the bloody matter with you?"

Blood pours from Joe's nose straight into his mouth. I can't handle gore. Everything tilts like we're riding some carnival Tilt-A-Whirl. I've never fainted in my life but vomiting is a distinct possibility. I need to get a grip and save Bran from committing murder.

"You little shit." Gaby flies from out of nowhere. Bran jumps up, dazed and still dangerous.

Joe rolls into a half curl and chokes out a sick, wet, rib-rattling cough. My mouth fills with saliva as vomiting threatens to become a reality.

"What have you done?" Gaby says with a hiss.

"That fuckhole crossed the line. He's cheating on you again. I saw him with—"

Gaby slaps Bran—hard—across the face.

His head flips back like a Pez dispenser and when he rights himself, his face is shuttered.

"Hey." I shove between them. "I don't know what's going on but Bran's—"

"Messing everything up." Gaby is in towering heels and still shorter than me. She gives her husband a disgusted glance before trading inscrutable stares with her little brother. Then she readjusts her hat to a jaunty angle and does the last thing I'm expecting—she smiles.

"Get fucked, brother," she says between clenched teeth before stalking away, head high, leaving her husband gagging on the ground.

Police and security push through the crowd.

Bran touches my elbow. "We're out. Right now." He grabs my outstretched hand and we flee in the opposite direction.

18

BRAN

*A*re you going to clue me in what the heck is going on?"
Talia chases me through a rosebush. The skin-tearing
thorns don't slow my stride. Her cheeks are flushed and she's getting breathless. I should slow down.

I should do a lot of things.

"Come on, talk to me. This Wolverine behavior is excessive,
even for you."

"Joe." His name hurts my tongue, like a stone in my boot.
"Motherfucking bastard."

"I hope not literally."

She's trying to coax out my humor. I hope she likes disappointment. I break for the exit and we collide with the loitering crowd
sucking air on the footpath. I push my way through, a fish swimming upstream.

Once we break into the clear, she gives it another go. "You
nailed the punch line—pardon the pun—but I missed the setup."

My words can't go as fast as my feet.

"Honestly, Bran—"

"You want the bloody blow-by-blow?" Her tart tone detonates the fuse inside me. I can't hold back the explosion. "Fine. Here it goes. Jocko was under the stairs, exploring some chick's tonsils with his slimeball tongue. Probably didn't think anyone could see. I'd never have noticed if we weren't standing in that exact spot. The more's the pity."

"Whoa, whoa, whoa. That's crazy. Gaby deserves to know what happened. Once she understands you were—"

"Don't kid yourself." I rub my cheek. My sister took Tae Kwon Do when she was a teenager. She still has bloody keen skills. "Denial is a beautiful thing."

"What are we going to do?"

There's an old school pub on the corner; crowds pour onto the second-floor veranda. The tables on the footpath are coned off. A perfect place to forget myself. "I don't know about you but my plan is to get obliterated."

"I don't think that's a viable solution."

"It's genius."

"Stop, please, I need you to look at me."

I walk right around her. "Don't you get it? I punched out my brother-in-law in public."

"A beat-down might be a more accurate description. You were a gladiator."

"Gaby cares too much about saving face. She'll pretend everything in her sham of a marriage is abso-bloody-lutely fantastic. In the past, she's tried to defend me but not this time. She'll side with my parents. They'll close ranks against me—every last one of them—my so-called family."

"I'm here. Don't shut me out. We'll deal with this."

"Talia, why can't you get it? Sometimes I don't want to deal."

Talia's mouth opens and shuts. She doesn't know how to respond, because deep down she understands. Now and again it's too fucking hard to face yourself.

"Fine," she says. "I've got your back."

I take her hand in mine. "Don't let go."

She gives my wrist a kiss. "I won't."

I've got nothing to lose.

Except her—this—us.

And that's pretty much everything.

———

We pub-crawl through Flemington, down into North Melbourne. The inner-city bars fill to capacity as everyone and their senile great-uncle are out on the town. Cup Day is a state holiday, and one massive piss-up. The crowds, with their drunk-ass banter, stop my ears and blank my thoughts. Talia looks at her watch again but I'm not nearly done. Not by a long shot. Going home now means silence. A silence that screams, *You're hopeless. A bloody disappointment. A discredit to the family name.* No matter how just my cause, when it comes to my family, I can't get a damn thing sorted.

My phone buzzes in my pocket while Talia's in the bathroom. I ignore it but someone's a persistent bugger. I check the screen. Dad. Bloody hell, I didn't even know he had my number.

"Yeah?"

"Brandon? Where are you, mate?"

Mate? Don't make me laugh.

"A pub."

"I heard there was a disturbance."

"You heard right."

"Can you make your way back? I need to speak with you."

"Negative."

"Son."

"I got to jet. Whatever it is can keep until morning. Don't bother waiting up." I get a text from Davo right before I shove the phone into my pocket; apparently his place is going off.

I kill the pint in three long swallows but my stomach still feels run over by a bulldozer.

"Did you hear?" Talia drapes over my chair back and plants a kiss on my cheek. "Chip on His Shoulder won. That's a good sign, right?"

I don't have the heart to tell her that in real life, those guys never win. We rage until our heart lights extinguish.

"Grab your bag, we're out."

She releases a relieved sigh. "We're going back to your home?"

"That's not a home; it's a structure where I used to live. And, no, we're headed to the Docklands."

———

"Hey, hey. You made it." Davo wipes his nose, amped, clearly on something. He's already looking past us at the next lot coming in the front door. "Beers and champers are in the fridge, hard stuff at the bar, anything you want."

"No worries."

He heaves his arm around me in a gesture that's half mateship and half trying to keep standing. "Dude, I'm so pissed."

Talia's smile is more a grimace but I ignore her, walk toward the bottles.

I dragged her here for one reason. I'm a coward. I don't want to go back and face Dad or the rest of them. What was he even going on about anyway? He doesn't speak to me, at least nothing approaching an actual conversation, in years and suddenly I'm supposed to engage in a deep and meaningful? Maybe he's going to throw me a bone, a spot in the family business—a cushy desk job where I'll be paid to stay quiet. Bought off to keep the fucking peace.

Not going to happen.

"What can I get you?" I ask Talia, who's busy checking out the space. Davo's family connections greased his path into corporate finance and this massive converted warehouse apartment. The walls are original brick, exposed pipes run along the ceiling, and the cement floor is sticky with grog.

"Water's fine." Talia tugs my sleeve. "Being here—is this really a good idea?"

"We'll hang with my old school mates for a bit." I pull her in for a quick kiss and get her cheek. "It's almost dark. Everyone will crash at the house soon. When we get back, I'll switch our plane tickets. We can head home tomorrow afternoon."

"Sounds like a plan, Stan." She eyes the front door with undisclosed longing.

People ebb and flow from the loft in a steady stream. Guys are wearing their ties around their heads like ninjas, knocking back shots like they'll have had a crap night if they don't wake in the gutter.

What are we, five years out of Geelong Grammar? Nothing's changed, not really. Bloody depressing how the same girls fall into each other, laughing fake-hard over inside jokes no one else gives two shits about, vying for center stage.

"I don't want to be here," Talia mutters.

"We won't stay long."

She looks around with a pensive expression. "I keep waiting for Jazza to put in an appearance."

Jazz—my former friend who dicked around with Talia when she made it clear she wasn't interested.

"Please, I want to go."

"Soon." Because what else do I say? I'm lost? Yeah—that's great. Get Talia sucked into my own pity party. She's got enough on her plate without being force-fed my whiny bitch poison.

"I'm underdressed."

"You could outshine these girls from inside a burlap sack."

"Brando!" Kylie, a chick I've had every which way, calls out. "You forget my number?"

"Here we go," Talia whispers.

Kylie sidles close in a cloud of heavy floral perfume. She ignores Talia and purses her lips in a pout I used to find sexy.

"Kylie, meet Talia—my girlfriend."

Kylie's plucked eyebrows jump to her bleached hairline. "The rumors are true."

Talia looks like she's about to unhinge her jaw and bite off Kylie's smirking head. I'd advise against such tactics. If memory serves, my girl would only get a mouthful of hot air.

"Remind me where you ran off to, Adelaide? Wagga?"

"Hobart."

"Tasmania? What's it like living in Dullsville? Are there actually inbreeds trying to hide their second heads?"

"You're an original."

"You must totally miss Melbs."

"No."

"But in all seriousness, you shouldn't be a stranger." She makes sure Talia bears the brunt of her naughty smile. "We have history, me and this boy."

"Join the club." Talia releases my grip to pour herself a G & T, heavier on the gin.

"Kylie! Kylie! Kylie!" The crowd on the veranda chants her name.

"My loyal fans." She curtsies to the salivating guys. "I promised the boys a game of Century Club."

"That wise?" From memory, Kylie weighs fifty kilos dripping wet. Her plan to take a beer shot every sixty seconds for a hundred minutes seems like a recipe for a hospital visit and stomach pumps.

"I've drunk you under the table, too, don't forget. And had you on a few others."

"For fuck's sake." Talia glares into her glass and stalks away.

"Bloody hell, Kylie."

"Oh, come on, Brando." Her eyes are harder these days. "Any girl with you needs to know the drill. You're a player—you play."

"It's not like that with her."

"Yeah, whatever. So later, you want to—"

I walk away from her midsentence. Talia can't be left alone in this place. I've been to enough of these parties. The Amazonian jungle can't be more cutthroat. The vibe here is hunt or be hunted; except in the end, rather than killing the prey, we fuck it in one of the back rooms.

Talia's not in actual danger; she can hold her own in the take-no-shit department, but there are quite a few randoms hanging around. Ice sluices through my chest as I duck under a dude balancing a case of beer on one shoulder. Everyone is off their faces. Where is she? This was bloody stupid to come. Selfish to bring Talia and act like my old scene had anything to offer anyone.

How did I ever hang with these guys and stand myself?

Oh wait, that's right, I couldn't.

Talia is across the room, leaning against an exposed beam. Some neckbeard is invading her space. I stalk closer. Give me a bloody break . . . is he smoking a pipe?

"Whaddup?" The phrase sounded better in my head than in actual reality.

The guy dribbling pipe ash down my girlfriend's cleavage sneers through his thick-rimmed glasses like I'm this big hassle.

His name is probably Phineas or Brooklyn, the type to try and paw into a girl's panties by demonstrating an extensive knowledge of Reddit.

"Need help, mate?"

Nice private school accent, wanker.

I lean in. "Does your version of help include my knee in your face?"

"Settle down, Gin Mill Cowboy." Talia reaches out and—unbelievably—ruffles my hair. She gives me an indulgent smile, like I'm an ill-tempered puppy growling down a chew toy. "Doesn't that Kylie girl have a new tramp stamp to show you?"

My brain sloshes through the grog, processes that tone. What's with the evil death stare? Okay. She's pissed—bloody angry pissed. Make that flamethrower and bazooka pissed.

"Far out, it's Brando! No way, Brandorama? Hey, Brando, over here!" Three girls squeal over the back of a white leather couch. One I don't recognize but the other two, it takes me a minute because they have clothes on, but yeah, I know them.

Neckbeard and Talia stare at me like downvoting Romans in the Colosseum.

Feed this one to the lions.

"I changed my mind about that refill." Talia passes Neckbeard her glass.

"Right-o."

"Hold up, Phineas." I grab his arm.

He frowns at my hand. "The name's Jordan, mate."

"Who said anything about being mates, mate?"

"I don't think you are in the position to argue, *Brandorama*." Talia steps between us. "Besides, haven't you issued enough beat-downs for one day? Jordan is a grad student in history. I'm going to have a quiet drink. Enjoy the Charlie's Angels."

"Talia—"

"No!" She shoves off my hand. "I told you I wanted to leave. Repeatedly. Now I'll see you when I see you." She shrugs at Neck-beard. "Sorry, my boyfriend can be a bit much."

"I think I'll go grab us those drinks." Jordan retreats.

"Keep on walking," I call out.

"Will you stop? This is getting embarrassing. Jordan's not trying to explore my Mason-Dixon line. We were discussing Port Arthur, for God's sake."

The Tasmanian penal settlement.

"I'm sure he'd love you to visit his penile colony."

"Seriously, did you travel through a time portal and reconnect with your bratty five-year-old self?"

"Why are you even humoring that Hipster Jesus? Port Fucking Arthur! Can't you see he's knocking on doors to find the one that opens your legs?"

"Right. Because why else would anyone want to talk to me?"

"Look around you, this party, everyone is here for one reason."

"I'm curious, what did you say to Kylie to get her to sleep with you, back in the day?"

If I flip a coin, what are my chances of getting head?

"I'm not like that anymore."

"And I'm not falling for that tired old chestnut. We're all lots of people. You just don't like that particular version."

The brokenhearted part who slept with half of Melbourne? No, that dickhead sucks.

She gives this heavy sigh, one that's pulled straight from her bones. "People don't change, Bran. Not really. Not deep down. We slap on new masks and hope for the best."

She tries to push past me but I catch her waist, spin her around to face me.

"Stop. I want space and you're going to give it to me."

"Five minutes ago you couldn't leave fast enough."

"That was before I realized you'd slept with everyone here."

"Hardly."

"How many of these girls have you been with?"

"Captain—"

"Go on, noodle it out."

"This is stupid."

"Okeydokey, I'll take a guess. Five?"

At least eight.

"Talia, leave this shit alone. I'm with you. I love you."

"I'm tired of your ghosts, Bran. I need a drink. Correction: I need multiple drinks. And then I want you to get me the hell out of here like I begged for the moment we stepped foot in this place." She beelines to Jordan.

She wants to get all earnest about nineteenth-century prison systems with a dude who uses convicts as foreplay?

Fine.

Fucking live it up, Talia.

A girl passes me, trying to unsuccessfully unscrew the top off a rum bottle.

"Here, let me help, love." I pop the cap and take a swig.

"Hey!"

"Finders keepers." I stroll to a lounge chair, flop with my feet on the armrest, and keep drinking. Too sweet; I'm not a rum fan. Talia's right, my past happened and there's not much I can do. My story is depressingly familiar. Once upon a time, a lonely boy fell in love. All was great until he got his heart ripped out of his chest, drawn and quartered, and then run through the garbage disposal. For a time, I found distraction—lots of distraction—but I always let the girls know the drill. A straight-up, no-strings root.

And for the record, there weren't many complaints.

The faces jumble; the girls' colorful cocktail dresses swirl into one blurry kaleidoscope. Whoever chose the music is an idiot. When I examine the bottle, there's less than I expected. I check the bottom for a hole because I don't feel a thing.

Numbness...

Maybe that's a bad sign.

I drop the bottle on the ground but it's hard to balance, so I let it tip. Amber liquid spreads over the creamy rug like a Rorschach test.

Everyone looks strange if you stare hard enough. Someone touches me from behind. A hand suggestively slides over my thigh. I throw myself to my feet and tear in the opposite direction. Talia. I catch sight of her, still yucking it up with Jordan the Neckbeard.

She's midsentence when I grab her waist and throw her over my shoulder.

"Bran!"

I steady my balance. "Let's leave."

"Put me the hell down. We are not reenacting some crazy-ass *Clan of the Cave Bear* moment."

I half stumble and crash us into a wall. A frame falls, the glass shattering. She uses the opportunity to climb off me.

"You're so wasted."

"I'm not." At least that's what I want to say. It came out more garbled, like, "Nyahh."

"Crap, Bran. I can't take you home like this." She stares at the wide staircase disappearing into a second level.

I'm not sure what happens next but it's quiet. We must be in an upstairs bedroom, but I can't figure out how we got here.

"Pretty, pretty Talia." I collapse on the duvet. "Is this bed too short?"

"It's only a double, but you're lying on it the wrong way. Here we go, there's a pillow."

"You like him?"

"Who?"

"Jordan."

"Sure, he's okay."

"Want him?"

"I'm not even dignifying that with an answer."

"Go on—say it, I fucked up. I'm fucked. Do it, get the lecture off your chest."

"Wow, okay. Two firsts." She's removing my shoes. "One, I have never seen you this drunk. The other, I've never known you to be so needy. I'm enacting Prohibition, starting now."

"Not needy." My God, do I need her. "You're angry."

"A little. But I'm mad at myself too. I shouldn't have let you turn into a train wreck. You had a terrible day. Get under the blankets. I locked the door, so this is our room tonight."

"I like bed." No pillow ever felt so good. "Talia?" I open my arms.

"Oh, all right." She stretches against me and rubs my hair, the way I love. No one else ever touches me so gently, like they don't need a tit for tat.

"Feels good."

"You need water."

"All I want is Talia." I half sing the words.

"Bran, I got jealous tonight."

"Me too."

"The difference is you got jealous over a gay dude. I was jealous over girls who acted like you were their private mechanical bull."

"Gay?"

"Yes, Jordan, Neckbeard, was a hundred percent obviously gay. Kind of makes you look like—"

"A jackass." The room starts to rotate. "Though if I were gay, I'd turn for you."

"That's not how it works, but I appreciate the sentiment. I'll grab that water."

"Don't go."

"You really need a drink."

"Please, stay."

"Okay, for a few minutes. Then water, deal?"

"Dealsies."

"You are kind of a cute drunk."

I smile into the sheets.

"Bran?"

"Uhn?"

"You are super trashed, huh?"

"Yeffff." My communication skills are shutting down fast.

"I need to talk, even if you don't remember."

I will remember Talia next to me. Talia in my bed. Talia in my head.

"I get jealous, Bran—of you—so much that I can't breathe. I can't compete, can't catch up. And by being down here, in Australia, I keep falling farther and farther behind. This whole marriage thing scares me. Because even if it doesn't mean, like, the same thing as an actual marriage, I think it sort of does. I mean, we love each other and want to be together. So how is our supposedly fake but totally legal marriage any different than a real and totally legal marriage? It's not. This is real, Bran, and I haven't seen marriage go well for many people. I love you, I do. I love you so much. But I am not sure if this is the right path. I have this chance for an interview—"

What she's saying sounds important but I'm sinking. Sleep washes over me before she takes her next breath.

19

TALIA

*M*orning sun dapples the loft in golden ribbons of light. I zip my skirt while people scuttle outside the one-way window like determined ants. Why's everyone awake so early? Oh, right, it's Wednesday—a workday. The Cup was a disaster on an epic scale. A body shifts in the unfamiliar bed. I turn to see Bran's head ram under a feather pillow and allow my gaze to travel those lean but strong shoulders. Impossible not to admire the way his upper body's perfect upside-down triangulation whittles to a hard abdomen, and or the point where that arrogant arrow of black hair disappears beneath tangled silk sheets. His combination of unexpected vulnerability and patent sexiness sends heat surging through my breasts before a sharp pain stabs my midriff.

Beautiful, angry boy.

Sleep proved elusive after Bran passed out last night. I paced through the dark hours like a nocturnal animal until the party sounds long abated into silence. Why must he break himself against the world? What's wrong with keeping a low profile, avoiding attention—live life with the attitude of *move along, nothing to see here?*

He mumbles an incoherent sentence as if to argue my thoughts.

I creep toward a blank notepad on the chrome and glass desk against the opposite wall and scribble a note, placing it beside him on the bed.

> *Going to catch up with a friend. I'll be back at your parents' place by dinner.*
> *I love you.*
> *PS. Drink water.*

I ease into the hall, careful to hold the knob until the door shuts. I pause, cautiously alert, but there are no disturbed sounds inside. Bran needs to sleep it off. I'm confused and yesterday only further muddled my thoughts. There's only one person in this city whose company I'm up for—Marti, my imperturbable neighbor from my tenure at Melbourne Uni's Foreign Student Hall.

She came out from Montreal for a study-abroad year, and her time in the country is down to the wire. Luckily, she's still around. Marti embraces life with all its mayhem. Today, I can use a dose of her confidence.

The living room is an obstacle course of insensible bodies, the air thick with sour alcohol and Chanel. I pick my way through the gauntlet like I'm in a battlefield, trying to avoid a land mine.

Oh, shit!

An empty champagne bottle slides underfoot. I wince as the clattering glass echoes along the industrial epoxied floor.

To make matters worse, Kylie peers from the balcony, smirking at my not-so-stealthy retreat. Did she rise at dawn for a makeup reapplication? She looks perfectly refreshed in a canary yellow dress, cut mid-thigh.

"You're up early." She takes a sip from her espresso cup.

"I'm meeting a friend for breakfast."

"What's with Americans and their breakfast?"

"Most important meal of the day."

"Food before noon makes me want to spew."

"Oh, okay, great. Duly noted."

She glances over my shoulder. "And where's Brando?"

I hate that she calls him that.

"Asleep. He went pretty hard last night."

"Won't be the last time. Maybe I'll bring him something in bed."

"I doubt he's hungry."

"Who's talking food?"

"You know he's my boyfriend, right?"

She giggles without humor.

Why am I still standing here? I remove my ragged nails from the fleshy part of my palm. "Look, I really need to go."

"He's going to break your heart."

I rock on my heels. "Excuse me?"

"It's what he does. Although"—she taps her index finger against her chin before casting those full lips into a wicked smile—"you know that already. Don't you, bad girl?"

"Huh?"

"You want to bring him to his knees. That's the plan, isn't it? Far out, but can't say I blame you—an interesting challenge. Succeed and you've made the conquest of the decade."

"This may be a hard concept for you to grasp, but Bran and I—we don't get off game-playing."

Snap, bee-yatch.

"Right." Her tone is dry, her teeth small. Too small. I cling to that single flaw with pitiful eagerness. "You guys have it all sorted. What with your drunken fisticuffs last night and you sneaking away at the crack of dawn."

Hopefully my front door slam serves as an eloquent reply.

I catch a tram to Carlton. The closer I travel to the Melbourne Uni campus, the more the city loses its anonymity. Strange to be back at ground zero, the place where Bran and I got together. Marti asked to meet at the Bean Counter, the cozy student-oriented coffee shop across the road from Bran's former flat. I stop on the sidewalk, peek through the high hedge, and glimpse the terrace's mildewed white brick. My heart gives a forlorn thwack; aching vibrations tingle through my limbs.

Why didn't I wait for him to wake and come along?

Because I wanted a break from feeling all the feels.

When I stress, my brain gets bad, like all the different sections scream, drowning me with intrusive thoughts, hyperawareness, and compulsive urges. OCD catches me like a riptide, pulling me farther and farther from shore. I'm slipping, kidding myself I'll ever be well. In my heart of hearts, I know the truth—I'm a hopeless basket case.

Why does Bran even bother?

He has his own drama and still tries to rescue me. What if someday I cling too hard, like a drowning person, and drag us both under?

Perspiration dampens beneath my arms and in my bra, despite the relatively cool temperatures. I can't fail and let my defective brain ruin this relationship like it's done to everything good in my life. I take a shallow breath, knowing I need to refuse performing rituals—no counting, no tapping. I brace my stomach and let the current pull me. If I stop resisting, eventually the powerful urges wane and I can swim to shore.

Will I always make it back?

Will Bran continue to wait for me?

Kylie bounces into my mind—beautiful and bright. What if Bran returns to sanity, realizes he doesn't need a freak show American occupying his life?

I mean, marriage?

To me?

What was he thinking?

What if Kylie's sneaking into his bed this very second?

I should go back.

No. I need faith. Bran isn't a cheater. Let Kylie try her worst, crawl naked on all fours, purr like a kitten—he would kick her out under no uncertain terms.

Right?

Right.

Oh, really? He is a guy with a pulse. Kylie could make a Lazarus from a dead man.

The girl's like a platinum-blond cyborg specially designed for a career as a *Maxim* cover model. She probably bathes in pheromones every night. How else to explain why she oozes sex appeal from every perfect pore?

We're slut-shaming now? Nice one. Way to stay classy.

Marti's hot-pink ponytail is visible through the Bean Counter's plate glass. She's got her back to me, hunched at a small round table. I have a million and one problems. If I can't trust my boyfriend not to ball sex kittens, that's a million and two. I have to trust he'll keep true to what we have, that I'm something worth wanting.

Time for a little faith and to see my friend.

I fly into the coffee shop before I can rethink my decision and tackle Marti with a massive backward hug.

"Talia! Bonjour, hi! Whoa, okay, I missed you too."

I plant a big, messy wet kiss on her cheek before plopping into the opposite chair.

"You have no idea how good it is to see you this morning."

"You come alone?" Marti looks around, her features contorting into a puckered frown. "But where is your *petit ami*?"

I shrug.

"Uh-oh. What is happening?" When I'd texted Marti to catch up, I'd left out any drama.

"I needed some girl time."

"Pffffft. Go on—how do you say? Spill out the beans."

"I need caffeine first." I go order. After knocking back a triple-shot soy cappuccino, I muster the energy to fill her in on the Cup Day calamities and resulting Lockhart craziness.

Her brows furrow. "Bran…you sure he is not an idiot boy?"

"Aren't we all idiots in love?" I let my chin plop into my hand. "Didn't Shakespeare say that?"

"If not, he should have."

"Here's the problem—I'm not sure whether we're a comedy or a tragedy."

"Maybe it is best to be both."

"Here, here."

We clink mugs.

"Enough with my boring crap. Fill me in on your world. How's Lucy?" Marti's been going hot and heavy with Lucy, a barista and scrappy London East Ender, since she arrived in Melbourne.

Marti's gaze wavers to the counter.

"Is she working? I didn't see her."

"No," Marti whispers. "But quiet, these walls have ears."

"Um, okay."

She checks the time. "I have an appointment in twenty minutes. We will talk on the way."

The sidewalks bustle with foot traffic. We cross the bottom section of Lygon Street. The shoddy Asian takeout shops bustle with hungover students. My stomach rumbles. Noodles sound rather delicious.

"I moved to a new place, on Cardigan Street," Marti says, cutting through a park.

"Sounds cozy."

"I'm sick of Melbourne and eating cheap curry."

"Really?" The downtown skyline emerges through the trees. "I miss it."

"What? The self-satisfied hipsters? The trams that want to run you down? The awful weather that changes every four seconds? At least in Quebec you know the weather is shit."

"What about the coffee? It's amazing here."

"Pfffffft. They act like they invented the drink. Turn here."

We veer up a side street. "Where are we going?"

"My wax appointment."

"Je-sus." I laugh under my breath. "Why am I even surprised?"

"I support rainforests but that doesn't mean I should grow a jungle between my legs."

Marti has a certain gift in rationalizing even the most off-putting things.

"I'm taking this to mean things are all still good in the hood with Lucy. You were rather coy at the Bean."

"*Non. Okay* is not the word I would select." Marti has mastered the eloquent shrug. "I return to Montreal before Christmas."

"What are you going to do?"

"I go home. She stays here."

"Harsh."

"I am only twenty-two. Time to move on."

"You can do that?"

"*Oui*. That is the way the cookie smashes, no?"

"Crumbles?"

"Ey?"

"The cookie crumbles, that's the expression."

"Pffffft."

"Don't you want to stay together?"

"Milk does not stay good past the expiry date. Why should love?"

"That's a pretty gross metaphor."

"At first, everything is sweet deliciousness but wait too long and, phew." She wrinkles her nose against an imaginary stench.

"But the alternative is way worse."

"I am speaking only for me, Natalia. You live your life. I live mine."

My stomach contorts itself through half a dozen sailor knots. Maybe I drank more than I thought last night. I'm growing queasier by the block. Is the sidewalk riddled with more than the usual cracks? I try not to step on one but I'm going to fail. These short, fast breaths only make things worse.

Slow down, inhale through the nostrils and breathe into the belly.

Marti pivots in front of a pink storefront. "Ah, here we are."

I lurk behind while she checks in with the waxing parlor's perky receptionist.

"And will you be partaking in any services this morning?" the woman chirps, handing me a menu.

"You know, I've never given much thought to landscaping."

"You have a boyfriend?" Her just-us-girls wink elevates my terror levels to code red.

"Um, yeah? I mean, yes, I do, but I fail to see what—"

"Trust me, doll. Mow your lawn and he'll go wild."

"He will?"

Marti snickers. I stomp on her toe but it doesn't do much good, steel-toed combat boots and all.

I scan the services. "Wow, okay, the Vajazzle. Might you expand on that for me?"

"Vajazzling? Sure, not a problem! A highly skilled beauty therapist removes your vaginal hair, and once everything is nice and smooth, she'll affix body crystals to the skin."

So pretty much exactly what I was afraid of.

"And people do this?"

She gives me a puzzled look.

"Real, actual people people, not...you know, porn stars." I whisper the last two words.

"Do I look like a real person?"

"Yes." She looks like a rather nice person, actually—neat, with a fresh complexion. Your classic girl-next-door type.

"I personally find the effect quite cute, very feminine."

Okay, make that a classic girl-next-door who happens to rock a glitter pussy.

"Oh."

She taps her nails on the counter and gives me a thoughtful look. "How long since your last bikini wax?"

"Um, never?"

She and Marti exchange scandalized expressions.

"Never?" Marti echoes.

"Ever?" the receptionist adds in hushed tones.

"No! Hot wax? Down there? I mean, not that I judge, whatever floats your boat, it's just never made my to-do list."

"But a bikini wax is like brushing your teeth, no?" Marti says. "Part of the maintenance routine."

"Not for me."

"Of course not, doll. To each their own." The receptionist picks an imaginary hangnail with a bemused look.

"Seriously, I'm not a prude."

"My friend is *au naturel*," Marti says.

I yank her ponytail.

"You're all sorted." The receptionist nods to Marti. "Please take a seat and Leticia will be ready for you shortly. Can I offer you a tea or coffee?"

I glance back at the seating area. Women flip through magazines. Regular women. One looks like a fortysomething teacher, the other a young corporate mover and shaker.

Bran's never commented about my situation down there, acted like there's anything abhorrent with female body hair. I mean, it's not like I'm smuggling a baby yeti in my undies. Still...I close my eyes and picture Kylie's smoky eyes and radiant confidence; she probably bathes in wax on a biweekly basis.

"How much?" The words croak as I speak them.

"For?" The receptionist doesn't look from her nail filing.

"A wax."

"Depends on what type."

She's not going to make this easy, thinks I'm mocking. I dial up my most sincere expression, trying desperately not to picture her blinged-out honeypot.

An impossible feat, thanks to my overactive imagination.

"We specialize in the French wax, the Brazilian, and the full Brazilian."

How international.

"Out of curiosity, what's the difference between a regular and the full?"

"The full removes all the hair, and the regular leaves you with a landing strip, very tasteful."

"I'll bet."

Marti joins me at the counter. "Everything okay?"

The receptionist gives me a long look before leaning in on her elbows. "Trust me, you aren't the first newbie I've ever seen. But they all come back."

"They do?"

She nods. "The effects go down a treat at home. The men go wild."

"Really?"

She drops her voice to a confidential whisper. "The first time I ever did it, my boyfriend ate me out like a champ. I couldn't get him to stop."

I almost cough out my spleen.

Marti pats my back. "You do what feels right. If you cannot be the master of your own vagina, what can you rule?"

"I'm thinking, you know, why not shake things up a little?"

Bran will expect me to be angry about last night. Why not turn the tables? I'm not the jealous, self-conscious type. I'm Talia Amaze-balls Va-Jay-Jay. This has nothing to do with the fact I need to compete with all those faceless ghosts he's screwed. I'm empowered. Not pathetic.

I'm so fucking pathetic.

The receptionist flips through her appointment book. "Looks like there's been a cancellation. We have an opening the same time as your friend. What shall I put you down for? A bikini?"

"Let's do the Brazilian."

"Very good. Full or regular?"

"Go big or go home."

"So full?"

"Sure."

"With the Vajazzle?"

"I'm not going that big. Let's stick with the wax."

"No worries."

The door to the back cracks open and a delicate woman emerges, her hair swept into an elegant bun. "Marti?"

She doesn't look so scary.

Marti pauses beside me. "No peer pressure."

"I'm all good." I flash a thumbs-up. Apparently I am also an outstanding liar.

"Leticia?" The receptionist tips back in her chair. "Can you tell Oksana she has a ten-thirty?"

Five minutes later, I'm stripped from the waist down while a woman roughly the same age as my nana rubs talcum powder over my girl parts with thick fingers.

Is every wax strip going to peel off another layer of my feminism?

But really, what purpose does pubic hair serve? Isn't it merely a vestigial relic from the Ice Age when women needed to keep their goodies warm?

"Hey, uh, excuse me, Oksana?"

"Hmmm?"

"Can you talk me through the game plan? Break it down so I'll have a sense of what to expect?"

I appreciate Oksana is a woman of few words. When we entered the small room, she ordered me to strip off my skirt and panties and climb onto the table covered by crinkly paper, not unlike a doctor's office.

She snorts like I'm an unbelievable idiot. "I remove the hair."
Her accent is thickly Eastern European.

"Yes, of course you do, that's why I'm here." I flash a winning
smile but her dour frown throws cold water on my attempt at good
cheer.

Holy crap, what am I doing? Trying to make my vagina different in the hopes it keeps my boyfriend interested?

Yeah, pretty much.

Seriously, though, everyone does this. *I'm* the outsider by not
taking part. I hate being a deviation.

This is going to happen. No take-backs.

"Here's the deal, Oksana. I've never done this before, okay?
And I'm not a girl who is big on surprises."

"Bend your leg to the side."

"You washed your hands, right?"

"I'm a professional."

"Will it hurt?"

"I'm ripping hair off your *vlagalishche*. What do you think?"

I wince as she lathers the most private crevice in my body with a
lashing of hot wax. "So you're going to—"

"One, two, three."

"Holy everlasting shit." I suck in my cheeks. It feels…exactly
like snatching pussy hair from the roots.

She pats my quivering thigh, revealing a millimeter of human
emotion. "Many woman say this is harder than birthing a baby."

I fight the urge to cross my legs. "You're not instilling
confidence."

She comes at me again and I have to grip the table to keep from
jumping off. Finally, there's a blessed pause.

"Natalia?"

"Mmm?" My voice is reedy; I'm still shocked I've gone through with this.

"Turn over."

"What?"

"All fours now and spread." She lifts tweezers.

"Are you shitting me?" She can't honestly expect to do what I think she's about to do.

Her frown accentuates every dour crease. "I never shit."

"I believe you." I obey because I don't have the strength to resist. I'm disappointed in myself. Marti is here because this pleases her. I'm here because I'm still not comfortable in my own skin.

And despite everything Oksana does, this is the truth that hurts the most.

20

BRAN

*Y*esterday was shithouse and today's forecast isn't promising. Talia abandoned me unconscious in the Docklands with nothing but a cryptic letter. I woke to twin nightmares—a tongue drier than the Strzelecki Desert and Kylie Martin dripping ice on my chest. I told her to get stuffed, bailed quickly, and spent the equivalent of a week's grocery budget on the bloody fare back to Portsea.

I stare listlessly over the cabbie's shoulder. The backed-up traffic on the Nepean makes me miss Tasmania's quiet two-lane roads. Who is Talia meeting? Face Fungus Jordan?

Fucking hell.

Her whereabouts are a mystery I can't unravel with a head like a bucket of smashed crabs. The cherry to this situation is the particularly stellar pain concentrating behind my left eye socket.

My options are simple: spew or sleep. I opt for the latter.

The cabbie vanishes before I punch in the gate code. A narcoleptic snail could beat me down the driveway. The clouds are as gray as steel wool—a low-pressure system builds over Bass Strait.

I pause at my parents' front door. I'm not exactly sure what a gird is, but my loins need one to survive the imminent "Bran, you've ruined the name of this family, *again*" lecture.

The house smells wrong. Stale smoke and burned toast overpowers Mum's fragrance sticks.

Gabriella glances from her crappy sitcom and ashes a cig into an empty wine bottle. She's still dressed in yesterday's gown, her eyes black-ringed with smeared makeup.

No doubt Western stare-down music will play if I stand here any longer.

She sighs. "Come back for more?"

"No."

"I've been a right bitch these past few days, huh?" She sounds scratchy like she shredded her vocal cords screaming or weeping— probably both.

"No comment." She's normally a bit high-maintenance but her attitude has run seriously amok.

"My marriage is falling apart."

"I didn't realize how bad things were between you and the douche."

The moniker earns me a wry smile. "This wasn't supposed to be my life."

"Oh, Gabbles, I'm sorry—"

"God, Spunk." She throws her head back and shouts, "I'm such an idiot. I kept deluding myself that he—Joe—would match this fantasy in my head. All the stereotypical signs stared me in the face: the out of town trips, endless guy nights, late phone calls. He even started doing his own laundry. How thick can I be, honestly? I bloody deserve this."

"Don't say that."

"He kept a list on his phone of all the—what do I even call them? His pussy. He showed me the names last night. There were dozens." She laughs in a way that makes me wish she'd cry. "Guess how many people I've had sex with? In my life?"

"You're my sister. That shit's—"

"Three."

"Serious?" Not that I particularly cared, but she spent years as footy player arm candy. Those guys weren't exactly lauded for their wholesomeness.

Her expression is all *Et tu, Brute?* "Everyone thinks I'm such a moll."

"I don't."

But I guess I used to.

She sniffles. "Talia's a lucky one. Your lying skills are complete crap."

"Tell me what you really think." I collapse on the couch and loop my arm around her shoulders but the gesture is awkward. This family isn't big on touching.

"No pity." She shies from the contact. "Please, just…don't. I'm one hug away from shattering."

"Fair enough." I feel relieved—and instantly guilty. "Where is everyone?"

"Mum and Dad never came home. Joe's at the dentist—lost a tooth."

We both glance at my ravaged knuckles and the dried blood-stains on my sleeve cuff.

"Thank you, for what you did at the races yesterday. I should have had the guts to kick his ass myself. Instead, I froze as if my knickers were out for everyone to judge. I hate him but I hate me more."

"He doesn't deserve you."

"No. He doesn't." She lights another cigarette and kicks this morning's paper on the coffee table. "Have you seen this?"

Crikey, there's a grainy shot of me going starkers on Jocko.

I cover my face with my hands. "Mum will have an aneurysm."

"Yep, pretty much. She and Dad are probably holed up in a suite at the Sofitel wondering if we still qualify for late-term abortions."

"One big happy family, huh?"

"Don't do it." The momentary humor extinguishes from her eyes.

I shift to the edge of the cushions. "What?"

"Marriage."

"It's a not-a-marriage."

"I'm serious, little brother. Stay far away from anything remotely matrimonial."

"I don't think—"

"That weird little American, you love her, don't you?"

"Yeah." I drum my fingers on the leather cushion.

"I mean, really, really love her? Like she's the Kate to your Will, the Lois Lane to your Clark Kent, the…the…I don't know, Moriarty to your Sherlock?"

"I'm going to take a guess that you haven't read much Sir Arthur Conan Doyle."

"I'm hungover and not in the mood to take your crap."

We don't talk love in this house. I don't even know how to have this conversation.

"My point is, marriage isn't a game."

"You want to lecture me? Fine. Go ahead, expert." Maybe if I'm a big enough ass, this awkward conversation can cease. I want to pass out, escape.

"You little—"

"Or wait, never mind, I should ask Mum and Dad for advice, is that it? Those two have gone the distance, hey?"

"Don't try to run me down with your badass bastard tactics. Cut the angsty teenage crap. It wasn't cute when you were fifteen and it's considerably less so in your twenties."

"Fine, get to the point sometime this century."

"I'll spell it out for you in easy words. Talia? The girl's so not ready for what you want. *You*? Even less so."

"Don't get in a tizz, Gabbles. Marriage is a piece of paper. Doesn't change anything."

"Doesn't it? Well, excuse me, you're not Sherlock after all. You're a regular Einstein."

"I need to keep us together. I'm trying my best."

"What do you want, little brother, a participation medal? You need to figure out how to be a grown-up, not just play one on TV."

A pop song ringtone blares from under the cushions.

"Christ, answer the bloody phone already."

She groans. "You never quit, do you?"

"My ears are imploding."

"There isn't a person on this planet I want to talk to."

"Gabbles—"

"Dammit, Brandon!" She yanks out her phone in a huff, checks the number, and punches the screen. "Mum?"

Gaby's stony gaze catches mine. "Pardon?" Her expression is one of growing horror. "Can you repeat that? Is he..." Her voice fizzles to ominous silence.

"What?"

She shushes me with impatience, transfixed; her fingers grip the phone so hard the tips turn a bloodless white. "No!"

I can't take it. "Gab—"

"Right. We're coming straightaway." She flinches from the phone like it's slicked with hot grease. "Dad…" Her voice drops out. The gap in her speech is a schism in my brain.

I'm on my feet, backing away. Never mind—don't want to know.

"He's in the hospital. We have to leave now. Mum said…he's not good."

———

"Dengue fever?" I kick at the Royal Melbourne's spotless linoleum, taking perverse pleasure in every black scuff.

Mum's face is devoid of her usual heavy makeup. She looks older but also younger, in this weird way. Maybe because her features are finally free to contort into humanizing expressions without all that fucked beauty crap. "Your father has been unwell for two weeks. Severe ephemeral pain. Drastic weakness. We thought it was a bad flu he couldn't shake. Last night, after we checked into the Sofitel, he vomited blood." The way she describes the events, in her faint accent, it's as if she recites the plot points to a substandard movie.

Gaby lets loose a keening gurgle—the dubious halfway point between a cackle and a wail. Turns out my big sister was right after all. My parents had hunkered down in their favorite local five-star to avoid their disappointing offspring.

My dad is gravely ill.

This is a time that calls for high-level emotions to be on tap, ready to gush forth in a frothy cathartic stream. It would be normal to feel *something*, right? At least a sensation stronger than cotton-mouth. Jesus Christ on a slice of toast, I'd commit bloody murder for water.

Mosquitoes carry dengue fever. When you ponder the situation, Dad got astonishingly unlucky. Here is a guy who spends his life sequestered in boardrooms. How did a rogue insect enter his temperature-controlled, hermetically sealed sanctum? I ignore my headache from hell and continue to question Mum. "Are there any current outbreaks in Singapore?"

"He was in Port Moresby, remember?" Mum snaps like we're an actual family. As if I have the slightest clue about their comings and goings.

"Dad? In Papua New Guinea?"

Has the shock made her forget we are almost strangers? Even in the best of times, she was never a huggy, make-me-a-cup-of-Milo-and-tell-me-all-about-your-day-darling mum. I reconciled to our relationship ages ago, a purgatory bound by genetic material and the merest whiff of obligation.

"Right, the new project." Gaby nods slowly, comprehension dawning on her face. My sister works for Lockhart Industries, and I forget she speaks to our parents more than once a year—twice if one is lucky enough to avoid plunging to the Indian Ocean in a fiery plane crash.

"What was Dad doing there?" I ask. "He never gets his hands dirty—not with actual dirt, anyway."

"The way you carry on, it's ridiculous." My mother's blue eyes match the ice block wedged in her chest cavity. A memory kicks in. I'm eight and she's an hour late picking me up from swim lessons. My feet were numb. I'd started crying when her BMW pulled into the Peninsula Aquatic Center's deserted parking lot.

"Where were you?" I had asked.

She'd winced when I backhanded my dripping nose. She winced at everything I did or said.

"I was meeting a friend at the Baths." A beachside restaurant in Sorrento.

"You forgot me?"

She'd stared in bewilderment, like I was this strange little person invading her life.

"Mummy—"

"Whining is a sign of weakness, Brandon."

I was nothing to her but a responsibility to be fed, clothed, and polished in a manner suited to our status and wealth. There were vague intimations Mum had a less privileged upbringing in Argentina. I don't know specifics—there was an instinctive knowledge not to speak of South America. Never ask if I had any living *abuelos*. I knew only one grandfather—Grandpa Lockhart, who handed me a hundred-dollar bill at Christmas dinners, saying, "Go buy a kick in the arse." Dad laughed every time.

Bitterness ferments my blood. "Funny, though. Dad could die from a tiny insect in a place he tried to exploit. Not funny hilarious, maybe, but funny—"

Smack!

Mum slaps me hard, right across the same bones Gaby cracked yesterday.

"Fucking hell, what's with the women in this family beating me about the bloody face?"

"My actions were a mistake. Joe deserved what you gave him and then some," Gaby retorts. "But you earned that one. Do it again, Mum."

"We are making a scene," says Mum, who loathes public incidents worse than her prodigal son. "You love listening to your own voice, Brandon. You always have. But right now you will hear me.

Your father was in Papua New Guinea setting up his charitable foundation."

"There's a new one. What are we talking about? Open Pit Gold Mining for Peace?"

Mum arches a brow. "So much you don't know. So many things you assume."

Assume makes an ass out of u and me.

A doctor approaches. "Mariana Lockhart?"

My mother gives a curt nod, sits, and crosses her legs. "Yes. My husband...how is he?"

I try to treat the doctor's words like a wave, no point fighting, let them wash over me. Mum's fists ball against her mouth and Gaby's face is braced between her hands. I maintain eye contact, stare at the doctor like I'm coping, because someone has to.

"Dengue fever is endemic in warmer climates, particularly the remote region where Mr. Lockhart was traveling until recent days. Unfortunately, there is no specific treatment. This isn't like a bacteria that might respond to a course of antibiotics. Our options are limited. All we can offer is supportive care. His fever has spiked, and keeping him comfortable is a challenge."

"But will he...is he..." Mum can barely get out the words. "Is he going to—"

"What's the prognosis?" I butt in.

The doctor frowns, never a good sign. "The variation to how people respond to this illness is drastic. However, given Mr. Lockhart's health and temperament, it would be quite unusual for symptoms to develop into a situation we'd classify as a fatal illness."

Pays to be a hard-nosed bastard.

The pressure, still pounding over my head and shoulders,

abates a little, like maybe the surface is within reach if I kick hard enough. "Can someone wait with him?"

"We don't allow more than two visitors at a time." The doctor looks over our sad little trio.

Mum openly sobs. Gaby can handle her far better than me. Besides, neither of them look like they'd inspire much confidence in a critically ill man.

"I'll go," I say, standing. No doubt Dad will fight harder if he thinks the alternative is going out to the sight of my face.

For such a larger-than-life person, Dad's form is small on the bed, shoved full of IVs. He's sicker than anyone I've ever seen. I fiddle with my green sticker, the one that means I can remain in his room after visiting hours. Talia texted me as soon as I updated her with the news. Turns out she was in Carlton. She'll be here soon. My stomach knots and I dig my knuckles into my tense lower back.

I need her.

Occasionally, Dad's eyelids flutter and he blinks like he can't quite decipher what's happening. Must be a shock to be the center of the universe one minute and then wake as a sick bloke who can't take a piss without a catheter the next.

"Brandon?" he wheezes. His voice is less controlled than I've ever heard. A red rash rings his mouth.

"Yeah. Hey, Dad."

His gaze skims the room and he coughs wetly, clearing his throat.

"It's only me. Sorry."

"I feel like shit warmed over."

"I've seen better-looking cane toads."

His chuckle fades into a wheeze.

"Rest, all right? I'll tell Mum and Gabriella you're awake. They'll want to know."

"Wait—sit."

I'm half standing from the hard plastic chair. My ass hurts. But my dad, fuck, he's the type who if he orders sit, you bloody well listen—even if he's nothing but an unwell old man.

"What?"

"It's time for a talk, son."

My brows shoot up on their own accord. "Right now?"

"You have anything better to do?"

Long pause. "No. Natter away."

I'd ducked Dad's halfhearted attempts for a chat, suspicious he'd offer me a company job, a tokenistic bribe to control my life.

Turns out I was way off the mark.

My grandfather is a bigger bastard than I'd previously credited. He didn't trust Dad with his company, so he never vested him with controlling shares. The board drives the strategy and decision-making, always has. Dad profited nicely and never got in their way. Still, he says I inspired him, made him question his legacy.

I'm light-headed. Maybe I better place my head between my legs.

"I'm in the beginning stages of developing a foundation. There's a pilot project in Papua New Guinea building solar-powered generators."

"Mum said you contracted dengue fever visiting the work site in Port Moresby."

"I did."

"You're seriously taking an interest in…what did you call it? Philanthrocapitalism?"

"Financial innovation to create social impact."

"Venture philanthropy." The words stick to my tongue. "Sounds dubious."

"Works fine for Bill Gates. His foundation sees significant returns eradicating malaria." He adjusts his position with a slight wince. "Stop staring like that."

"Like what?"

"Like you're trying to figure out if I'm one of the good guys or not. Life isn't that neat, mate. Sorry. We all make compromises. You'll learn."

I cross my arms. "Who made you the Ghost of Christmas Future?"

"Would it surprise you to know you're a lot like me? How I was at your age?"

"Doubtful."

"Quick to anger. Faster to judge."

"Trust me, Dad. You don't know a whole lot about my life. Who I am, what I want."

"I'd like to learn more, if you let me."

"Why now, after all this time?"

"I used to believe growing older happened to others, not to me. But time's a finite resource—and one I've squandered where you are concerned."

"You chose Lockhart."

"I chose family."

"A corporation isn't a person." I glance at the door. Where's a bloody nurse when you need one? "When I was little, all I wanted was…" My heart pounds in my ears. "Be honest. How much has Lockhart despoiled over the years?"

"Idealism is a luxury of youth."

I snort. "Nothing is ever perfect, but wouldn't it be nice to know you aren't actively profiting from making the world a shittier place?"

"Yes."

"Wait…what?" I didn't anticipate actual agreement.

"And I want to enlist your help."

21

TALIA

I dial Bran's number and he answers on the first ring. "Talia."

My ear practically melts into the phone at his gravelly accent.

"Hey. How's your dad this morning?" Bran hasn't left his side for two days.

"Better." Never exactly verbose, the stress from his father's illness clipped his language skills to the essence. Still, from what little I decipher, his tone doesn't sound quite so closed.

My insides soften. "I'm out in front. It's a beautiful day. Can you come down for a little while?"

"On my way."

Trams and heavy car traffic careen along Royal Parade, one of the city's major thoroughfares. Melbourne Uni sits across the street and the Department of Lands, Planning and the Environment's redbrick façade peeks behind lush hardwood trees—Bran's old branch before he transferred to the University of Tasmania for honors.

Warming awareness spreads between my shoulder blades.

I pivot, my gaze riveted on Bran's grim face as he emerges from the hospital's front door. He frowns at nameless pedestrians congesting the sidewalk, his hands slung deep into the same gray slacks he wore to the Cup. Pretty students slow on their way to class, give him obvious double takes to which he seems oblivious. He's all slouching confidence with dark scruff enhancing his carved jaw. The brilliance in his contemplative green eyes is vibrant enough to catch my breath even from a distance. Suddenly, Brando, his aggravating school nickname, makes perfect sense. When that enigmatic remoteness combines with a glimmer of throat-aching vulnerability—holy hell, does he channel young Marlon Brando.

His posture relaxes when he spots me behind a crowded bike rack. That smile—*gah*, what can I say?

The boy slays me.

My cells ignite, and tingles radiate from my belly, spread through my limbs, growing more intense with every step. The pull is strong, like we're implanted with magnets and can't stop moving until we touch. His mouth seals over mine and even though the kiss is gentle, he groans.

His lips brush my neck and he sucks softly. "Fucking hell." His gruff words rumble through his chest, vibrating into my bones.

"It's only been twenty-four hours." I turn lightly away, my reaction almost too powerful to bear. "I was here yesterday, remember?"

"I miss you."

"Me too." I take his hand and pull him toward the crosswalk before we get arrested for indecent acts. We amble along Grattan Street, skirting the campus perimeter. "I thought we could grab coffees at Union Hall and seek out a patch of grass with a shady tree."

"Whatever you like."

"You've had an intense few days. I want to make you happy."

"You are." His fingertips slide to my wrist and he rubs his thumb over my pulse point. "Seeing your face, that's enough."

We gather supplies and find our tree in a quiet square near the ornately Gothic Old Art building. I lean against the trunk, cross-legged, while Bran sprawls, his head resting on my thigh. No one sprawls like Bran. All that lean strength, he's like an exotic jungle cat, able to project utter languidness while conveying the sense he could snap to attention in the span of a single breath. I play with his hair, addicted to the silky thick texture, and he gets all heavy-lidded. Maybe he'll drift to sleep. From the look of those sleepless rings bruising beneath his eyes, he could use an hour, or twelve.

"How is everything?" I received Bran's alarmed texts about his dad while having lunch with Marti after the waxing debacle. Luckily, her place is mere blocks from the Royal Melbourne Hospital. For the last two days, she's let me crash in her room and I've wiled away hours prowling the wide leafy streets around Parkville and Carlton, waiting for the odd moments when Bran is available. We've only had the briefest snippets together, enough time to check in, kiss, let me fret over his lack of eating, and worry about his evident exhaustion.

All the drama after the Cup doesn't matter. Not in the face of life and death.

"My dad..."

I fiddle with my cowl neck as his silence lingers too long. Apprehension twists my gut. Even though I barely met Bryce and think he's an utter asshole for the cold years he spent rejecting Bran, the man is his father. Finally, I speak. "How bad?"

"Sorry. I didn't mean to cause alarm. Not that he did a whole lot to deserve your sympathy. The doctor said the news is all positive. His fever is down, so this morning he received a platelet transfusion. Should be on the mend soon."

"Whatever bad things I think about your parents are out-weighed by a single positive—they created you. For that, I'm willing to forgive a lot. Besides, he's trying and that's to his credit."

He traces my chin back and forth in a soft, hypnotic rhythm. Our eyes meet and he takes a deep breath. "There's so much to digest. My dad—his personality, everything, is still the same but now I understand him . . . at least a little. But whatever. This is probably a near-death scare. He'll resume his typical hard-nosed bastard ways within days."

"Or maybe it's the start of a new dynamic."

"He wants to discuss me serving on the foundation's steering committee."

"You sound less than enthusiastic."

"What if it's all green washing? Sounds good on paper but underneath the whole idea is jack, a big PR spin."

"Don't let it."

"Why would I want a bloody thing to do with Lockhart Industries?"

"It's your family."

"This opportunity to do good only exists because such terrible things were done under that name."

"Here's a chance to turn the past on its head."

"I keep thinking about what you said, at Davo's place."

"That night was a hot mess."

"People don't change. We switch masks."

"I shouldn't have been so black and white. We can grow."

"I think shit happens. Sure, maybe sometimes a bit can be used for fertilizer, but it's still shit."

———

There's a hot breeze blowing in from the interior deserts. I struggle to leave the cool air-conditioning of the Lockhart's compound, but Bran's been swimming laps for almost an hour. His dad is due to be discharged later today.

I slide open the glass door, dance over the sun-heated decking to the pool edge, and kneel. Bran powers toward me in a butterfly stroke. As he breaks from the water, every shoulder muscle's in stark relief. Cut deltoids, ripped trapezius—almost makes a girl wish she'd studied harder at human anatomy. I tap his head when he goes in for the turn.

"What?" He heaves himself half out of the water, breathing hard, eyes hidden by black-tinted goggles.

"Hello to you too."

"Sorry." He reaches out and strokes my ankle. "I've been moody."

"Any second you're liable to confess writing really bad emo poetry."

He gives a dismissive snort.

"Wait, is that a smile I see?"

"Talia."

"A teensy-tiny little smile?"

"You're incorrigible."

"Oooh, been playing around in the thesaurus again?"

He pushes up his goggles, revealing his eyes—I could happily spend weeks debating his irises' exact shade of green. "I'm sorry."

"About what?"

"Being this way."

"I'm going for a run to the national park. Keen to get your ass kicked by a girl?" My forced grin is all style and zero substance. Bran could leave my poky eleven-minute miles in the dust without sweating a single drop. Still, I want to cheer him up so bad.

"Nah. I'm good."

"You sure?" I don't do a good job hiding my disappointment.

He gives a curt nod, shoves down his goggles, and kicks off in a backstroke.

I'd mistakenly believed forging a tentative connection with his father would rally Bran's spirits, but instead there's a serious case of two steps forward, one step back going on. The boy's cold and fragile, my impossible snowflake.

His avoidance strategies blow mine from the water. He's deep in the foxholes shooting down my increasingly tentative advances. The new Lockhart Foundation? Bang. The Sea Alliance? Bang. Bang. The Peace Corps? Cue rapid fire. I'm starting to feel like one of those silhouetted body targets at a shooting range.

He refuses to believe life's not one big war game. I've only stumbled through the darkness myself and still teeter dangerously close to the edge. It would be so easy to stumble into the void and spiral in a tailspin of anxiety and compulsions. So far I'm resisting but I'm not that strong or resilient. I need my beautiful, angry lover to come to the table but instead he sulks in a corner shoving aces up his sleeve. We need to talk about our future. How long can he fight me on this?

Or maybe the real question is—how long will I let him?

The temperatures have soared since breakfast. I've got to get out if I want a chance for much needed exercise and mental clarity before the thermometer redlines over a hundred degrees. I lace my shoes and stick my head back outside. Bran's in freestyle mode and doesn't look up.

"Good-bye!" I yell.

Nothing.

What a shocker.

I stretch under the shady palm by the gate and start off slow, weaving through the tiny, über-quaint downtown, past the pier where we'd once spent the better part of a lazy afternoon making out against the pilings. The road veers to the west and I kick it in on the hills. Yes, Bran's going through tough times, but that doesn't give him the right to hit the pause button on my life. I've probably screwed myself from any chance with the Peace Corps. I rescheduled the interview twice already. My last opportunity is tomorrow morning. Time to get off the fence. I've avoided making any decisions. Simply gone to ground, ducked and covered, pretended I was happy this way.

But I'm not. The day's come to dig out my big-girl panties. Bran can be a mad goldfish but I'm sick of endless circles. I want to be in the river, hurling wildly toward an unknown sea. The idea frightens the everlasting crap out of me, but if I don't believe I can make it on my own, I'll sink. I love Bran but I want him swimming beside me; otherwise we will cling too hard, end up drowning. We need to help each other reach the distant shore. I know, to my bones, it's better there—full of trust, faith, and joy.

The road levels and I greedily gulp air and around a half dozen flies. I beat my hands about my face. A cool change is meant to come before dusk. I can tell rain's forthcoming because the bugs are going nuts. Any time I slow, more flies make my skin their own private party ground. Good motivation to light a fire under my pace.

There's a map in the distance. Great—should tell me how far I've got until I reach the Heads. I want to stand over the dangerous rip sucking out the entrance of Port Phillip Bay. My tongue sticks to the roof of my mouth. Forgetting to pack water was a serious fail. I'm flagging and more flies kamikaze my eyeballs. My heart drops when I read the marked sign...another two and a half miles to the road's end. Not far, but far enough in this heat, with these flies and zero hydration.

An official park bus pulls up and the driver throws open the doors, peers at my beleaguered state. "Need a ride?"

My entire body inclines toward the blissful air-conditioning. A ride? Well, that's a horse of a different color. I'll see the Heads after all.

"Sure, that would be excellent."

"Ten dollars."

"What?"

He points to the sign. "Says right there, for the bus fare."

Freaking highway robbery.

I pat my pocketless running shorts. "I don't have any money."

"Sorry, love." He goes to shut the door.

"We'll take two seats, thanks." Bran steps around me, brandishing a pale orange bill.

"Where the hell did you come from?" I climb into an empty seat in the back. The bus is deserted. Scorching conditions must be sending saner people to the beaches, not jogging over sandstone cliffs.

"You told me where you were going. I finished my swim and caught up."

"You're not even breathing heavy. That's so not fair."

"Want a drink?" He passes me a stainless steel water bottle.

I unscrew the top and try for a restrained sip but gulp half the contents. I should say thank you. He didn't exactly rescue me, but if he hadn't shown, I'd be plodding the asphalt, covered in flies. Still, he's been blowing so hot and cold. I'm suffering from temperature whiplash.

The driver drops us off at the end of the point and says he'll return in an hour.

The panoramic setting is brilliant; the cliffs run the gamut from burnt orange to beige. The vivid blue water ranges from deep indigo to an inviting turquoise that's calling my name.

"Let's trailblaze down to those tide pools before I become a puddle."

Bran jerks his thumb to the signposts along the fence reading: DANGER! KEEP OUT!

"This whole area used to be one big military range. Unexploded ordnance hide all over the shop."

"Even on the beaches?"

"Everywhere."

I eye the perfect water with longing. "Why hasn't anyone tried to dig them up?"

"Too hard? Too expensive? Too many?" Bran shrugs.

"Well, it's stupid no one's done anything about the problem." I'm sweaty and irritable and verging on the kind of mood where everything is wrong—all wrong, all the time.

Bran indicates where the bay hits the Strait. Chaotic water churns past—the famous rip. "Tasmania used to be joined to the Australian mainland by low wetlands. Where the Heads stand plummeted a giant waterfall. That's what makes the area dangerous to this day. The depths drop from about ten meters to almost a hundred right offshore."

"Are you trying to woo me from a bad mood with fun facts?"

"Maybe."

I bump my shoulder into his. "More please."

"Look around, see all these old ammunition bunkers from the war?"

Boxy concrete structures emerge from the thick coastal scrub.

"They look ready for a siege."

"The first Allied shots from World War One were fired from here at a German freighter trying to escape Melbourne."

"Wow. You're a secret history buff."

"I read the sign back there, the one you passed while cursing the lack of beach access. Want to explore one?"

"A bunker?" I eye the cement-reinforced hole to our left. "My claustrophobia says no."

"There's shade in there."

The noonday rays are doing their level best to infuse me with three kinds of skin cancer. Even the flies are giving up the fight. "Screw claustrophobia."

We duck into a low chamber where darkness and silence reign supreme.

I peer around the gloom. "Think snakes hang in here?"

"Nah. They're cold-blooded. Want to be out in the sun, soaking up the good stuff."

"Right. Better we stay here." My eyes begin to adjust. "This place is pretty amazing. Think of the men who must have come through here."

"Hundreds."

"All waiting for an enemy who never appeared."

Bran wraps his arms around my waist in an easy, intimate motion. "I'm sorry for the last couple of days. I'm screwed in the head after talking with Dad. Sometimes when you get what you want, it's harder than expected."

"Preach," I mutter, remembering my Peace Corps interview in the morning. I relax my shoulders into his hard chest and my head rests lightly against his jaw. I inhale, greedy for his smell, even partially obscured by sunscreen and the faintest trace of chlorine.

Africa and Bran—impossible to hold such discordant realities in my head at the same time. Yet, I'm sure, like I'm never sure, this could work. "I think that—"

His tongue lashes my ear and my sudden moan bounces around the tight space. He matches my ragged breath, rasp for rasp.

"I want you." His low growl elicits goose bumps up my arms. He slides a hand under my elastic waistband.

I hook my fingers into his forearm. "I'm all sticky."

"Like I care." He inches lower and freezes. "What the hell?"

God, his fingertips on my exposed skin—is there supposed to be this much more sensation? My toes curl in my athletic socks.

"I waxed the day your dad went into the hospital. We haven't done anything since and it slipped my mind."

"Why?"

He surveys my new landscape and for a second all I can do is suck on my top lip.

"Why, Talia?"

"I was worried about you and your fath—"

"No. Why are you bare?"

He's into my wetness and everything clenches with anticipation.

"Don't you want me to change things up, be exciting?"

"You don't think you excite me?" His tone drops, the husky accent epitomizing sexiness. He seizes my wrist with his non-exploratory hand and presses my palm into his stirring erection. "You rock my world."

"Really?"

"Off the foundation."

"You liked my hair?"

"Abso-fucking-lutely." His answer is immediate and indisputable even as he kisses me with sweet slowness. "How many times do I need to tell you? I love you and your hair, wherever it grows."

Tears smart my eyes. "I got jealous of ghosts."

"Don't apologize, Talia. If you want to be bare, fine. Go for it. But not for me. I'd never ask you to change."

"That's not true!" The words break with unexpected vehemence. I push away, breaking his hold. "Deep down, that's exactly what you want—me, but different."

"How? I've asked you to see a therapist because that was your doctor's recommendation."

"I'm not referring to my defective brain. I mean you wanting me scared, faithless, like you."

"What?" he says hoarsely.

"You freak whenever I try to hash out the possibility of going long distance."

"Not the Peace Corps again. I'm not in the mood."

"Big surprise." I give the wall a halfhearted kick. What am I going to do with this boy?

"I'm in the mood for this." He spoons me from behind, sucking my neck with deep, knee-weakening kisses even as I wrestle the urge to lob a frustrated elbow into his midsection.

"Sex isn't a conversation."

"Says who?" He backtracks into my shorts and cups my velvet smoothness. "There's no more honest dialogue."

"I want actual vocal cord engagement, not you finger-banging me cryptic messages in Morse code."

His pressure on my clit is freaking exquisite. I moan despite my best efforts to the contrary.

"Sorry, Captain. I don't know Morse and I never bang. However"—he continues his clever swirls—"I *am* adept at cursive, received high marks for penmanship."

"You don't play fair. Now I can't move, or breathe."

"Hmmm"—he pulses his fingers and I instinctively tremble—"looks like you can move."

This crazy noise squeaks from the back of my throat. "Don't stop." I grind my hips against his slow, insistent rhythm. "You and me, we need to stop building our own bunkers and quit waiting for invisible enemies."

He's silent.

"Please, seriously consider the Sea Alliance position. You're not happy with academia and definitely not ready to join this new Lockhart Foundation. For where you're at right now, being a full-time activist would give you a proper channel for all the anger howling around inside you."

"Talia—"

"I really want to interview with the Peace Corps." I'm not raising my voice. I speak slow, with precision, as if excellent pronunciation and a serene expression will clear his sullen expression. "I keep delaying the conversation because I'm afraid to upset you but I'm tired of land mines—"

"Enough." He cuts me off with a kiss. Kisses my eyes, my furrowed brow, my chin, my throat, my shoulder, and slips a finger inside, pressing the right spot to set me off. He's punishing me, flaunting my own body's betrayal.

"Just because you can make me come doesn't mean you own me."

"Sure about that?"

I'm up against the wall and with a guttural sound he's inside me in a blazing thrust. I bite his lip, hard, and he bites back, only a little softer. His heavy-lidded gaze is pure savagery and I like it. This is no rhythmic release, no gentle give and take. We claw at each other in mindless fury, two starving people fighting over a scrap. I'm too exposed, too sensitive. His strokes are rough but I rock harder, demanding more turbulence. He responds with perfect force. I come my brains out and my only retaliation is to grab his head, force his face to me as he hits his own climax. I refuse to break our gaze as he rides out the feeling, pumping himself dry. A rainbow of emotions play over his face in quick succession: anger, lust, fear, and wonder.

He lowers me and I stagger against the rough stone. My internal muscles are tight and furious, strangely ready to go again. "This is craziness."

"Why do you want to blow us apart?" His words are raw, savage.

I saw too much; he's got to reset the mask. Fuck that, he's still smeared between my thighs.

"I'm not saying that." My shoulders contract. I ache to pacify him but I hold my ground. "We can both get what we want and still have the other."

"I'm so used to battling everything and everyone." His voice cracks. He seizes my hips and tugs me close, stomach to stomach, his forehead pressing mine. "What if I can't trust the alternative?"

"Which is?"

"Love." Self-loathing drips from the word.

My anger vanishes in an instant. "I'll fight for you." I press my lips to his damp cheek. "I'll never stop fighting for you."

22

BRAN

I arrive to Knopwoods Retreat. The popular Hobart pub is deserted midweek. No sign of Talia. Big surprise. People have all these misconceptions, saying shit like "I'm so OCD," referring to their preferences for punctuality or cleanliness. I could grow old waiting on that girl and I'm the one who does the dishes, picks up wet towels, or makes the bed. I cook too. Maybe I should be the house husband.

Husband.

I try to shake the unease. This plan is going to work. We'll get married and Talia can find work, gain skills, and advance herself. Me? I'll tough it out at university. Maybe it's not the greatest, sure, some days I even hate it, but this is the strategy that will keep us together.

She and I left Melbourne on a stalemate. Things seem okay on the surface, but like an iceberg, I'm unsure how much lies beneath the surface. I need to get us through another couple days. The not-a-wedding is coming down the pipeline. We're booked for the first of December, my twenty-fourth birthday. Tonight is

Talia's—she's twenty-two. According to her this means we're both Sagittarius, fire signs. I have no idea what the fuck that's supposed to mean except more flame translates into increased heat and I need to keep everything from exploding.

Tonight we're scheduled to have cruisy drinks with Friendly Phil, her history professor, and sit around his old man campfire listening to stories from his life. Talia relishes that stuff. Friendly Phil seems to serve as a substitute parent figure while her own are MIA in their respective midlife crises.

I dig out my phone. No updates from Dad. Apparently, our reconciliation didn't extend to actual post near-death communication. Suppose I'll wait for his next move.

Or maybe I should man up and give him a ring tomorrow, check in, say hi.

I Google around for a bit. Karma's blog is updated for the first time in weeks. He writes about the coming Weekend of Action in the forests. Imminent conflict seems likely in the protracted standoff between loggers and environmentalists, with the protests garnering international attention. A peaceful rally is set for two days from now.

"Sorry I'm late." Talia appears in a windblown flurry, cheeks bright from her ride. "It's blowing a gale out there."

"Hey, Pretty." I'm startled by her enthusiasm. She's glowing.

"Like my new outfit?" She spins and strikes a pose.

"I think you forgot to wear pants—not that I mind."

"It's a shirt dress." She leans in for a kiss. "Mmmm, you taste like apples. What are you drinking? Cider?"

"Sit down and I'll grab you a pot, birthday girl."

"Hey!" She grimaces. "You promised not to make a big deal."

"Aren't you supposed to wait until you're at least twenty-nine to hate on birthdays?"

She wrinkles her nose. "They feel so, I don't know, weird. I'd rather celebrate something better than an arbitrary benchmark in a ceaseless trip around the sun."

"Should I cancel the fireworks display?"

"Hah."

"The mariachi band?"

"A regular comedian."

"How about a few drinks and we'll go home and eat my chocolate cake?"

"Shut up, you baked?"

"Yeah, wearing some apron I found in the cupboard that said 'Barefoot and Pregnant.'"

She busts out laughing. "I would have paid money to see that."

"So we have a plan. Drinks, a little chatty chat with Friendly Phil, and then you, me, and a date with some frosting."

"I dig how you think."

She seems cheerful. Could everything settle down, return to normal?

Phil shows and we pocket the sexy talk. I love how Talia slips from being a naughty good-time girl to the guileless innocent next door. I sense Phil disapproves of me, like I'm this rogue slopping dirty paws all over his precious ingénue.

But then he's never seen Talia perform a striptease.

I catch her gaze across the scratched pub table. She deals me a knockout smile while waving her hands, keeping a running monologue at Friendly Phil. I settle back into my chair and pretend to avidly follow the conversation, but my thoughts drift to the previous night. Talia had slipped downstairs while I was working past midnight.

"Hey," I'd said. "Happy birthday."

She placed a finger to her lips.

"Right, sorry. Forgot your weird aversion."

She sauntered forward until it became obvious she was wearing makeup. She doesn't need it, but the fuck-me-hard black eyeliner made her look like a gypsy princess.

"What's going on?"

"I miss you."

We've been careful with each other, skirting each other like nervous cats. After our conversation at Point Nepean, I took a page from her playbook—don't want to acknowledge a situation? Pretend like it never happened.

Talia had propped a foot on the kitchen counter and her red toe polish threatened to smite me down. "You stopped looking at me."

She's right—because I'm afraid of what I'll see. Disappointment? Disillusionment?

"Talia…I don't want to hurt you."

"You need to see me." She unbuttoned her nightshirt, proffering a teasing peek at her black bra and hip-clinging panties.

I swallowed hard.

"Remember who I am—the girl who loves you. Who only wants what's best."

By the final button, I was done for.

"What happened?" The concern in Talia's voice snaps me back to the present faster than a bullwhip. She levels a pensive stare at Friendly.

He clears his throat, dabs his lips on a bar napkin like a

grandma blotting her lipstick. "There's been a—how to best put this—a hiccup with the rollout for the new website."

"Okay?"

"As you've no doubt noticed, with a change in government, refugee issues are growing contentious. This morning we were notified of a significant cut to our annual budget. Enough that it's going to cause organizational pain. It looks like we won't be able to proceed with the website overhaul. Our basic services must take a priority."

"Yes, yes. Of course." She rumples her hair. "Um, what about my videos?"

"Shelved for now."

Talia slumps, elbows resting on the table.

"That sucks, sweetheart." I massage her tight shoulders. "But hey, don't forget you worked your ass off on your thesis. You're going to graduate."

"And," Phil hastens to add, "the footage isn't going anywhere. We will use the material at some point, once the political climate shifts."

Talia plasters on a forced smile.

"It's fine to admit disappointment," Phil says. "Everyone on the board is upset by recent events. And I want you to know that I, and the rest of the team, acknowledge and value your hard work."

"Thanks, Phil." Her voice is bright and she's gotten her posture back under control. But her muscles remain tense under my hand, a sign everything isn't what it seems. "I appreciate you keeping me in the loop. Services are more important than a website any day."

"Good show! I knew you'd understand."

Phil leaves after his celebratory—or anticlimactic—beer.

Talia taps her empty glass. "Can you order me another cider? A pint this time?"

I return with two.

She lifts hers in a mocking cheer and tosses back the contents.

"Drowning sorrows?"

"Nah, those suckers just grow gills." She squishes her face, shakes her fists, and relaxes. "There, that's out of my system. I needed a quick adult temper tantrum but I'm purged."

"There's no shame in feeling let down. This opportunity meant a lot to you."

"Those videos were little windows into real people's lives. The participants opened up, and that's not easy. Now it's for nothing."

"Aren't they going to be stored? Phil said—"

"Realistically? By the time there's any funding change, the footage will be dated. This project is dead."

I'm not going to change her mind or cheer her up tonight.

"Well, how about toasting your arbitrary twenty-two years orbiting a flaming ball of hydrogen and helium?"

"Thank you very much. And a tip o' the hat"—she jerks the rim on my cap—"to you and your own upcoming birthday. Excited to qualify for your senior concession card?"

She loves teasing me for being two whopping years older.

"Steady or I'll make you hear about the time I bought five bags of groceries for a fifty-cent piece."

"I'll bet the women were prettier back in the day."

"And the air cleaner."

"The world safer."

"People kinder. Do you want your present?"

"Twenty-two spankings against the bar?"

"Why didn't I think of that?" I slide the gift across the table.

"Serious? You were under strict orders to buy me nothing." She turns the present over in her hands.

"I thought that was a bad boyfriend test."

"What?"

"You know, where you tell me not to do something that's exactly the opposite to what you actually want. If I listen, I'm a bad boyfriend."

"And here I thought I was the weird paranoid one. Nice wrap job, FYI."

The book's sealed in brown paper that I held in place with gaffer tape.

"I'm not a big believer in wrapping paper."

"You'll be fun at Christmas." She gives me a rueful smile and rubs the package. "What could it be?" She opens it carefully. "Pablo Neruda? Hey, fantastic! Thank you."

"I wandered this used bookshop in Salamanca the other day. The book fell from the shelf, opened right to that page I marked."

"Here?" She tugs the red bookmark I'd slotted in place.

"Yeah, it was you all over."

"Deep, sexy, devastatingly mysterious?" Talia pretends to toss back a headful of long waves.

"Read it."

"'I love you as dark things are loved.'"

"You like?"

"It's beautiful." She keeps her head down. "I need to tell you—"

"Blast, Talia. The bother about funding cuts drove the real newsflash straight from my skull." Friendly Phil is here again, breathing like he jogged a block. "The Peace Corps called today asking for a referral. Sounds like a sure thing. Congratulations."

"Oh, great." Talia flicks me a nervous stare. "Maybe we can talk tomorrow regarding the specifics." She speaks with perfect annunciation. She only does this when she's terrified about saying the wrong thing.

"Oh, it's not worth a whole separate conversation—"

"Phil—"

"Talia." I ball my fingers under the table.

She rubs her pint like a magic genie might burst forth and grant three wishes. "I was totally transparent about having the interview. You never even asked how it went."

"Apparently peachy."

"I didn't know their office would move so quickly."

Quickly?

"Have they made you an offer?"

"I guess so. Yeah. Yes. They did."

"When?"

"I got the e-mail about an hour ago. I was going to tell you."

"See here, Brandon—"

I level a look at Friendly Phil that promises one thing: slow, certain death if he's not cleared out ASAP.

Message received if his blanch is any indication.

"Oh, the time. I must run. You two appear to have much to discuss."

"Nice." Talia's visibly annoyed. "Way to scare off an old man who wants nothing but what's best for me."

"I'm pretty sure I'm the one with the monopoly in that particular field."

"You're a freaking Socialist."

"What about our plans? The marriage thing, the visa—all that?"

"Tell me, are you honestly happy with what you're doing? I mean really, truly happy?"

"I'm happy with you."

"And the rest? I'm talking about school and the direction of your life."

"Why do you always make everything so hard?"

She pushes from the table and her half-filled glass douses the poetry book. She mops it with her sleeve, tucks the cover under her arm, and tears for the exit.

I follow, giving a finger salute to the two guys at the bar cheering our display with catcalls and whistles.

She's not gotten far. In fact, she's stopped, on the curb, staring at stars hidden by the streetlight. "You're right. I do make things hard."

"I was being a dick. I'm sorry. It's just... we're so close... need to push through this last little hard bit and then it's all good."

"But..."

"Spit it out. Are you tired of me?"

"No! No way." She reaches for my hand and I give her more than that. I wrap myself around her. I'd cut out my heart and present it on a silver platter if she asked. "But I know we are strong enough to handle the distance. If you go for the Sea Alliance and I accept the Peace Corps offer, we'll be pursuing our goals while supporting the other. Bran, what I feel for you isn't going to change, no matter where we are in the world."

"You don't know that."

"Of course I do. You are my ketchup, remember? There's no way I'll ever quit ketchup."

"Unless you decide chutney's better."

"Impossible. My heart will be tied to a grumpy ass chained to a humpback whale in the Southern Ocean."

"I mean, it sounds fine and good but watch: I ran a marathon. Easy to say—hard to do."

"But can't we do difficult things? Because this is real." She gestures to the space between us.

All I see is emptiness.

"We shouldn't test our relationship to prove we're hard-core."

"We're not. We're testing our relationship because despite the challenges, we know we never want to be with anyone else."

"Fucking hell, when it comes to you, I'm softer than puppy kisses."

"Sick."

"What's the matter with puppy kisses? Girls dig that shit."

"Quick, someone get this guy a romance advice column," she shouts to the empty street.

Is she joking? I can't tell, so I shut her up with a kiss. My next sentence is interrupted by her little smooches. "How. Can. You. Consider. Leaving?"

She musses my hair. "This *is* nice. This is always nice."

"It doesn't get any better than me and you."

"That's the whole point. I love you enough to want you out there chasing your dreams."

God, do I wish for a little faith. But deep inside I'm still this ignored little kid who everyone forgets about unless he gets right in their face.

"Tell me we can do this," she whispers.

It's her birthday. I don't want to break out the cold truths. She's playing a dangerous game and doesn't want to consider the consequences.

"I'd do anything for you, Talia. Any-fucking-thing you ask, except go long distance. I can't do that."

"Are you threatening me with Meatloaf lyrics?" Her lips turn down when I don't return her smile. "You're serious? Deep down, really, truly serious?"

"Been there, done that. Not happening again. I've told you before, I don't make idle promises."

"You're not being fair."

"Welcome to life, Talia. I told you before—we all have lines. This one's mine."

"I can't believe this. I would never, ever make threats about ending us."

"There's a difference between threats and facts."

"This is bullshit. I'm not Adie."

There, she threw down the Adie gauntlet at last. The girl from Denmark. My first love. The one who atom-bombed my heart. Hid a baby. My baby. A baby who died without me there.

"No, you're not Adie. But I won't—I can't—go through anything like that again. Don't ask for the one thing I can't give you." I'm starting to yell.

"Settle down."

"How the fuck can I keep calm when you want to be somewhere else? What about this marriage thing?"

"Yeah, about that thing?"

Her tone shrinks my guts.

"What's wrong?"

She looks away, mumbles under her breath.

"Sorry?" I step forward, forcing myself into her personal space.

"It's the coward's way."

My heart forgets to take the next beat. "Marriage?"

"For us, at this point in our lives?" She gives me a quick glance. "Yeah, kind of."

I throw up my hands. "Nice one."

She grabs my fingers and clutches them tight. "You're the one who insists on calling it a not-a-wedding and a not-a-marriage."

"Only so I don't freak you out."

"Oh, right. Because you want this."

I shake free of her grip. "Yes. I do."

"You want an actual grown-up marriage built on love, trust, and mutual respect—or you don't want to share me with the world?"

How do I recover from that?

"Bran, you occupy such a large part of my headspace that I get lost. I love you. I want to be together more than anything. Yet you encircle me so tight, there's no room to branch out. We need space to grow together."

I got nothing.

Nothing.

No thing.

"Let's go." We pedal home in silence. She mutters that she's going to walk the bike up the hill near our house. I leave her dismounting on the footpath and push through the burn, climb the steep grade without gears. My leg muscles work almost as hard as my brain. I wait at the top, ready to test my best idea.

"There's a protest in the forest, starting tomorrow."

"Yeah, I saw the headlines."

"Karma invited us."

She frowns. "That's terrible timing. We have a lot to talk about, to decide."

"Let's go."

"You're looking for a distraction."

"No, I'm not."

"Trust me, I'm an expert in not dealing. If it wasn't a big ol' forest protest, it would be going out drinking or balls-to-walls surf sessions."

"A piss-up versus protecting old growth is nothing alike."

"I'm not saying the issue isn't important. But for you and me, it would divert from *our* bigger problem. We need to discuss the Peace Corps, see if you can still get on the Sea Alliance."

"I'm trying to share something here, from my history. Protests can be inspiring, a recharge. We could both use a boost. You take interest in topical issues, right? This is an opportunity to connect."

All true. My interests are legitimate. Tasmania's old growth native forests deserve the highest levels of environmental protection. I'd love for Talia to experience firsthand direct action activism—see if it's her thing.

And yeah, fucking sue me, I want to buy time.

I need to figure out how to convince Talia the Peace Corps idea is a fail. There has to be a way to achieve what she wants here, near me, not six thousand miles away.

"Come on. All I'm asking for is a little time-out, Captain. Think things through a bit."

She relaxes, clearly relieved. "Really? I'd love to have your support."

"Yeah, sure."

And now I know I can do it—lie straight to her face without blinking.

I'm a fucking bastard.

23

TALIA

I don't spend Thanksgiving night wrestling a big-ass turkey. Instead, Bran and I drive the winding country road into Tasmania's wild southwest. For the first time since arriving in Australia, I'm a little homesick. Sunny is a twenty-first-century Luddite, so I never hear from her beyond the infrequent candy care package. Her most recent letter detailed how an agent expressed interest in her graphic novel. Beth works for a tech start-up, so her communications are more frequent, except all she ever talks about is her job, how their top-secret project will supposedly revolutionize social media.

I suck my bottom lip as jealousy corsets my ribs. I'm stoked for my friends' successes but hunger for my own accomplishments—hard to celebrate a mundane feat like not flunking out of college. My upcoming graduation is all fine and good, but that simply puts me at the starting line. If people had to put bets on my future success, the odds would be huge. I mean, my little refugee video project didn't get off the ground.

Bran's grip tightens on the wheel as he takes a tight hairpin turn. Motion sickness and frustration roil my abdomen. We can't even have a conversation about our respective futures without hitting all his hot-button trust issues. Instead of addressing the problems in any remotely healthy way, he's retreated to a denial cave and rolled a boulder over the entrance. I'm quite familiar with that particular cavern; the place sucks, full of dangerous falling stalactites.

Bran's conned himself to think marriage will fix what's breaking us. Why does he refuse to realize that's why so many fail?

I love this boy with a fierceness, but his way will only lead us to a miserable dead end. His fear surrounds me like a strangling vine. Somehow he fails to see that the harder he holds, the more he chokes everything good about us. I see that now with eye-wincing clarity. Yes, I'll be able to work in Australia with a visa. But that's not even the point anymore. There's a bigger issue at stake, one I'm only beginning to grasp—his lack of faith is blocking our brightness.

Our opportunities—Africa, Antarctica—have so much potential. Instead, I'm stuck with two bad options: keep quiet or open my mouth and send our lives crashing down like a row of dominoes.

It's not fair.

If he directed the same energy to opening up, moving us forward as he does to closing us down, he'd be amazing.

We'd be amazing.

Instead we hurtle into the fog. A sign warning of the last service station flies past. The road narrows and houses evaporate as the eucalyptuses rise impossibly high. Intermittent clear-cut scars reveal distant craggy peaks. I'm tired of distractions. We need to be at this protest like a random root canal. The radio silence screams in my ears. I want to hash out the situation but I'm afraid. What's worse is

I think Bran's subconsciously manipulating my anxiety to press his advantage. My teeth set on edge and I start counting mile markers, probably dangerous territory but the well-worn ritual is as comforting as a favorite blanket.

Hand-painted placards sprout along the road.

SAVE ANCIENT FORESTS.

STOP THE DESECRATION!

NO COMPROMISE.

Bran's already internalized that last one pretty well.

Two guys with bandanas tied around their faces flag down our car as we pull into the protest encampment. Bran rolls down his window and discusses logistics on where to camp and park. The Kingswood's headlights reveal a sheet strung between two gigantic tree trunks. The image is of a single hand, held in a universal stop sign over the hand-lettered words YOU SHALL NOT PASS.

I snort at the *Lord of the Rings* reference. Clearly, Karma walks among us. We locate a level spot to set up a tent before the drizzle increases into proper rain.

"Here." Bran passes over a long, thin bag. Apparently he entrusts me to click together the tent sticks, poles, whatever—a promotion.

"Thanks."

"Catch." He tosses me a headlamp from his gearbox. "You'll need this tonight."

"Fine." I pull the lamp's strap over my woolen hat and click on the weak light, rummaging through my backpack for a rain jacket.

I guess we are reduced to monosyllables.

He comes from behind and touches my lower back. "Hey. How are you feeling?" He knows I get all hurly on twisty turns.

"Still a bit yucky." I relax into his touch. "Carsickness is a bitch."

"Why don't you walk it off in the fresh air? I'll get everything sorted."

"You sure?"

"I love playing with gear." He unrolls a Therm-a-Rest like it's the best fun ever. "When you get back, there'll be peppermint tea waiting."

I can't hold back a small smile. "Okay, thanks. Back soon."

"Love you."

"I love you too." *Even if I'm tempted to kill you sometimes.*

I weave through the tents and steer clear of the drum circle. Instead, I side-walk down an embankment, sinking in soft soil and slipping over coarse, woody debris. My breath condenses in wispy puffs and the light reveals trees that would probably take a dozen bodies to encircle. They remind me of the redwoods. Another sharp homesickness pang stabs my throat. I swallow, hard. There's nothing in California for me anymore. My friends, sure, but everyone's busy with their lives. Pippa's ashes swirl around the Pacific, Mom's in her Hawaii never-never land, and last I heard, Dad scored a last-minute gig circumnavigating the Galápagos.

The ground disappears and I trip, landing hard, one knee down, in a puddle. Crap, wasn't watching where I was walking. The conversational din and the distant drum circle are muted by rain splattering ferns. I wandered farther than intended.

Come on, focus.

I need to pay attention. Can't wander willy-nilly in unfamiliar forests. What about big bad wolves? Scratch that—wrong continent. Big bad snakes?

A low growl rumbles from behind a fallen tree. My squeak is shrill as I vault straight back into the puddle. Water splashes over my boot tops and soaks my socks. My headlight catches familiar pale eyes.

"Fucking hell!"

"Borrowing from the Brandon Lockhart phrase book?" Karma reclines against a tree fern.

I smother my envy toward his snug-looking rain pants and focus on how much I'd like to kick that smug smile. Sometimes violence is the answer.

"Wow. Exactly who I wanted to see."

"Yeah. I'm sure."

"What are you doing out here?"

He shrugs. "Truth?"

I'm surprised he seems genuine. "Sure, okay."

"I don't know how things will go tomorrow. Everything relies on the situation remaining peaceful but there's a contingent here I don't trust. Dudes more excited about starting shit than seeing it through to the finish. They're creating a power struggle among the leadership right when we need to be most united."

I remember the two guys who met us at the camp entrance— their skittish posturing and the bandanas blocking their features.

"What can be done?"

"Not much at this point. I blame myself in part. The main antagonist is Weasel, my so-called friend. I'm starting to wonder if he—" Karma breaks off, his dreadlocks bumping over his shoulders as he shakes his head. "Got to hope for the best, right?"

"Sage advice." I turn, preparing to slog back to our tent.

"Talia?"

I freeze at the unease in his voice.

"Tomorrow—stay near Bran, okay? Especially if it looks like it's going to hit the fan. This isn't his first rodeo; he'll know what to do."

The morning breaks cool and gray, with—big surprise—more rain. Intermittent showers lash the nylon as I snuggle close to Bran. Karma trailed me back to camp last night and the three of us hung out for almost an hour. Surprisingly, it didn't suck. Karma treated me with a weird brotherly fondness. Even Bran commented on it.

"Why does everyone think I'm such a hater?" Karma had thrown his hands in exasperation.

"You do seem different." *And less unpleasant.* I had clutched the tea Bran brewed as if the mug were my personal space heater.

"I'm telling you—it's being out here, in the forest. Admit it, man, the office is a toxic environment."

Bran grunted in reply, avoiding my gaze. Hard to admit you despise something when you're desperately trying to convince yourself it's the best solution.

He stirs as I run my hand over his chest, circling his tattoo. How can he ink a symbol for infinity on his skin and fear we won't last forever, no matter where we are?

I curl my toes against the sleeping bag. My bladder gets heavy, until I'm forced to seriously consider stomping into the cold and hunting down a covert pee location. There's angry shouting followed by a *ka-boom*! The explosion's echo ricochets around the surrounding mountains.

"What the fuck?" Bran's at the tent flap before I can duck. "Stay here. I'm going to scout."

"No way in hell. We stick together."

"Talia."

"Bran."

"I'm against this."

"I'll make a note in the official record."

We lace our boots and walk. Bran plasters to my side. We aren't the only ones drawn out by the ominous sound. In the dawn light, I'm surprised by how many people are here. The forest floor is covered in a festive tent rainbow while hundreds of feet in the canopy the protest tree-sitters dwell in what can only be described as a modified Ewok village. Some have been there for nearly a year. Karma is support crew, responsible for getting them food and ensuring the solar-powered technological equipment stays charged—a challenge in a rainforest. Still, it's vital to ensure communication channels to the media remain open.

Karma rushes from the direction of the most recent explosion. Surely he didn't have anything to do with—

"We got a problem, dude. Weasel." Karma pulls up short before Bran, panting. "He and a few others set a pipe bomb in an abandoned bulldozer."

"Anyone hurt?"

"No. They're lucky they didn't blow themselves to hell. The media's all over it, though. Fuck. This is supposed to be a day of peaceful protests. I'm starting suspect Weasel's a nark."

"For real?" Bran stiffens.

"What's that?" I ask, not following.

Bran folds his arms. "He's getting paid by someone to come out here and start shit, discredit the protests. That's a serious charge, man."

"If he's not a nark, then he's got shit for brains. Either way, I'm beating his ass."

"Want help?"

"Sure." Karma waves me back. "Go to the tent, Talia. Things are going to get out of hand."

"That's what I told her." Bran's face looks grim.

"This isn't *Little Women*. No way am I staying home to tend the hearth while you chase some asshole with homemade bombs." As soon as I say the words, there's another popping blast. More shouts. Alarmed parrots wing past in a swooping ruckus.

"Bloody hell." Karma breaks into a run.

Bran and I give chase. I link my hand in his. "Don't let go."

He squeezes my fingers. "Not a chance."

We reach a murky grove where a logging road is broken off by an old blockade. Heavy machinery is parked in a neat line, the closest truck swarmed by five guys dressed in black like ninjas—or cockroaches.

"Fuckwits," Bran calls as police sirens wail in the distance. "There are hundreds of people here for peaceful protests."

"Not to mention media from five different countries," Karma adds. "What are you idiots thinking?"

"Stand back," cautions the one who's taller than the rest.

From the canopy come unintelligible shouts from the tree-sitters; they don't sound happy.

Karma jabs a fist toward the platforms. "Those folks have been up there for months, rain and shine, putting in the hard yards. That takes heart, commitment. Keep going and no one will report how the soul is being cut from an ancient forest or how all the animals are getting poisoned. The only stories will be how violent hooligans blew apart company equipment."

The sirens' piercing wail increases.

"Back off," the tall one shouts.

"The only people you are hurting are the good guys," Bran fires back.

"That's exactly the plan, isn't it, traitor?" Karma throws his hat on the ground.

"Sorry, mate." Weasel shrugs. He lifts his fist in a signal.

"Go, go, go!" The ninja team scatters and there's a clanking sound as their explosive falls from the truck.

"Grab him!" Karma yells as Weasel whizzes past Bran and me.

"No—Bran, wait!" I shout.

He turns, releases my hand, and charges, head down.

The bomb detonates right as Bran tackles Weasel, both of them disappearing into a tree hollow. I'm flung from my feet and land, disoriented, with the taste of blood in my mouth—must have bit my tongue.

Karma half rolls to his side and spits. "You okay?"

"I'm really dizzy."

There are heavy footsteps. Boots move into my field of vision.

Thank God, Bran.

Wait, aren't Bran's boots brown? Not black.

"You are under arrest for attempts to destroy property by explosives."

24

BRAN

*T*wo cops yank Karma and Talia to their feet. I release my chokehold on Weasel. The evil asshole scuttles into the undergrowth as I claw back up the hillside.

"Talia!"

"Bran." She looks around wildly. There's blood running down her chin. Karma seems dazed, has a three-inch gash on his forehead.

"Take me instead," I shout, running toward them.

The cops ignore me.

"Didn't you hear a word I said? Take me, not her."

"Doesn't work that way." The cop keeps pulling Talia.

She stumbles over a log, whimpers.

"Can't you see you're scaring her?"

They're going to take her away. That can't happen. There's nothing I can do. Wait—I need to get arrested too. Go with her. Karma's already getting thrown in the police van ahead.

"I'm trespassing, right? Arrest my ass."

The cop stares straight ahead.

"Stop," Talia hisses, keeping her head down. "Just stop, Bran."

"I'm not leaving you."

"A little late for that."

Fucking hell. I let her go, instinctively chasing the bad guys. I failed her.

She trips for a second time and this time I rush the cop. "Seriously, treat her gently."

A forestry security guard barrels in and I don't see the fist coming. I hit the ground hard. My head explodes in white light. Swamp gum branches sway hundreds of feet away, and beyond the distant canopy is a small patch of blue. The wet ground soaks into my back and I blink, returning to myself.

Talia.

I climb to my knees as she's pushed into the van.

"Talia." I scramble in her direction. She turns and her lip does this wobble that breaks my heart.

"Are you okay?" she shouts.

"Don't worry about me. What about you?"

She looks scared as hell.

"I'm going to get you out of there."

She mouths, *I love you.* The windowless door slams before I can respond. What have I done? She can't cope with this situation. I needed to be there for her and I blew it so hard.

Everywhere I look is chaos. The peaceful scene from this morning vanished. This place will regroup. The real believers, the ones who built this camp, will remain. The fuckwits who get off on destruction will move on, find another place to raise hell. Or return to their suburban families, grow old, and laugh about the days they played radical. Or was Karma right? Is Weasel a nark, paid by underhanded company operatives to start shit and discredit the movement?

Fucking whatever. Right now all I can think about is Talia, speeding toward Hobart in the back of a police wagon. Handcuffed. Terrified. Alone.

My face is wet. I swipe the warm stickiness and look down. There's blood on my hands. I tear up the mountain, holding out my phone, trying to catch the elusive signal, working my way through my contacts.

What are my options? There's only one—a thing I said I'd never do.

Takes me less than a heartbeat to reconsider.

"Gaby?"

"Bran? Is something wrong?"

"I need Dad. I have to talk to Dad. No one's answering at the house. Or his cell. Or Mum's." A terrible thought occurs to me. "Are they...Has something happened?"

"They flew back to Singapore last night. They're probably still on the plane."

"Oh." Of course. Not like they'd call to keep me updated on the blow-by-blow of their movements. Why should they? We haven't had anything approaching a normal family in, well, forever. Looks like even a brush with death and a half-ass hug aren't going to change a whole lot.

No time to stew on shit.

"What's going on?"

"Talia."

"Oh, God."

"She—"

"She left you, didn't she? I knew it. I told you, Bran. She wasn't ready."

"I—"

"You probably think you won't ever get over it. But you will. Remember last time? Adie?"

Why is Gaby dragging her into the situation? Adie has nothing to do with anything, not anymore. Talia burned out whatever darkness my ex left in my heart.

"She—"

"She's so young. So are you."

"Will you shut your fucking mouth for two seconds?"

"Don't take it out on me, Spunk."

"Talia and I didn't break up. She's been arrested."

"What?"

"She's in jail. I need to get her out."

"Oh my God, what did you do to her?"

My sister assumes it's my fault—and worse, she's not wrong.

Talia warned me about her misgivings in coming here. I brushed her off, desperate to escape into something bigger than myself. Instead, I might lose the one good thing I've ever found.

Fuck.

No good can come from me freaking out. I explain to Gaby in short, curt sentences what happened in the forest. I tell her everything except the most important part.

I let go.

I let her go.

And now she's screwed.

I punch a nearby boulder. My knuckles crush the stone and the skin rips open. The pain makes me forget my next breath. It hurts like hell, but not nearly enough.

"What was that?"

"Nothing," I say, shaking out my hand.

"Don't you get crazy. Promise?"

I force a bitter laugh. "Too late."

"What's Dad got to do with this?"

"Lawyers, money, connections."

She's quiet a moment. "Everything you hate."

"Yeah, pretty much."

"He should be landing soon. Give it another hour or so. I must say I'm shocked."

"None of this was Talia's fault."

"No, not that. Figures you'd land your sweet girlfriend in jail. No surprises there. I'm surprised you're going to Dad. To go through with this—wow. You do love her."

"That's what I've been saying."

"This is the first time I've actually believed it."

I get Dad on the phone within the hour. If he's surprised to hear from me, he doesn't show it. He listens to my case. I keep it short. No point retracing the well-worn "I'm such a fuck-up" trail. He says he'll make a few calls.

After I hang up, I turn the phone over in my hand. Here we go. I've gone and bent over to the Lockhart machine.

This decision has the potential to fuck me, hard.

I wind up my arm, ready to hurl the phone off the ravine, but a logging truck rolls below. The eighteen wheels shake the earth and knock some sense into my skull. Destroying my phone will hurt Talia.

Besides, it's ringing.

"Hello?"

"Brandon?" The voice is unfamiliar. Australian, but polished. A posh, private school accent. Takes one to know one.

"Yeah, this is Bran."

"Daniel Rivers, attorney for Lockhart Industries."

"My father filled you in?" That took what, two minutes?

"The basics. I'll need your version."

"You can help?"

"I'm the guy paid to move mountains."

He probably means that literally. How many lawsuits has this dickhead been involved in that have destroyed whole ecosystems? He's probably got third and fourth houses paid for by fucking shit up since before I was born. And now I've got to take what he's giving me and like it.

The shittiest thing is, I feel grateful.

For the next twenty-four hours, Daniel Rivers and I have a bloody love affair. I'm surprised to find the guy's not a dickweed after all. He works for Dad's new foundation and has kids, twin girls, studying medicine in New South Wales. Apparently sometimes they're a giant pain in his ass. He isn't the soulless money grabber I'd feared. Instead, he seems borderline human. When he calls in the end, telling me that Talia is getting released in two hours, he sounds nearly as relieved as me.

I drive to the shop and buy Talia food. I'm sure they fed her, or whatever, on the inside, but I don't know what else to do. The helplessness grates. I didn't do shit besides clutch the phone while Daniel Rivers dribbled me information on the hour. Should I try ringing her parents? No—I won't do anything but worry them. Better we do it tomorrow, once she has a night to get some sleep.

I reach the Hobart Police Station early. Fantasize about ripping down the walls, busting her out. But I'm no hero, not here. I fucked up everything. And tomorrow we're supposed to get married.

Call me crazy but there aren't not too many girls who'd be stoked about being in jail the day before their wedding, even if the marriage is a not-a-marriage.

Fuck, fuck, fuck.

I stalk around the cars until I notice an officer staring in my direction. He's daring me to be the world's biggest dumbshit and break into a vehicle, right in front of the police station.

I sit on the Kingswood's hood and watch the sun travel the sky. I'm going to make this up to her. We can go away. Christmas is coming. Maybe we could hike the Overland Track. And then there's New Year. The lineup at Falls Festival, the big concert out at Marion Bay, is killer. Anything she wants.

I broke my life rules for her, without thought or hesitation. Because when you love somebody, really love them, there are no rules. You do anything for that person. You find a way. And if there is no way, you get out your bloody ax and hack forward, making a path. There is no room for impossibility, not when you've done the most radically unfeasible action in the universe—hand over your heart, place it into another's hands for safekeeping.

I hold Talia's heart with me; I carry it deep in my own heart.

Finally, my phone clock says it's time.

Well, thirty minutes away but close enough.

There's one last thing I need to do before I go inside. I scroll through my phone contacts and hit SEND.

"Lockhart."

"Dad?"

"Brandon?"

"I wanted to say thank you."

———

The thick metal door opens and the moment our gazes latch, proper lung-functioning resumes.

My legs tense from adrenaline and the balls of my feet press on the linoleum, ready to sprint.

Something is wrong in Talia's expression. Her features shift in a way I've never seen, and that checks me. Better to ignore the gut slam. I can't begin to know how it's been for her these last two days. However bad it's been for me, whatever hell I faced, hers was tenfold worse.

We should put off the whole marriage plan a few days. Chill out and rest. Return to normal. She must be freaked out about losing her visa. Thanks to Daniel Rivers and his legal magic, we don't have to worry about any of that.

She walks forward in stiff, jerky steps. I can tell from the way she holds her chin she wants to be strong. So I don't grab her and hide her from the world the way I want to.

"Hey," she says, like this is normal. Like I'm meeting her at the university library rather than the bloody jail.

My hands migrate to her face. "Talia."

Her whole beautiful face crumples faster than an old tissue. She braces her hands on my shoulders and each breath is deep, shuddering. A breath you'd take if you'd almost drowned and instead found yourself tossed onto a beach.

I pull her to me and grind away whatever is in my eye.

"What about Karma?" she whispers.

"What about him?"

"He can't stay in here."

"Right." In my haste to get Talia, I spaced on Karma. Some great friend I am. Guess Daniel Rivers isn't finished with me yet. "I'll put in another call once you're sorted."

Her fingers grip my threadbare T-shirt and she presses her face into my chest, right next to my heart. "You smell like home."

"That's exactly where I'm taking you."

"How did you get me out? They said I'd be deported. That my right to ever visit Australia was put into jeopardy."

"Everything is going to be fine."

"But how? That's the part where I'm so confused."

"I went to my dad."

"What?"

"What choice did I have? My pride? Over you? No way. You win that contest every time."

"Bran...I have to tell you something."

That look she's giving me skewers my bravado. I'm flayed to a naked weakness and am afraid, scared to death of this small, exhausted girl.

"Let's get you home first."

"About tomorrow—"

"Dad's lawyers have been working on it. Everything is fine. The charges against you were dismissed. We can still get married. Or wait a few days. Whatever you prefer."

"I hate leaving Karma in there."

"I'll fix him."

"It doesn't seem fair that I'm out and he's in."

"He'll understand. You were my priority."

"Kiss me. I've been cold—so cold these last few days."

I do exactly as requested, but I can tell her heart isn't into it.

She doesn't speak until we reach the house. "I want to go to sleep and forget the last forty-eight hours ever happened."

"I'm sorry."

"You don't need to keep saying that. All I want is dreamlessness. A long, dark stillness of the brain."

When we get inside, she dashes for the stairs.

"Hey."

She pauses on the top step.

"What are you doing?"

"I need time. For myself."

She shuts the bedroom door, and just like that, she's gone.

25

TALIA

December

J'm curled in a fetal position on the shower tiles. The spray runs over me but I can't wash away the fear souring in my mouth. Even though I've turned the water to temperatures that are making my skin flare into shades of pink and red, my teeth won't stop chattering.

Eventually, the water cools and I get out. I towel-dry and slip into clean underwear—taking a moment to enjoy the bliss of clean cotton between my legs. I crawl into bed. The sheets are cool against my skin. I couldn't sleep in jail. I haven't slept in two days except for catnaps; even then my body seemed to snap back to consciousness after realizing it was letting go. My dreams are restless, my synapses firing off a memory kaleidoscope from the past few days.

*"You look like you are about to crawl out of your skin." Karma
sits across from me on the way back to town.*

"Handcuffs? A windowless van? Fucking A—could we get any more claustrophobic?"

"Ever been in a divvy van?"

"What's that?"

"What we're riding in—a divisional van."

"I thought it was a paddy wagon. Same difference, I suppose."

"So you've never been arrested."

"No! Of course not."

"Here's how this is going to go. Don't say a fucking word. You have a right to silence in this country."

"We do too...I think. Isn't that what they always say in the movies?"

"This isn't Hollywood. All you tell them for now is your name and residential address."

"You've done this before? Been arrested? Gone to jail?"

"I grew up in a station."

I snort. "Figures."

"My dad was a copper in Gippsland—big rural region to the east of Melbourne."

"Police? Huh, that's not something I'd have guessed."

"You'll be fine, you know."

"What if I'm deported?"

"You think your Daddy Warbucks is going to let anyone remove a hair on your precious head?"

I close my eyes and refuse to speak to him the rest of the way. Instead, I concentrate on the way my stomach clenches every time we take a corner too hard. When they open the doors in Hobart, I vomit against the curb.

"Karma is getting released." Bran presses his hand to my forehead. "Can I get you anything? Water?"

"Do we have any black currant cordial?"

"Probably."

"A cup of that, please. And a hug."

He pulls me hard against him and I drift away again.

Karma and I are in separate cells, side by side.

   "You still rattling around? Must be past midnight."

   "Can't sleep."

   "I can't either—you keep tapping your feet against the wall."

   "Can I really be deported? Blocked from ever returning?"

   "Your boyfriend's father probably owns half of Canberra. The prime minister will be called in to handle this personally."

   "What about you?"

   "I'll look after myself."

   "Can you call your family?"

   His laugh is bitter. "Fat chance. If my old man knew I was here, he'd throw away the key."

   "Jesus."

   "I'm bored. Tell me a story."

   "Are you serious? I'm freaking out over here."

   "What did you ever decide to do about your big Africa plans?"

   "Nothing."

   "Bran's not hip to the gig."

   "Something like that."

   "He'll get over it. Trust me."

"Yeah, right."

"You're doing him a favor. Blaze the trail and he'll be forced to follow."

Bran comes back with an ice-clinking glass. I was too nervous to eat or drink much in jail. I'm almost too nervous now. I reach for my laptop bag.

"What's with the computer?"

An invisible fist thrusts into my stomach. The tightness spreads into my lower ribs. "We need to talk."

He hands me the glass and sits on the bed. I can't bring myself to take a sip. Not yet. "The Peace Corps offer…Malawi—"

"Wait—"

"I'm going to accept."

"No."

"I'm saying yes to me, and I'm saying yes to us. We can do this. Our love is big enough for the whole world. The direction we were heading won't work, not right now. It would warp us into something unrecognizable."

"You don't know what you're saying. You're exhausted."

"You're right. But this is our shot, to live a life that is truly extraordinary, to lift each other somewhere better."

"You don't need me to remind you we're supposed to get bloody married tomorrow, right?"

"Why not make tomorrow be the start of something bigger? A commitment bigger than this whatever not-a-wedding."

The look on his face hurts like hell. My throat works overtime to swallow the lump there. Every muscle in my body aches like I've been run down, backed over.

"How exactly do you see this playing out?"

"I don't know. All I know is I'm sick and tired of worrying about enemies that might never eventuate, fears that may never come true. If we have what I believe in my deepest heart we have, then this is a lifetime kind of love. So why be miserly? When we sit together someday at eighty, we can tell stories to grandkids about how you sailed around in the Antarctic and then came to visit me in Africa. We backpacked to Zanzibar. Climbed Kilimanjaro."

"I've broken every rule for you, every last one. But not this. I can't fucking do long distance with you. Trust me, I've been there, done that. You think it'll be great but in reality the situation will grind us to dust."

If he keeps talking like this, I'll cave. "I'm never sure about anything but I'm positive about this. You have to believe, Bran."

"Believe what?"

"That you are loveable." My voice breaks. "That I will love you near, that I will love you far. You don't have to be scared."

"I'm not going to stand here and listen to a bunch of bullshit."

He slams out the door.

My stomach roils but I lift the cordial and down the whole glass. Then I open my computer.

I keep my breathing slow, measured. I even try to smile at my reflection in the window.

You can do this. Make him believe.

26

BRAN

*T*alia cracks the bedroom door. "Brandon?"

She's never called me that.

"You accepted."

"Yes. I told you I would. And I did."

I collapse against the banister and press my hands to my forehead, like if I squeeze hard enough, I can push her words from my skull.

"You're leaving."

"Yeah," she whispers.

"Can't hear you."

"Yes—but only technically. Remember, I'll get time off. I can visit. You're able to stay with me, too, as long as you want, after you finish with the Sea Alliance."

"Go ahead, say it."

"What?"

"End this, end us. That's what you want, right?"

"No!"

"Don't you fucking lie to me, Talia. Not you."

"We can make this work." She reaches out.

I recoil like she offers a bouquet of cobras. "You are not allowed to touch me."

Her fingers hover midair. The inches between us might as well be the Mariana Trench. "If you'd listen for once, try and see my perspective—"

"Everything is crystal clear."

"Will you stop? Let me speak for a sec?"

"I loved you with every ounce of my shitty soul. I was ready to give you my whole life."

"That's just it, Bran."

"I'm not good enough?"

"I don't want to take your life to make us work. Or give you mine. I love you too—so much I might explode. Enough that I know we can do this. Chase our dreams yet stay together. Come on, take a leap of faith."

"You want faith? Bloody hell, did you ever pick the wrong guy..."

"Tell me you don't love me enough to believe, to take a chance."

"I haven't taken chances with you? I worked my guts out to make this work and you want to play Russian fucking roulette. Will Talia and Bran go the distance from separate continents? No? Bang, we're dead."

"But if I'm right, we'll prove something to each other."

"I don't need to prove shit. I know the truth."

"It's okay to be scared. I'm freaked out too."

"Not nearly enough." She's my anchor. I fly up the stairs, grab her hips, lift her against the wall, knock my forehead into hers so she can't look anywhere but my eyes. "You said you'd always hang on. We swore that to each other."

"Bran—"

"Don't break us. Don't you do that, Talia."

"I—"

"Why can't you shut up?" I kiss her. I'm an ass, a coward. When have I ever been anything different, down deep? I'm a cheetah who painted stripes over his spots. Her lips soften. Hope claws from my heart as she offers a breathless moan. I fold my arms around her in a protective cocoon.

The last few days were insane. Okay, sure, she got cold feet. There were moments the world seemed to disintegrate into thin air.

She tears open my pants and my hands are everywhere. Her nightshirt loses a button but she doesn't seem to mind. Our urgent soundtrack undercuts every movement, ragged inhalations followed by groans torn straight from the dark center of the universe. We collapse, a knot of sweat-slicked flesh. There's no room for anything measured or gentle. Her mouth tastes like apples and mint. Maybe I should slow down, savor, but I'm like that bloody kid in the Dickens novel.

Please, can I have some more?

We kneel, face-to-face, breathing each other's breath. Streetlight filters through the skylight's frosted glass, shrouding her body in a pale glow. She looks like a hallucination, or a ghost. There's an indistinct growl, distant thunder. She pushes the space between my shaft and navel with the heel of her palm. I tip back against the floor and she crawls on top. Shadows cling to her body, a night angel coming straight for my soul. I grit my teeth when the wetness between her thighs slides against my leg. I start to shake and so does she, all over. Vibrations hum between our bodies and she shifts her weight, grinding in a slow deliberate rhythm, the way that's good for her.

"I want...I want everything," she whispers, working harder.

"It's already yours." I lock my forearm over my eyes and let her use me.

With a slight pivot, her pelvis sinks, descending to my hilt.

Eyes, meet skull.

Outside, rain unleashes in a furious downpour.

"Gorgeous."

Her pretty lips crook in a half-smile. "You're not so bad yourself."

I hiss through clenched teeth and her knees grip my hips as she rides, pressing into my pubic bone. She leans all the way back, hands braced on my shins, exposing every beautiful inch.

Fucking hell. Talia on top, there's nothing better. Nothing.

I shudder hard.

"Bran." She dips her torso over mine and there's this wet suction sound from the sweat misting our bellies. She grinds harder and our kisses grow wetter. Her tongue traces the roof of my mouth.

"God, Bran. Oh my holy God."

It's like she wages war on my body and I'm not putting up any defenses. I don't even want to win a battle. I just want her. With me. Always.

Her head rocks back. What happens when we come together— there are no bloody words. You don't throw this away. "It's not going to be better, Talia. Not with anyone else."

"I know that." It sounds like she wants to add "you idiot" to the last part.

With her every rock, I'm coming home, so why does it feel like good-bye?

We inch closer and closer to the brink; the drop is just there, right ahead. I dig in my heels and fight against the inevitable because if she slips from my reach, I'll free-fall. For a second we hang in midair, like a cartoon character right before everything falls apart.

She screams.

I snarl.

We're coming.

But where the fuck are we going?

My head knocks against the floorboard, my dick still pulsing from the aftershocks. She pulls away, clutching her pajamas to her chest, and pads into the bathroom. My brief spark of hope fizzles as rain clangs against the tin roof. The sweat misting my chest and stomach cools. She rings a cab.

She emerges from the room, dressed, with her two bags.

This is happening.

"Are you fucking for real?"

"I'm staying in a hotel tonight. I'm going to book a flight that leaves tomorrow." I can't decipher her features in the dark. There are familiar planes and angles but nothing concrete. Is this what she's destined to become—a faded memory?

"If I stay here—with you—it will mess with my head and you'll talk me out of leaving. You'll literally screw me senseless. I need space tonight. But I know we can do this."

Rage cuts through me with white-hot heat. "We're breaking up."

She starts to cry. "Why are you saying this? I love you."

"Stop fucking lying to yourself!" I fly toward her and she jumps back.

"I love you." She's hysterical, covering her face with her hands.

"I hate every fucking lying lie coming out of your lying liar mouth." I punch the wall over her shoulder.

"I'm not...I do love...I believe...I—"

"Enough." I'm scoured clean. Empty doesn't begin to describe the hollowness in my chest. "You want to fuck and run? Fine. Get out. Go. I won't try and change your mind. But know this, once you walk out that door, you and me? We're finished. No take-backs."

"If you really love *me*, not the idea of me, you'd never make me choose."

"What was I? A stunt. A kick? A twentysomething adventure so someday when you're back in your same boring hometown with your same boring friends living your same boring life you can brag how once upon a time, long, long ago, Natalia Stolfi had herself a great big adventure?"

"Stop and think. You want to join the Sea Alliance. This is your chance. You still have time."

"Sure, I could do that. But I wanted you more. That's where we differ. If given the choice, I choose you, Talia. I always choose you."

"We shouldn't have to choose. We have a whole lifetime. I don't want to ask you to sacrifice your dreams for me, not ever. Why can't you pull your head out and see that I'm breaking us apart to keep us together?"

I brace against the wall. "You want to leave. So go."

Her boots click closer to me and so I fold my arms, bury my face. There's a long pause.

"Tell me the truth about one thing."

She runs her hand over my back. "Okay."

"If you hadn't gotten arrested. If I hadn't dragged you to the protest, tried to bring you into my world, would this have happened? Would you still be leaving?"

"Yes." The resulting silence lasts longer than the age of the dinosaurs. "Please, Bran, say something, anything. I want to take part in your interests but I want my own too."

Sure, makes sense. But I can't agree. Literally, my mouth won't form the words.

Her shoulders slump. "Forget about it."

"We don't share that particular talent, sweetheart."

Headlights flash through the front door windows. A car horn blares.

"That's my cab."

"So it seems." She won't even let me drive her away. I've blown it so hard it's like I'm touring a bombsite, unable to wrap my head around the devastation. "Tell me leaving is going to make you happy."

"Leaving will make me happy," she whispers.

"Is that what your mom said?"

She starts to noiselessly cry. "Please try."

"Can't." Cue my own waterworks. I grind a fist into my eyes.

The taxi honks again.

"We can make this work. You and me, we're different, right?" She vaults forward, wraps her arms around my waist and leans into my bare skin like she belongs there. Which she does.

Grow a fucking backbone. She's leaving. She's not who you thought. Kick out the pedestal and be done with it. Stop the bleeding.

Every cell in my body wants to reach for her. But my brain has me on survival mode lockdown. I can't do this. In another minute, I'm going to fall on my knees, wrap my arms around her legs, and beg.

I clear my throat. "Go then."

"Kiss me."

She thinks her lips will work mind-fuckery on me. She's right.

There's one last warning horn blast from the cab.

"I . . . I have to go."

"You don't."

"Stop!" she whispers.

"You're breaking us. You. No one else." A storm whooshes through my body. I'm hanging on to a spiraling hurricane.

"I'm trying to save us but you're too stupid and myopic to notice."

"Break us down to rebuild us into something stronger?"

"Yes, that, exactly."

"Good-bye, Talia."

"Please, stop!"

"Truth hurts." It's funny, saying something cliché—so why isn't anyone laughing?

"I lo—"

"No. You don't." I throw down a spindly hall table. Glass breaks, probably a bloody antique vase. I kick a porcelain shard into the wall. "If you loved me, you'd never go through with this."

Her eyes are huge, two moons.

Sorry, sweetheart. I'm no bloody astronaut.

I throw on my boxers and run. I'm outside, in the yard, at the back fence. There's nowhere else to go, so I collapse to my knees and keel forward, face in the dirt.

Right where I belong.

———

One swing of my ax and the wood cleaves into neat halves—not unlike how Talia treated my fucking heart. I'm three seconds away from puking or ripping open like a mutant alien. Fine by me. I can use my guts to hang myself from the apple tree—fitting conclusion to tonight's gong show.

A light in the cottage next door flicks on and outshines my head torch's feeble glow. "Bloody 'ell, dickhead, it's past midnight," the neighbor hisses from a side window.

I ignore him and seize another log. Swing and chop, swing and chop. That's all I can manage. Reverberations ricochet through my locked shoulders, an ache that fails to override the bone-deep pain. Sweat streams down my clenched back. Empty beer bottles pile to my left and a mountain of kindling grows on my right.

"Mate?"

Dude, better to leave ax-wielding psychos well enough alone.

"You all right?" The guy's voice grows hesitant, unsure if I've got a few kangaroos loose in the top paddock. I refuse to answer. Eventually, the lamp clicks off.

Alone, raging in the dark, exhausted, devastated, my self-control frays to a single strand of whipcord. Got to keep my hands tight gripped on the rusted handle, ensure I don't pull an idiotic stunt—like grabbing my keys. Chasing her down.

"I held on," I mutter. My eyes sting with a fierce burn. "Fuck-ing held fast."

Tough shit.

I still lost everything.

27

TALIA

I fly to Santa Cruz in a series of mind-numbing flights: Hobart to Sydney to Los Angeles to San Francisco. My tear ducts are broken by the time I clear customs. Somehow, incredibly, life continues. Breathe in, breathe out, and I'm here, surviving without a heart. Every morning I wake, lock the bathroom door until it feels right, and stare in the bathroom mirror. Each time I am surprised to find myself still here, staring back.

I speak about that last, terrible night with Bran only once, with Sunny, on New Year's Eve. She's letting me crash in her garden studio behind her grandma's house while I wait for my Peace Corps posting to begin in a few weeks. We hide out at Cowell Beach, avoiding the drunken shitshow raging up and down Pacific Avenue.

Sunny's features briefly blaze into view as she inhales her joint. I work through a box of Junior Mints. Weed, sugar—we all have our vices.

Beyond the waves, sea lions bark on the rocks. A few intrepid surfers ring in the year with a night session. I can't decode their bodies in the dark but there are occasional whoops and hollers. I bite my lip. I'm not going to cry. I've shed enough tears for Bran to irrigate Death Valley. I thought we would work, no matter what.

By the time I reached Santa Cruz, his phone was disconnected and his university e-mail disabled. I try to believe he'll come around but it's hard, like diamond hard, without the luster.

"Wait, wait, wait. Holy shit, T! He *punched* a wall above your head? Why didn't you knee him in the junk?"

"He wasn't threatening *me* with violence."

"No excuses. Good thing he's far, far over the rainbow. You're done."

I know. We are.

"It's better this way, trust me. Someday you'll see."

"He hasn't e-mailed or called. Just the one postcard."

The card arrived at Sunny's address, which is the one I left him, a few days before Christmas. He'd scrawled two words: *Going south.*

My sweet boy did it; he joined the Sea Alliance.

"You look like shit, honeybunch."

"I feel worse."

"Fucking Bran."

"Don't say that."

I drop onto the sand beside Sunny and she passes me the joint. I take a single, lung-stinging puff, shove away a fleeting lung-cancer fear, and exhale.

"Why do you insist on defending him?" She sounds genuinely curious. "I mean, Brandon Lockhart is the type of guy who's fun to fall into bed with, but that's it, *no más.*"

"I…"

I've heard people toss around the term *other half* and it always sounds like an expression served with a heaping side of barfaroni.

Bran and I, we share the same soul and end up yanking it back and forth like two people with a single blanket on a cold night.

I can't help but hope he'll catch his mistake, want to tuck me back in.

"Sorry, Sunshine. I can't give you a reason that will make sense."

She smooches my forehead. "You were going along, minding your own business and—*bam!*—out of nowhere he careened into your life, a total sideswipe. But you'll get back on track."

"Do you believe in true love?" I say, turning to face her straight on.

Sunny kicks the sand. "What about Tanner? Ever think about him anymore?" Her voice is strained, in a weird way that I can't put my finger on. Maybe it's the weed.

Tanner—my sister's big love. The guy I nursed a major crush on for my entire teenage existence. The guy I drunkenly lost my virginity to a year after her death.

"Why are you bringing him up? He's ancient history."

"You make my point."

"Which is?"

"People move on. It's what we do, as a species, how we survive. Someday you'll realize this guy was an accident. Nothing more."

———

I'm teaching English to sixty children who sit on a dirt floor. After nearly two months I'm squeezing the dregs from my shampoo bottle and have run dangerously low on tampons. Time to make a resupply trip to Lilongwe, the Malawian capital city. After a bumpy three-hour ride in a flatbed truck, I reach the Happy Days Hotel, a concrete guesthouse and agreed upon flop pad for Peace Corps volunteers in from the field.

This is the place where us wide-eyed newbies can rub shoulders with the more experienced crowd, those who've stuck it one, two, or even three years. These guys have a steely end-of-the horizon stare and the ability to discuss worms burrowing from their eyeball without a shudder.

In fact, seems you don't get respect in the Peace Corps until worms emerge from somewhere in your body. The crazier the better.

Guess there's no surprise the in-country volunteer dropout rate is close to one in two.

I'm determined to stick it out, even if it means coating myself with hand sanitizer and ordering in a self-help library. I love my students' exuberance and my work site right near beautiful Lake Malawi. Everything here is totally different. The food. The language. The clothing. The smells.

Nothing to trigger painful memories.

No one is around when I drop my bags in the sparse hostel room. I unpack my mosquito net and check and recheck for holes. That's when I hear the moans coming from next door. I'm not alone after all. Lilongwe is the place for volunteer hookups—people are determined to make Happy Days live up to its bold promise. The bed hopping reaches epidemic proportions.

I do my sleeping alone. Turns out I'm remarkably gifted at the cold shoulder. Guess I learned from a master.

I trudge to the Peace Corps head office and guys look right through me. Street heckling, a usual part of my day-to-day at home, is unknown here. No one tells me to "smile" or calls me "beautiful." I've lost fifteen pounds since arriving and the local menfolk prefer more voluptuous women.

I stride past the compounds; high walls lined with broken glass bottles surround fancy houses, and armed guards linger out front. A little boy in a hot-pink shirt that hits near his ankles, bedazzled with the word DIVA, chases after me. Western clothing donations are sent here from all around the world. It's not unusual to see a guy squeeze into a tummy-revealing Little Mermaid halter or a teenage boy fronting tough in a Barbie tee.

"*Mzungu!*" cries the boy. "*Mzungu!*"

White person.

The word is a soundtrack to my day.

Outsider.

I close my eyes for a second and see Bran's face, right there, always with me.

Time is supposed to heal, but in this case, I'm not sure what remains under my scar tissue. I scan my body, starting at my scalp. So far I'm coping okay. I stopped taking medication before leaving because mental illness disqualifies you from fieldwork. No one did any hard-core background check. This is the Peace Corps, not the FBI. I did manage to avoid getting prescribed Lariam for an antimalarial—heard that drug can totally mess with your head.

All I can do is hope for the best. For me.

For him.

I walk into the Peace Corps office and the receptionist calls out, "Natalia! Mail for you."

Sunny and Beth must have sent another care package.

An envelope is on the counter. For a second I wonder if it's from Mom. Maybe she's decided to stop being MIA at last. I lift the note and at the sight of the familiar block letters, my stomach pays a hasty visit to my ankles. The stamp is from New Zealand and the date is over a month old.

By the time I make it to a chair, my hands are shaking so hard I can barely tear the paper.

Talia—

I hope the fact that you are reading and not burning this letter is a positive sign. This is old-fashioned but I don't have a choice. Your UCSC e-mail must have been deleted after you graduated. Luck's on my side today—there's a documentary crew visiting the ship with a reconnaissance helicopter. They say they'll mail this letter for me but I've got two minutes to write. Here goes nothing.

I am so fucking sorry.

Do you still care? I do. I made you a promise to hold on. This is me holding, Talia, to the chance you'll give us another go. I confused holding with death grip. You were right. I lacked faith, freaked out that if you left, your love would vanish.

But I can't live a life expecting disappointment or fearing ghosts.

I get who you are—to your bones—and the simple fact this crazy-ass world can hold such an amazing person within its gravitational pull should be more than enough to give me confidence.

You had every right to want to claim your own life and independence. I should have been the guy to love and support you. I wasn't but will never make that mistake again.

They're saying I have to stop writing. Fuck, there's still so much to say. I talk to you all the time in my head. Do you ever hear?

I have no clue what the next steps are, but there's got to be a way. So here's the million-dollar question. Will you give

us another chance? Let me prove I can love you no matter the
distance. You are worth it. You are worth everything.

I don't know how long I stare at his hastily scribbled words.
He'd pressed on the paper so hard the pen tore through in a few
areas. I close my eyes and tears cascade over my cheeks. Bran
included an e-mail address for the ship under his scrawled signature.

It takes the length of a heartbeat to arrive at my decision. After
four deep breaths, I'm moving to the computer room. I know what
I want to say, what I've imagined saying a thousand times, but here
in the actual moment...

Please let me make the right choice.

Because this is the scariest thing I've ever done.

28

BRAN

February

I scan the horizon from the ship's bridge—blue, white, sea, ice.

There are times my eyes ache for a richer color palette. Fern greens. Ripe lemons. Lavender stalks. The sweet-tea brown of a pretty girl's eyes.

After Talia left, I dropped out of honors and joined the Alliance. She was right, as usual. I needed this, wasn't ready to settle into the academic track. I have too much anger inside me. This work helps to channel the emotion into something productive, like activism, where injustice, greed, and rash destruction are my targets.

Every day is full with the right sort of mission, defending the fragile marine environment. We are trolling for the commercial whaling fleet at present. So far no luck but there's a general feeling on board that we are closing in and everyone's buzzing from the tension. These days down south are grueling but the work's good— important. As crew, I keep fit and focused from rigorous ship maintenance. Nights, though, when it's only me and my head—those are a different story. Can she feel me? Does she know I always think about her?

"How's it?" Right Hook, the first mate, strolls in, the same build and temperament as a water buffalo. He's South African, and a temperamental bastard, but guess I don't have much cause to complain.

"Going well." As a lowly deckhand, he's allowed to shuffle me off with a menial task.

"Am I supposed to tell you something?" He squints in my direction.

"Don't know, are you?"

"Oh, right." He nods, relieved to have located the errant thought. "An e-mail came in for you on the general inbox."

I fight the urge to climb the ceiling. "Mail, for me?"

"Yes, Princess. Maybe it's an invitation to the big ball." Right Hook raises a pair of binoculars to his eyes and turns away. "Com-Ops taped it to your door."

There are two likely outcomes. Dad is relapsed.

Or it's her.

She's made a decision.

Since hitting the Antarctic coast, I've watched countless glaciers calve. The same ice sheets I'd studied so abstractly now rise in all their white-walled magnificence and when they break, there's a thunderous reverberation you feel in your molars.

The same phenomenon is happening inside my brain.

"Who sent it?"

Right Hook snaps his chewing gum. "Some girl. Your fan club was moping below. Don't know what everyone sees in your skinny ass."

"Where—"

"The e-mail is taped to your berth's door as per standard procedure."

I'm out before he can do something totally within character like order me to go swab a deck or inspect the produce in the galley for mold.

"Please, please, please." I'm praying. The knowledge nearly slams me from my feet. Never, not even when I was strapped into a fucking jet, minutes from crashing into the Indian Ocean, have I prayed.

Sure enough, a printout is folded and taped to the center of my door.

"Courage," I mutter, and peel away the tape.

Do I have the guts to unfold the message? My breath stutters like a car running on its last fumes. Right now the possibilities are infinite but any moment my dreams might detonate. Bloody hell, this could be a paper hand grenade.

We had stood at an abyss. Talia offered to build a bridge but instead I jumped into the blackness. I fell and fell until I realized that with this girl, failure's never an option. At last I bottomed out and discovered the one thing I never expected.

Hope.

It's a thin little sprout—spindly as shit—but alive, sending roots into my soul's bleak lunarscape.

I open the door to the dormitory and roll into my bunk, not trusting my legs.

"Please, Talia," I whisper. "I made so many mistakes. Let me put us right."

I must have opened the note the same moment as a solar flare or a gamma ray burst. Maybe the earth shifted magnetic poles. I'm flat on my back, mind sailing beyond time and space. When I return to my body, I reread the note. And once more for good measure.

Will you give us another chance? I'd asked, expecting nothing and everything.

Will you give us another chance? I'd asked, when I'd lost the right to make requests.

Will you give us another chance? I'd asked, because when you truly love someone to the dirtiest, dustiest bits of their soul, you need to believe in the impossible.

Will you give us another chance?

My laugh is also a sob. I press the paper to my face and kiss the most precious fucking word in the English language.

"Yes."

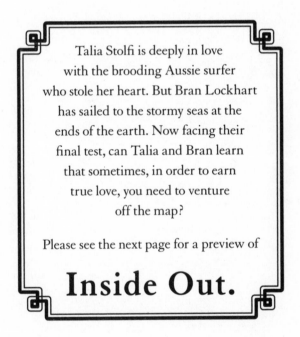

Talia Stolfi is deeply in love
with the brooding Aussie surfer
who stole her heart. But Bran Lockhart
has sailed to the stormy seas at the
ends of the earth. Now facing their
final test, can Talia and Bran learn
that sometimes, in order to earn
true love, you need to venture
off the map?

Please see the next page for a preview of

Inside Out.

I

TALIA

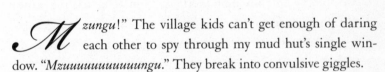

*M*zungu!" The village kids can't get enough of daring each other to spy through my mud hut's single window. "*Mzuuuuuuuuuuungu.*" They break into convulsive giggles.

Mzungu means "white person" in Chichewa, Malawi's national language. Since arriving in Africa as a Peace Corps volunteer, the word follows me throughout the day. It's taken the last three months in-country not to cringe at the term and to accept the truth stamped in my pigment. I am an outsider.

"Hey, *mzungu*!"

I uncurl from child's pose, push off the straw mat, and wince. Yoga therapy isn't doing much in the way of curing my abdominal crampage. Still, I manage to make it to the front door. "Boo!"

My barefoot students scream with delight and scamper toward the shoreline. Lake Malawi is one of the largest in Africa. Mozambique is on the other side, the distant hills obscured by a hazy plume, as if the water itself is on fire. Weird. Maybe it's going to rain? The wet season is long over, but this country is nothing if not unpredictable. I swipe my hand over my brow. The noonday sun is pleasant, nowhere near hot enough to justify this much sweat. My mouth fills with saliva.

Great, here we go again.

I shuffle around the side of the hut to the latrine in the back-yard. Eighteen steps. Twenty at most. I enter just in time, thighs quivering from the effort and get quietly sick for the fourth time today. How the hell did I catch a stomach bug? I'm anal-retentive about using a water filter and iodine purification tablets. Still, there was clearly a breach in my defenses. Local families have taken turns hosting me for dinner since my arrival in a sweet, generous gesture of hospitality. It doesn't take an expert in cross-cultural communication to know it's impolite to drill people on their household food preparation methods if you're the guest of honor. No matter how teeth-clenchingly bad you want to do exactly that.

My stomach roils, painful to the point that a moan escapes. I brace my hands on my knees and pant. What if parasitic worms are hatching in my stomach or burrowing through my liver?

I step back outside and linger in the mango shade, resisting the urge to scratch the welts speckling my arms. Mosquitos are eating me alive, so taking antimalaria medication has become an accept-able nightly ritual. The dark cloud over the lake drifts closer. A trio of local women skirt my yard, swinging plastic utility buckets and handwoven baskets. Their lively chatter makes me miss my best friends, Sunny and Beth. I wonder what they're up to? I've avoided their e-mails since Bran and I got back together.

To say my girls aren't Bran's biggest fans is a rather epic under-statement. In December he morphed into a Big Bad Wolf, shredded my heart as easy as a straw house. After a cooling-off period—literally, in his case, as he joined a marine activist organization dedicated to preventing illegal whaling in the Antarctic—he wrote an apology and asked for an opportunity to set things right.

I've seen Bran at his worst, know his best, and somehow reconcile the two. He's broody, unpredictable, and twists my brain like a pretzel, but my love for him isn't a word, it's an involuntary, instinctive act, like breathing. Our connection is the one thing I trust in this far-too-fragile world. Despite his past wounds, he craves heart-peace as much, maybe even more, than I do. When he finally mustered the guts to step up and show courage, there was no way I could say good-bye. I want to believe he has a chance for happiness.

I need to trust we both do.

The women notice my stare and slow their pace, brows knitting. I haven't been at my site for long. The mandatory three-month volunteer training in the capital, Lilongwe, wrapped a few weeks ago and here I am. Home. Sort of. The village is quietly assessing me, and I'm not exactly putting my best foot forward. This is my fifth day out sick from teaching. Hardly a confidence booster.

I raise a hand in forced cheer that the women return with shy waves. Once they're safely out of sight I double over. It takes serious diaphragmatic breathing before I can hobble back toward the refuge of my bed.

The doorway provides a welcome rest stop. Fussy stomach aside, I'm glad I came to Africa, right? I mean, in a great many ways, I've gotten exactly what I wanted—plus a guy who loves me and has come around to accepting that long-distance relationships don't mean doom. I should be happy. Am I happy? Sometimes.

And sometimes not.

When we get what we want, the dream becomes real, and real life is never perfect. I realize some of my naïveté in joining the

Peace Corps. I think deep down inside I believed something would shift in me, in my life, like I'd wake one morning and it would be a whole new world. Instead, I'm still me. Just here, in Africa, teaching English as a Second Language in a rural school.

I adore my students and their sweet enthusiasm, but my assigned project? Not so much. ESL isn't the work I want to ultimately pursue. I'm no grammar whiz and get nervous talking in front of groups. Every morning I wake hoping today is the day where I'll stop second-guessing and start to thrive, and every night I fall asleep uncertain, listening to the mosquitoes' unrelenting hum.

I was having a twentysomething crisis when I applied to the program, running from big decisions on what to do with my life. The Peace Corps was one of many pipe dreams that floated around during my undergrad, and in a desperate Kermit flail I snatched the opportunity with both hands.

My Facebook feed was littered with people from my major squee-ing over cool jobs, internships, or graduate school admittance, and I wanted in on that success. The Peace Corps seemed like the perfect way to have an adventure while advancing my future. But just because an idea is good in theory, doesn't mean it works in practice. Now that I'm actually here, I can't shake the sense that I'm an imposter, a fraud. Am I an intrepid development worker, decked in head-to-toe khaki and ready for anything? Not by a long shot. I should like being here more. And I don't.

God, whatever, Talia. Pack away the tiny violin.

Got to stick it out because ultimately, I like the stigma of failing even less.

I shuffle to the plastic milk crate beside my bed. Inside are seven crinkled pieces of paper. I've printed each of Bran's e-mails. Our communication has been infrequent. He's not able to write much from the ship, and I have to hitch to Lilongwe to source reliable Internet access.

When we met in Australia during my exchange, I tried to convince myself he was a little adventure, some uncomplicated fun. The first time he touched me, my body went, "Ah, okay, *there* we go." Bran revealed himself to be the exact puzzle piece I was missing. I ease onto my bed and peer at the first dog-eared page.

Hey Darling,

Wait a second. My eyelids twitch and vision goes wonky. I blink to refocus.

Hey Darling,

What the hell? Words skitter in every direction. I try to give chase, but my eyes no longer operate in unison. Pain explodes behind my sockets like a hand grenade, radiating through my temples. I've never had a migraine hit with such sudden intensity. Maybe I'm dehydrated from throwing up so much. I fold Bran's note and tuck it inside my shirt, next to my heart as my stomach constricts again, from agony and mounting dread.

At one point or another, most everyone confronts debilitating sickness during their Peace Corps placement—practically a part of the job description. The other volunteers regard parasitic worms as an African red badge of courage. More power to them. Me? I'm content to play the coward.

The doctor blew off my vague symptoms—fatigue and nausea— at the health clinic this morning. He was nice enough, but the halls were filled with villagers suffering from actual diseases like AIDS and hepatitis. Part of me wanted to demand tests, but I've freaked out about so many phantom ailments in my life that a little voice kept whispering, *What if the sensations are all in your head?* Guess I should have rethought the decision to go home and sleep it off, because this feels different. Something is wrong, really amiss. I'm the Boy Who Cried Wolf who's finally in the shit.

Cracks fang over the hut's interior walls like sudden lightning. I hunch forward, dig my elbows into my thighs, and count them off in sets of two. I hate that I keep doing this but it's the only way to ground myself. I never sought appropriate cognitive therapy and stopped taking my medication because mental health issues posed clearance challenges to becoming a Peace Corps volunteer.

Sucking it up and trying harder, my two plans for coping, don't seem very successful.

I miss a crack. Shit. Now I have to go back and begin counting all over.

No! Not again. Stop it. Just . . . stop.

I wrench my gaze from the wall and push down the dread that if I don't count exactly right something terrible will happen. I breathe deep but the anxiety lingers, debating whether or not to grow into an angry monster or slink into my subconscious.

Better not to give it a choice. I need a mission, something to distract me. A tin pail sits in the corner of my makeshift kitchen, a grandiose title for what amounts to a table, rickety stool, and bowl of cassava. I don't have a shower—no indoor plumbing—but a sponge bath might be the thing. I'm exhausted, restless, and jittery from discomfort. Fresh air makes everything better, right? I shuffle over, lift the handle, and muster the energy to trudge outside to the nearby water pump, wincing in the sunlight.

Meghan, my neighbor, fellow Peace Corps volunteer and HIV-prevention coordinator at the clinic, is there chatting with other women in fluent Chichewa. Her upper lip is too heavy for the lower, and dips into an almost-but-not-quite frown at my approach. Pretty sure she secretly believes I'm a total wimp ass.

I take my place at the end of the line and hope it doesn't look like my intestines are contorting themselves in figure-eight knots.

Meghan adjusts the intricately patterned *chitenje* that wraps her otherwise thick black hair. These large fabric squares are cheap everyday wear in the village, and I have one tied around my T-shirt and skirt as a sarong. Envy constricts my rib cage as she balances a full-to-the-brim bucket on the top of her head with casual ease. I've yet to manage such coordination, much to the merriment of the village women. It takes time to learn the little skills that make you invisible. Aside from the glaring difference of my pigment, I'm still too conspicuous, prone to making a dozen tiny errors in a single outing. The teasing is never mean, but sometimes yeah, I wish I fit in better.

"What's up, T?" Meghan's sharp gaze takes my measure. *Can the newbie hack it?*

Africa has the highest volunteer dropout rate of any continent. There is no way I'm going to early terminate. The very idea is taboo. I gave the Peace Corps a two-year commitment. Here's my big chance to show my spirit animal isn't a scaredy-cat. I'm a girl with fortitude, spunk, and great gobs of mettle—need to dig deep and see this decision through to the flip side.

Meghan tries to hold my gaze, but I don't let her. Instead, I study the ant marching across my bare foot. "Sorry if I seem pathetic—can't kick this stupid bug."

She's from North Carolina, and her twenty-four-month contract finishes next month. After Malawi, she hopes to score an aid position elsewhere in the sub-Sahara.

"Got to keep on keeping on." Meghan squints at the horizon with a thousand-mile stare.

"Doing my best." I take a deep breath through my nose. When people toss out those empty phrases, I kind of want to pat their heads, with a hammer.

"Sorry I haven't checked in on you since getting back."

She's going all hot and heavy with one of the two clinic doctors, a lanky Médecins Sans Frontières guy from Belgium. They recently returned from a week-long getaway climbing Mount Mulanje in the country's south. She's strong and independent, exactly who I aspire to be. In the meantime, I crave her approval. I want her to think the best of me, even if that means hiding my worst. The fear. The uncertainty. The moments of sheer I-don't-know-what-I'm-doing terror.

I'm unable to speak as my abdominal knot tightens.

"Stomach again?"

A wave of dizziness tumbles over me. I nod, not trusting my voice.

"That sucks. Hey, we all get sick. Adjustment takes time. I had giardia three times my first year. Lost almost twenty pounds."

My own clothes hang off my frame. I've never been big, but I sported more curves than not. These days my body's flat, battening down the hatches, reduced to two dimensions.

"Lay low and rest."

"I'll brew a pot of ginger tea," I mumble. "There's a bag left over from my last care package."

"Good idea, and, hey, if you need anything, you know where to find me."

Wow. Quick, someone nominate my fake smile for a Best Supporting Oscar, because Meghan's answering grin makes it seem like I'm not this big bummer.

Screams rise from the direction of the lake—the good kind—laughter harmonizing with joyful squeals. The women around me abandon the pump and race to the water. The weird cloud from earlier hits the shore, breaks apart in furious wings and discordant buzzing. Flies. Everywhere. I swat my face, strength depleting faster than bathwater spiraling into a drain. Women and children swing any available container through the air, collecting as many insects as possible. No one passes up free protein in this region.

Pain lances my side, an invisible knife ripping through my torso. What's happening to me? No way anyone hears my useless squeak. My heart flops in an erratic rhythm as blue stars cascade past in a psychedelic stream. Flies hum in my ear, crawl over the back of my neck.

Help. Please. I need help.

My knees hit the soil and I pitch forward, grappling the *Hey Darling* letter pressed to my heart. Bran is my sanctuary. If anything will keep me lucid, centered, it's him, but the blackness pulls too strong, rushes through my brain like a wild flood, dragging me into the shadows.

———

"Talia? Talia, can you hear me?" That deep rumble could be mistaken for calm and in control until the under-the-breath expletive. "Fucking hell."

My fingers slide to a narrow wrist, a leanly muscular forearm. A flash of recognition. I read this body like braille. A name flits past, a firefly illuminating the darkness, but only for a split second.

Bran?

No way. That's impossible. He's on a boat in the Southern Ocean.

Can a hallucination brush warm lips across the side of my neck? I blindly clutch the strong fingers laced with mine, trace faint calluses. This contact is an anchor, holds me fast, safe from the hungry dark.

Bran.

A wordless prayer. For a moment, wild joy blooms. He's so close. I want to tell him I'm within reach, but speech is impossible, like trying to smile without a mouth.

"Don't bother bloody dying because I swear to God I'll hunt you down and drag you back."

Hot tears burn beneath my lids at the familiar accent. I clutch each word, his presence a safe harbor.

"Sir, I'm going to ask you again, step away from the patient."

"Not a chance," he snaps.

"I need to check her hematocrit and switch out the quinine." A woman speaks with unfamiliar cadence, hitting each consonant hard like she wields a hammer.

"Work around me." The pressure on my hand increases. "Don't worry, I've got you, sweetheart."

There's a sharp prick on my upper arm. Nothing compared to the pain dimly lingering in my memory's recesses—a skull-wrenching, chromosomal-deep agony.

Strange to feel so numb now.

There's an unpleasant tang to the air—disposable rubber gloves and disinfectant? A hospital smell. Claustrophobic panic wells in my throat.

"Damn it, Talia. Wake up." The fierce order is a tether out of this limbo.

My eyes open.

Bright. Ouch. Holy shit. Way too bright.

Everything is blurry without my contacts.

A hospital bed rail.

A shadowy outline of an IV pole.

A face.

The only face.

Bran moves with a suddenness that makes my heart skip. My limbs become aware of their existence, nerves revving to life. "You're back," he says quietly, firmly, as if there's to be no arguing the point.

He looks like someone pushed to the brink and kicked off the side. Thick, dark hair juts in odd angles. His eyes are chipped jade, but bloodshot and wild, ringed by sleepless bruises. A muscle bunches deep in his jaw, nearly undetectable beneath the days-old scruff.

He's beautiful.

But he's not supposed to be here.

Get lost in the Off the Map series

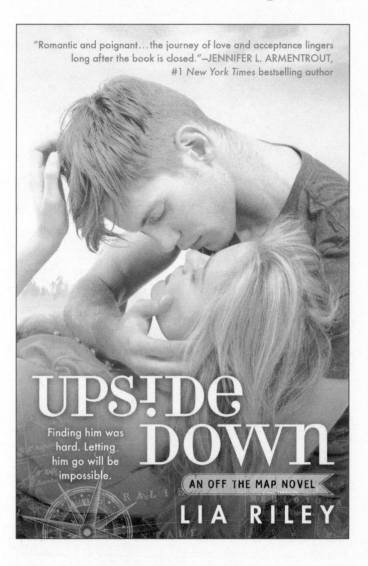

"Romantic and poignant...the journey of love and acceptance lingers long after the book is closed."—JENNIFER L. ARMENTROUT, #1 *New York Times* bestselling author

UPSIDE DOWN

Finding him was hard. Letting him go will be impossible.

AN OFF THE MAP NOVEL

LIA RILEY

Book 1 available now!